PRIMAL
ANIMALS

ALSO BY
JULIA LYNN RUBIN

Burro Hills
Trouble Girls

PRIMAL ANIMALS

A NOVEL

JULIA LYNN RUBIN

WEDNESDAY BOOKS
NEW YORK

First published in the United States by Wednesday Books, an imprint of St. Martin's Publishing Group

PRIMAL ANIMALS. Copyright © 2022 by Julia Lynn Rubin. All rights reserved. Printed in the United States of America. For information, address St. Martin's Publishing Group, 120 Broadway, New York, NY 10271.

www.wednesdaybooks.com

Horse skull case stamp illustration © Shutterstock.com

Designed by Devan Norman

The Library of Congress Cataloging-in-Publication Data is available upon request.

ISBN 978-1-250-75729-6 (hardcover)
ISBN 978-1-250-75728-9 (ebook)

Our books may be purchased in bulk for promotional, educational, or business use. Please contact your local bookseller or the Macmillan Corporate and Premium Sales Department at 1-800-221-7945, extension 5442, or by email at MacmillanSpecialMarkets@macmillan.com.

First Edition: 2022

10 9 8 7 6 5 4 3 2 1

For anyone who fears the flies; it's okay to be afraid,
but you're braver and stronger than you know.
Don't let them consume you.

OH, HOW SWEET IT IS,

THE TASTE THAT ONLY COMES FROM

A COCKTAIL MADE OF BOTH PLEASURE AND DISGUST....

PRIMAL
ANIMALS

CHAPTER ONE

The air is thick with flies.

"Horseflies," Mom says, as if in reverence. She closes her eyes and leans her head back against the driver's seat as we stop at a traffic light. "Now *this* takes me back." Mom inhales deeply, that sharp scent of horse manure and fresh-cut grass intermingling in the early summer air. A smile plays at the corners of her lips.

The blueberry oatmeal I had for breakfast crawls up my throat. The flies and their too-many feet, their nasty wings. It's too much. Too many eyes. Too much buzzing. They're angry little torpedoes, shooting themselves through the open car windows and bumping against my face, my bare arms and legs.

I feel hot and shaky all over.

I want to vomit.

But Mom doesn't seem to feel the flies. Not like I do.

Buzz-buzz-buzz.

The traffic light finally turns green. "Mom." I shake her arm, and she snaps her eyes open, gasping as if coming up for air. She sees the light, sees the look of horror splashed across my face, and that trace of a smile fades. She hits the gas pedal and swats frantically at the flies as if she's just noticed them. Rolls up the car windows. Flips the AC back on. Reaches out a freshly manicured hand to me in apology, guilt etched across her face.

"Arlee . . . ," she tries. Mom knows I hate bugs—flies especially—but she doesn't know just how much. I play it off like it's because they gross me out, but it cuts deeper than that.

I wish I could tell her why, but then I'd have to explain . . . and I can't.

"It's okay," I lie. There're still a couple of flies lingering in the car. Little hitchhikers, I tell myself. I breathe slow and deep. *They can't hurt you, Arlee. They're harmless.* I pretend I can't see or hear them—that low, thrumming, dull buzz—but my heart is racing all the same, pumping blood into my ears.

I want to scream.

Mom merges lanes. She swallows hard. "We're almost there, honey."

"I'm fine," I say, though far less convincingly. I squeeze her moisturized hand in reassurance, and she gives me a squeeze back.

"Are you sure you want to do this?" she asks. "Because I could just turn around and drive us home now." She grins faintly to let me know she doesn't mean it.

I nod and force a smile that I know she sees right through. "It'll be good, being there all summer. I was reading online about exposure therapy, too, you know? I can handle it. I'll probably come home in August and you could dump a whole vat of cockroaches on me and I wouldn't even flinch." I shudder at the thought. I'm rambling. I can't stop. I'm so anxious.

Mom chews at the bottom of her scarlet-red lips but says nothing more. She's so beautiful and glamorous in her perfectly winged eyeliner and emerald blouse, and it's kind of strange sitting next to her with my bare face and dirty, tangled blond hair. My jean shorts are tight around a belly I'm insecure about.

I catch a glimpse of myself in the passenger side-view mirror. Even though I just turned sixteen, I feel younger now, somehow, with my face free of makeup and my black-framed glasses on instead of the contact lenses I sometimes wear. I guess I'm going to have to feel younger for a little longer.

Because for the next two and a half months, I won't have access to eyeliner or curling irons. Not my laptop or even my phone. I can't use my meditation app to calm down if I get severely overwhelmed, or binge-watch Netflix into the early hours of the morning to try to distract myself from my own racing thoughts that keep me up all night. I won't be able to call Mom to vent if something stressful happens, or even contact Dad, though it's not like we still talk more than once or twice a year. I can't take long walks downtown at sunset and window-shop. Browse boutiques and sip iced coffee and then cool down in our cozy apartment after a day spent in the blazing sun.

No respite from the moths and mosquitoes and . . . *the flies* . . . those creepy-crawlies of my darkest dreams.

Good thing I packed two huge cans of Deep Woods bug spray.

I'll be on a strict daily schedule, up early each morning. Splitting my time between standardized test-prep sessions and camp activities like horseback riding through rivers. I'll be sleeping in a screened cabin in an extra-long twin bed, surrounded by the bodies of other girls.

There will be networking events with fellow ambitious students and a few guest camp alumni.

That's what I've been told. That's what the brochures all promised. Time to really focus on what I want to do next. Where I want to go to college, and beyond that, who I want to become.

Camp Rockaway is going to help secure my future. That's what the admissions counselor in the stuffy office with the knit sweater kept telling Mom and me, over and over, while I sucked on a disgusting candy from a dish on her desk that I felt too self-conscious to spit out, and Mom just smiled politely. That's why my father forked over half the tuition for me to attend, even though he's only been in and out of my life since eighth grade.

Mom spent four summers at Camp Rockaway from the ages of fourteen to seventeen, and ended up graduating summa cum laude from Dartmouth and with a distinguished law degree from Yale. She says she'd never be where she is now without her summers at camp. They helped her work her way up from nothing; now she's a real self-made woman. She met three of her best friends at camp, too, the women she has over for Scotch and soap operas every other month, the ones who've known me since I was a baby. They gift me things like Hermès bracelets and velvet scarves for my birthday. They came to so many of my piano recitals, including my biggest one ever, where each time they sat front row, clapping and sobbing with pride as if I were their own daughter . . . even though I barely knew them.

So, I know that Camp Rockaway is one of those chances you don't pass up, especially if you're sort of a fuckup like me with a less-than-stellar GPA. I screwed up big-time freshman and sophomore year, but that's over now. I can't focus on it anymore. I have a chance to boost my college application and get me in prime position to ace the SAT and ACT. I think of what the camp admissions counselor kept telling me, over and over as I sucked that too-sour candy: "We are drawing a blueprint for your future." Camp Rockaway is a work-hard, play-hard summer prep camp for bright kids with big goals. It isn't jail, or even boot camp.

So why does it feel like it is? Why is my stomach churning like a washing machine?

I push my glasses up the bridge of my nose and turn up the volume on the radio. Try to listen carefully to the lyrics, let my mind empty of all thoughts.

My right leg is restless. No matter what I do, I can't seem to calm it down.

We drive past weathered clapboard homes and old farms. Firework stands that sell sweet tea and lemonade. A field full of beautiful white horses. It's real country out here. I flip off the AC and roll down the windows, trying to coax out the remaining hitchhiker flies. The air out here feels different, cleaner. Sweeter. Mom steers us onto a rusty iron bridge. It's impossibly tall, and as I glance out the window, I see the vast expanse of bay blue stretching out in all directions, the water so dizzyingly far down. I squeeze my eyes shut tight. I already desperately miss Raleigh. Camp Rockaway is just a three-hour drive from home, but it's like we've been on this road forever. The deeper we go, the swampier it gets, and the taller the leaning trees loom, branches winding to the sky. It's like we're entering a different world.

Mom gives a dreamy sigh, seemingly oblivious to my simmering anxiety. "It's been over twenty years since I've been back down here. It's been too long. I almost wish I could join you and be one of your bunkmates." She laughs a little, though it's tinged with sadness. "You don't even know how much it's going to change you, Arlee. It really is going to change everything."

I nod like I understand, but I'm still not sure how only one summer is really going to change everything for me (even if it does give my test-taking skills a boost) or why she's making this place sound like some sort of quasi-religious retreat.

Mom's brows furrow when she finally notices my expression. "Honey? What is it?"

"It's . . . not, like, a Jesus camp, right?"

That cracks her up. A frantic laugh spills out of me, too, releasing some of the gut-crushing fear. She gives me that look, a sparkle in her eye—that *there's my girl* look she flashes my way whenever she's proud of me or I've said something funny—and rests a hand on my knee. I always swell with pride whenever I make her laugh like this. Whenever I do something that makes her glow.

"You're funny, Arlee."

"I try." I make myself grin at her, even though inside and out, I can't stop trembling. The short burst of laughter didn't last long in calming my nerves.

Mom squeezes my knee in the same solid, sure way she squeezed my hand. Her long fingernails pinch at my skin. "I know you're a little nervous, baby, but it's going to be good. So good. Things are coming that you can't even see yet. Believe me?"

"Yep," I say, "it'll be great," even as I feel my head shake in contradiction.

∘ ∘ ∘

We pull into the parking area—a grassy, open field littered with shiny cars of all shapes, sizes, and makes. BMWs, Escalades, even a few Ferraris mixed in among the normal sedans and SUVs. Young adults in bright red Camp Rockaway T-shirts—counselors, no doubt—mill about with clipboards in hand, greeting arrivals, helping to move our footlocker cases and bulging suitcases out of trunks and hoist them onto massive pull carts, which muscular attendants then haul up the hill.

Check-in time started at nine, but it's quarter to noon, so we're some of the last few arrivals. A part of me wants her to turn us around, *now*, and drive the three hours back to Raleigh. A part of me could also quite easily curl up in the trunk of the car and hide there for the rest of the summer.

But we're here now, and Mom's turned off the engine. I take a deep breath, slip my backpack on, and step into the radiant midday heat. I immediately feel like choking. Everything down here is alive and humming with energy. A sharp electricity. Insects

buzzing and voices chattering, the muffled sound of a pounding bass from just up the hill, beyond the huge wooden arch
that marks the entrance to the camp grounds. The faint smell of
woodsmoke.

Out of instinct, I look to my mother.

Mom steps out of the car, locks it, and slips on her Chanel
sunglasses in one fluid, artful motion. She has that serene look
on her face again as she soaks it all in: the heat, the noise, the
energy.

My heart hammers against my chest, blood pounding in
my ears. *It's okay*, I tell myself. *If Mom is calm, you have no reason to panic.*

Why should I panic?

Why would I?

The sound of the admissions counselor's voice rings in my
ears: *"Kids around the world would die to be in your position. . . ."*

"Well, hi there, camper!" A girl approaches our car, waving,
clipboard in hand. With her swinging blond ponytail and bright
white smile, she's already much too chipper for my liking. Her
sunny mood slices right against the edges of my anxiety, but it's
not her fault I'm so nervous. I can at least be nice. Make a good
first impression. She squints hard as she takes me in. "Hmm, I
haven't seen you here before. First time?"

Mom nods and rests her hand on my shoulder, her nails
pinching at my skin again. "First time," she says for me. "This is
Arlee Gold."

"Hi, Arlee! Welcome. I'm Anna, one of the girls' counselors."
Her voice is high and chirpy, like a little bird's. She scribbles something down on the clipboard, flipping through a few pages. "How
old are you?"

I open my mouth to answer but Mom cuts in first. "Sixteen.
A rising junior. She'll be in Unit Seven, if I'm not mistaken."

"Yep, looks about like it. That's my unit!" Anna chirps, though there's an edge in her voice as her blue eyes slice back up at Mom. Now I see it: her smile a little too wide, her eyes not quite matching her widened lips. The knife in her tone.

She turns those icy eyes directly on me. Everything inside me goes very still and quiet as the volume on the world turns down. All of the sounds of the chatter, the thumping bass . . . they all diminish. A strange feeling washes over me. It's peaceful, in a way, somewhat bright and beautiful, but there's something sinister there, too. Anna's smile widens, and it's like I can see her fangs. . . .

I blink and the moment is gone, and everything is loud and bright and electric again, and I stand shivering even in the heat.

What the fuck is wrong with me?

Mom pops open the trunk and Anna helps lift out my footlocker case and laundry bag stuffed with riding gear. Unlike some of the kids here, I packed pretty light.

I stare at the grass, fighting a sudden wave of shame, like it's my fault this happened again. It hasn't in so long. Sometimes I get these little glitches in the matrix of my mind, little blips in time where things go fuzzy and surreal. The last doctor I saw assured me that it's nothing, that my brain is perfectly healthy. Every test I took came back normal. It might be auras, he said, perhaps some kind of "silent" migraine. *An overactive imagination.* The pills he prescribed me didn't help. He never seemed to take me seriously, just made sympathetic noises and gently implied that I see a shrink.

"These moments, these lapses you have, they're likely benign and nothing to worry about," he said. "They're not real, Arlee."

But he didn't know . . .

He didn't know about what happened in the woods.

There's that familiar taste in the back of my throat, the one that always makes me shiver.

The taste of metal.

Stop it, Arlee. Stop! Just breathe. Remember the meditation app: four long in-breaths, then pause, four long out-breaths.

I slap at my face a little, trying to wake myself up.

"You coming, Arlee?" Mom calls. She and Anna glance back at me expectantly, and immediately I feel embarrassed for standing here, being such a fucking weirdo. Anna must hate me already.

Though her eyes no longer look menacing, and her white teeth no longer resemble fangs. Her smile is warm again, and she motions for me to follow them, so I do.

The entrance to the camp is up a small hill lined with towering poplar trees covered in vibrant green moss.

With each step up the hill, the smell of woodsmoke grows stronger, the thumping bass louder. Anna passes beneath the entrance arch, but Mom hangs back a second, stopping me in place with her hand.

"Look," she says, as if we're standing before some ancient, holy monument.

CAMP ROCKAWAY is carved into the top of the arch in swooping cursive, along with ornate depictions of an owl, a horse, and a deer. The animals seem to stare back at me with their wooden, knowing eyes.

"Incredible, isn't it?" Mom breathes. I'm not sure what to say, because while I know this place is so meaningful to her, to me it's just a sign, and it's not even that remarkable, if a little unnerving, so I choose to say nothing.

o o o

Lush.

That's the best word I can use to describe the grounds of Camp Rockaway. The grass is so green it looks spray-painted, and the sprawling front lawn where the Welcome Center sits is perfectly manicured, lined with sunflowers and milkweed bushes. The air is fragrant with pine, mingling with the earthy scents of sunbaked mulch and horse manure.

This camp is huge, judging by the detailed map they hand me inside the Welcome Center. At least a thousand acres, though much of it seems to be woods. There are eight clusters of cabins, called units, scattered across all different sections, half of them for the boys and the other half for the girls. There's a gigantic equestrian facility with a stable and training rings. Two amphitheaters, one small and one grand. Two massive outdoor swimming pools and every kind of sports court and field you could imagine, from tennis to soccer to archery. Crafting and fine-arts pavilions, complete with pottery wheels and a wood-fired kiln. A challenge course with a towering rock-climbing wall. A sand volleyball court, a yoga studio, and an indoor music-practice space. There's even an outdoor rink for in-line skating. I half expect to see a fucking roller coaster, too. At the bottom of the map, the Echo River slashes across the south end like a scar.

I can't help but wonder, like the total nerd that I am: *When will we have time to do test prep?*

I'm dizzy with the enormity of the camp, the endless possibilities that it seems to offer. I imagined something nice but sparse, like camping should be, but this place already feels so weirdly artificial. Like college meets Disney World in the forest. No wonder Mom pushed for Dad to fork up half the tuition money. Mom and I aren't close to rich—even though she plays the part well—and a whole summer here must cost a fortune.

It's nice and cool in the Welcome Center, a rustic but accommodating cabin of its own. It's where they sell all the kitschy Camp Rockaway apparel and gifts and, as Mom tells me, where the main office is located. A dozen or so parents in crisp polos and floral sundresses schmooze with one another over camp-themed hors d'oeuvres, chatting and joking about their own fond memories from back in their days at Camp Rockaway.

I notice a few of them throw shifty looks in our direction, but no one approaches to say hello. I sip nervously from my new aluminum water bottle, half tempted to say "fuck it" and grab one of the alcoholic drinks set out for the parents. Mom buys me a Camp Rockaway T-shirt, a lanyard, and two extra bottles of bug spray, all of which she tucks into my backpack for me. Then she clamps her hand down on my shoulder.

"Oh, Arlee, honey, look! Here's someone I need you to meet!"

I turn to see an older woman watching us from across the room. She's very tall, with a long, thin face and snow-white hair braided all the way down her back. She wears dazzling gold earrings, lavender pumps, and a cream-colored pantsuit. The crowd steps aside for her as she approaches, parents nodding in her direction and giving murmurs of approval and salutations, but she ignores them all in favor of Mom.

"Sam!" she says warmly, grabbing both my mom's hands in her own. The woman beams at her like she's a long-lost sibling. They air-kiss. I feel the eyes of the other parents on us once again, hear their faint whispers turn back to chatter as they continue to mingle among themselves. "Oh, and this must be Arlee." The woman gives me a quick once-over and nods, like she's appraising a new car. I'm not sure if I should reach out for a handshake, because she's still holding Mom's hands, so I just nod and give an awkward wave.

"Still wearing that Clive Christian," Mom chides as she pulls her in for a hug, and then I, too, smell the expensive, earthy perfume. They linger in each other's arms a little longer than I've seen most adult friends do.

"Oh, darling, they discontinued the kind I like years ago—
because *of course* they did—so I have to have it shipped in from
Berlin," the woman says, lowering her voice and grinning as if this
were some big, dirty secret. Mom laughs, and it's airy and light
and not her usual laugh at all.

I shuffle from side to side and it's only then that Mom seems
to remember that I'm standing there. "Oh, Arlee, forgive me, I'm
so rude. This is Caroline Rhinelander, camp director."

"A pleasure," Caroline purrs. As we shake hands, her gold
bracelets slide down her thin wrist and kiss my skin. "Arlee,
if you need anything at all, I'm in the office most days from
nine to six. Seriously, anything." She leans in close to me and
speaks in that same low, conspiratorial voice she used with
Mom. "Help transferring elective courses—don't bother with my
secretary, she gets impossibly scattered—or getting switched
to a new riding instructor or horse if they match you with an
unruly one. A phone call home. Anything. Anytime. Day or
night."

"Thanks" is all I can think to say, but Caroline's attention is
already turned back to Mom, her blue eyes twinkling at her with
utter adoration.

"You got my voicemail?" she asks her quietly.

"Of course," Mom says. "I'll get back to you Monday." They
both seem to communicate something else without words, and
with a swish of her hips, Caroline dips back into the crowd,
which once again parts for her like the Red Sea.

"Wow" is all I can say. "You've never mentioned her before.
Was she one of your bunkmates?" She's about ten years older than
Mom, though, if I had to guess, so it's unlikely they shared a cabin.

"Something like that . . . ," Mom says. She clears her throat.
"Okay, baby, I've signed you in. Everything is in order. Like Caroline said, if there's an emergency, just come here and ask to call

me. Whatever it is, no matter the time of day. This is where we say goodbye. I have to get back to the office."

"It's a Sunday," I point out.

Mom kisses my cheek, ignoring my remark. "You're gonna do great, kiddo." I do my best to look happy for her. She gives a strand of my honey-blond hair an affectionate twirl. "Being here brings back so many indescribable memories of times with my sisters. . . ." I assume she means with her bunkmates or fellow campers, possibly people like Caroline—I guess they became like sisters, so I don't correct her. Mom, after all, is an only child. "Anyway, I'm just so excited for you."

"Thanks, Mom. It kind of feels like you're dropping me off at Yale but, you know, I appreciate the sentiment."

She laughs again and gives my hand one final squeeze. "Yale is the next step, baby. Be good." With that, she turns and leaves just as gracefully as she came in, not bothering to touch a single hors d'oeuvre.

"Ready to go?" Anna chirps, and I startle. She snuck up behind me like she's been watching us and waiting in the wings.

"*Jesus*, you scared me."

She raises an eyebrow but doesn't apologize. "I see you met my mom," she notes.

"Caroline?"

Anna barely suppresses an eye roll, but I catch it just before she grins and nods, and it fully dawns on me how fake she is.

Anna beams and waves at the other parents, even shakes a few hands, cracks jokes with one dad, then swipes a couple pigs in blankets—they have little eyes drawn on with ketchup to make them look like campers stuffed in sleeping bags—before taking me back outside into the shimmering heat.

There's that bass again, the steady *thump-thump-thump* of the beat.

"Is there, like, a concert or something?" I ask, craning my neck to try to find the source of the sound.

"Some of our musical campers are getting early practice in for the Midsummer Concert," Anna says, chewing thoughtfully. She offers me one of the camper pigs, but I decline. My stomach feels sour and the taste of metal has seeped back into my mouth. "Let's get you settled in." Outside, away from the parents, I note, her voice is far less perky.

I follow her down a dirt trail that takes us past the tennis courts and swimming pools and sand volleyball court, cutting into a thick slice of forest. Cicadas buzz in the trees, making me shiver, and a tiny warbler darts past us. Once we're deep enough into the woods, Anna stops and lights a cigarette.

I just gape at her, then snap my mouth shut when she notices me staring.

"Shit." She chuckles. "I forget that you're new here." Anna taps some of the ashes to the dirt. "You don't know how it works yet. That's okay. You smoke?"

I shake my head rapidly, clutching at the straps of my backpack. "You can smoke here?" I ask weakly.

Anna fully rolls her eyes this time. She continues walking, me toddling along after her, the trail growing wider as we go.

I hear a shriek of laughter, and as we turn a sharp corner, we nearly collide with a group of girls. They walk close together, arms linked, decked out in designer-looking sunglasses, matching tie-dye T-shirts and Sperrys. All of them so effortlessly glamorous even without a hint of makeup.

One girl turns to glance over her shoulder as we pass them. Her friend whispers something in her ear, and they both burst into giggles.

Are they laughing at me? I stare at the ground and keep my eyes on my dirty sneakers, which now feel hideous and out of place. I should've insisted Mom take me to the mall or some downtown boutique and pick out better clothes.

I don't belong here. This was a mistake. I shouldn't have come.

There's more laughter and voices now. My heart thuds against my rib cage. As we pass a cluster of cabins, I feel other eyes on me, too. Shirtless boys with sun-kissed skin in all different shades. This one white guy—blond, covered in a smattering of freckles— raises his shades and stares after me with his mouth slightly ajar. They're all curious, I realize. Most of them know each other, so it's normal to give me a second glance. But the blond guy keeps watching me, and something about the way his eyes stay pinned to my body as his head swivels to follow the movement of my hips makes the blueberry oatmeal threaten to rise up again.

I take a long swig from my water bottle and trot to match pace with Anna. She may be a smoker, but she's somehow speed-walking along this winding path like she's been doing it her whole life, whereas I'm panting, wiping sweat from my face as I struggle to keep up. Several minutes later, more cabins and a campfire circle come into view, along with a smaller but just as beautiful wooden sign, done in sweeping cursive.

Unit Seven

"Here we are," Anna says dryly. "Your home sweet home for the summer."

There are girls everywhere. Girls by the campfire circle. Girls huddled together, laughing, talking excitedly. Girls braiding each other's hair. Girls playing card games on picnic benches. One girl even sits on a tree stump strumming her guitar.

Anna approaches two girls leaning against an old oak tree, clearly in the middle of some intense, private conversation. "New bunkmates," she says. "Your cabin."

The girls' heads shoot up. They both blink in surprise, like they've awakened from a dream. One of them points right at me and goes, "You're not Vidhya," as if this is some obvious fact that I should be aware of. She's supermodel tall and gorgeous, with long, black box braids that cascade down to her waist. She wears a fashionably bleached crop top and high-waisted denim shorts, an expensive-looking gold watch wrapped around her wrist.

I swallow down the lump in my throat. "No . . . ," I whisper, but I don't know if they hear me.

"Remember Vidhya dropped?" The other girl gives her tall supermodel friend a pointed look. She's about half her height, with short, sleek black hair cut close to her face and curves that remind me of ocean waves. Her sneakers aren't too different from mine. Dirty and scuffed. How they probably should be for a summer camp, I think. She looks adorable in denim overalls with a stained white T-shirt tucked underneath. When she catches me tracing the lines of her hips with my eyes, I turn away, pretending to be fascinated by two girls play-wrestling by the unlit campfire.

Anna squeezes my shoulder so hard that I wince. "This is Ar*lee*," she says. I instantly feel five years old again, an awkward little kid being introduced to these impossibly cool girls who feel years older than me.

The supermodel girl's face relaxes into a smile. She steps forward to shake my hand, and this warm energy just radiates from her, calming the storm inside my belly. "I'm Jane," she says.

Her shorter friend also extends a hand, and as we shake, looks me right in the eyes. "Winona."

"*Winnie!*" Jane corrects, playfully kicking at her ankle, then smirks at me like now I'm in on some private joke. Like I've somehow crossed the threshold into a safe zone, and I'm part of this. Part of something. My jaw unclenches. My shoulders relax.

Winnie laughs in agreement, and it's the most gorgeous laugh I've ever heard. "Ignore her. But it's true. All my friends call me Winnie." When she finally lets go of my hand, my cheeks burn, but she can't possibly notice because I'm already so sweaty and, no doubt, red from the sun.

"It's nice to meet you," I finally get out.

"Likewise." She winks at me and a rush flashes through my stomach. "Here, I'll take your backpack. You've lugged it far enough up this hill and honestly, it looks heavy as hell." She reaches for it—I don't even hesitate before handing it over, like I might normally do—then slings it over one shoulder. There's a pull to Winnie. Something fiercely magnetic and easygoing all at once. "Consider me your temporary camp bellhop, *madam*."

I giggle, and there's this twinkle in her eye that makes me want to know everything there is to know about this girl.

"We got her from here, Anna Banana!" Jane says. "You're officially off Arlee duty!" Winnie gives Anna a salute while Jane beckons for me to follow her into the cabin.

Anna gives a half-hearted salute in return, like the act took up more energy than she was willing to expend. "We're meeting at the campfire circle in thirty," she deadpans. "Don't be late. Seriously. You guys need to stop with that. It quit being cute, like, two years ago."

Before any of us can say another word, she's speed-walking back down the slope of the hill.

"I fucking *love* her," Jane gushes. "I want to *be* her."

"Aim high, I guess," Winnie snarks.

Winnie links her arm through mine and I practically melt at her touch, following her into the cabin. *This is it*, I think. *My new home for the summer.*

It's built into the side of a steep, forested hill, along with the five other cabins that make up Unit Seven. They remind me of birdhouses, or little wooden mailboxes, and ours is the farthest up the slope and closest to the edge of the trees. A little wind chime hangs from the awning, tinkling in the breeze. I step up the small flight of wooden stairs and go through the open screen door. Old wood floors creak beneath us. It smells like patchouli and fresh-cut grass and sunscreen. Through the screens that wrap all the way around and serve as windows, we have a gorgeous downhill view of the campfire circle, the archery field, and a small duck pond just beyond. Wooden bunk beds line each side of the wall. They're covered in colorful quilts and blankets. Though the camp did provide each of us with a basic set of sheets and a pillow, some girls brought their own more luxurious bedding from home.

A Brazilian flag is mounted on the beams beside one bunk, the wall area covered in photos of friends and family. On another beam hangs a trans-pride flag, and it instantly warms me to the place. I spot my footlocker, stored beneath one of the bunk beds with an open bottom bunk.

It's hot inside the cabin, but also cozy and comforting. Already it almost feels like home.

Winnie carefully sets my backpack down on my bare mattress, my sheets and pillow wrapped in plastic and perched on top.

I feel a surge of courage.

"So, should I tip you now?" I ask.

She blinks at me. "What? *Oh.*" She laughs, getting the bell-hop joke. She's quick. "Consider this one on the house, though feel free to leave a five-star Yelp review."

"You're so corny," Jane scoffs, but she's smiling. "This is you, Arles!" I guess I have a nickname now, too. "Well, you and Winnie." Jane hoists herself up the side of the bed to the top bunk and makes herself comfy on Winnie's plush comforter.

Winnie follows suit and beckons for me to follow. "There's plenty of room for all three of us." She offers a hand to help me up, and I shiver when her warm palm holds mine and helps lift me as I struggle to climb. I stumble a little and bump my knee, but eventually make it up there.

"Nice view," I say. "Definitely has a different feel from above. Though getting up here wasn't the easiest."

Jane giggles. "Oh, girl, you'll get used to it."

Winnie rips opens a bag of Swedish Fish with her teeth and pops one in her mouth. She feeds one to Jane and then offers one to me, which I accept gratefully. I haven't eaten since this morning, and my stomach is starting to rumble. "By the end of the first week, you'll be able to get up here faster than you ever thought possible!"

"And these hills," Jane agrees. "You'll get used to those, too. You'll get supermuscular calves and thighs in two weeks' time."

"So . . . where are the bathrooms?"

"Oh, down at the bottom of the hill," Jane says, midchew. She opens her mouth and waits for Winnie to feed her another fish. "That's where the showers are, too, obviously. It's all in one building."

"If you have to pee at night, use your flashlight," says Winnie. "Or you can just shake one of us awake and we'll come with you."

Jane waggles her perfectly waxed eyebrows at me. "Nighttime pee time is the best girl time."

The screen door bangs open and another girl walks in. "Hey, Jane, do you—"

When she notices me, she stops short, and her eyes go wide long enough to make me nervous. "Oh," is all she says. She just stands there, looking at me like I've sprouted two heads, while I feel my palms start to sweat again.

Jane scoffs. "Don't be rude, Olive. This is Arlee."

"Arles," Winnie corrects.

Jane tosses a Swedish Fish at Winnie's head. "She's *new*."

The girl gulps and nods. She drops her head, as if ashamed, her cheeks growing ruddy. "Sorry." She gives me a sheepish smile, eyebrows arched with guilt. "You just . . . I thought you would be someone else."

Like so many of the other girls I've seen here so far, Olive is stunning. She has short, coiled black curls and a heart-shaped face. She wears a stylish white tank top with red trim that makes me think of summertime in the seventies, her hands tucked into the pockets of her tailored, striped green shorts. She's like something out of a Polaroid dream, a flashback in time, and for some reason, she looks achingly familiar. . . .

I clear my throat. "Nah, I'm just me. Arlee Gold. Nice to meet you."

Her smile widens and her posture relaxes. "Likewise. Olive Williams."

Something clicks into place. "Wait. Is your mom Tiffany Williams?"

"Yes! Oh my God. Arlee Gold. You're Sam Gold's daughter!"

Holy shit. No wonder she's so familiar. Jane and Winnie exchange a look. In my periphery I think I see Winnie mouth, *Sam Gold,* as if the name carries weight and meaning.

"Tiffany Williams is one of my mom's best friends!" I blurt out. "They met here!" Maybe this summer won't be so bad after all. I have Jane and Winnie, and now Olive, who's basically my sister by default.

Jane and Winnie don't seem as enthused as me. Winnie has inched away from me slightly, to my dismay, while Jane has already clambered down off the top bunk.

Olive cocks her head at me. "Wait, why do you have your mom's maiden name? Did you change it or—?" She stops herself when she realizes she may be cutting into some uncomfortable territory.

I'm used to this, though—or at least, I was growing up. I shrug, reciting the story that always brings me a rush of warmth and comfort. "My mom kept her last name after she married my dad, and insisted I have the same one. He wasn't excited about it, but he gave in." I always thought it was really cool and feminist. Progressive, even. Now though, retelling the story gives me a new prickle of discomfort, especially with the way Olive is looking at me.

"Oh," she says. An awkward silence ensues for several seconds.

"What'd you need, love?" Jane asks Olive.

"Can I borrow your nail clippers? I forgot mine at home and this hangnail is about to rip clean off."

"Yeah, I think mine are still in the bathroom. Be back in a second, Winnie!" Jane calls. She and Olive link arms and waltz outside, the screen door slamming shut behind them.

She didn't say goodbye to me.

I sink deeper into Winnie's mattress. Did I do something wrong? Am I just so insufferably awkward? Winnie chews at her nails and stares at the ground.

"Everything okay?" I ask.

She studies her cuticles. "Your mom is Sam Gold? *The* Sam Gold?"

"Is . . . there another one I should know about?"

Now she's chewing at her bottom lip, too. She laughs, but it sounds forced. "No, no. Of course not. That's your mom. That makes sense."

"What does *that* mean?" I can't help the edge in my voice. I hear it, the defensiveness creeping in, but I can't stop it. "Why does that *make sense*?"

I immediately feel bad when I see the look of shock on Winnie's face. "Oh no, no," she says quickly, shaking her head. "I didn't mean to insinuate anything. It just . . . makes sense because you're the only other Gold here. That's all. She's the only other one I've heard of."

She's not telling me everything. There's something else . . .
a reason why she looked so anxious when she said my mom's
name. Why Jane did, too.

Why she's even heard of my mom to begin with.

There has to be.

The Sam Gold.

Chill out, Arlee. You're being fucking paranoid.

"But you've heard of her?" I press. "What did you hear?"

Was Mom a total asshole to the girls in her unit? A bully? It's
possible. Mom can be a firecracker when she wants to get her
way, though I wouldn't call her nasty. . . .

Winnie only shrugs at me helplessly. "Nothing. I've heard of
a lot of people who went here. Like I said, I didn't mean anything
by it."

She looks so genuine. Maybe I misheard her . . . or misunder-
stood.

My shoulders droop, the small burst of anger now gone.

I suddenly feel like crying.

"Arlee?" Winnie's face has softened. "Hey, it's okay. Please
don't worry about it. Let me help you set up your bed, okay?"

My eyes sting with tears of shame, but I nod as we unwrap
the camp-provided sheets, comforter, and pillow from their plastic coverings and pull out the extra blanket from my footlocker,
wrapping my bare mattress in a brand-new nest of rosy pinks and
white.

I always do this. Read situations wrong. Assume the worst in
people. This is why I have no more friends.

I turn away from Winnie so she won't see me wipe my eyes.
Won't see me cry. I think about the way Mom looked at me in the
car, her eyes full of hope. She knew I needed this summer in
more ways than one. A fresh start.

Just relax.

I unroll the comforter.

Nothing has happened.

Lay it flat on the bed.

Nothing is wrong.

Tuck the corners in nice and neat.

There we go.

Just be normal.

A few girls pop in and out of the cabin as we work.

"Winnie, you got any more candy?"

"Winnie, where's Jane?"

One girl says hi to me but tells me her name so fast I can barely register it. By time I start to ask her to repeat it, she's already rushed out again.

Another girl pops her head in briefly to ask Winnie another question—*what is she, the official cabin spokesperson?*—but doesn't say a word to me.

These girls don't know me yet, but I can't help but feel like an afterthought. I pretend to keep myself busy arranging my shoes beneath my bed.

I've always had some trouble with new people, and these girls talk and move so fast, with an ease and comfort between one another that extends back years. Of all my bunkmates, it seems like I'm the only new girl.

I grab the portable spray-bottle fan from my open footlocker and fidget with the foam blades, the thought ricocheting through my mind: *This is it. I'm really trapped here all summer. I can't go home.*

I shake my head as if trying to shake the thought out, swallow down the sadness rising in my throat, and plop down on my newly made bed. It's surprisingly comfortable, though the mattress is definitely on the creaky side and not as nice as Winnie's. Winnie joins me, her arm brushing mine as she leans back on her elbows and looks up at me with interest. It snaps me out of my angsty reverie.

"So, where are you from?" she asks. The way she smiles is so cute, almost crooked, the right side of her mouth rising a little higher than the left. She's already told me a bit about her home in the suburbs of Atlanta, something about her dad doing research for a major tech company. I should be paying closer attention, not letting myself keep drifting aimlessly into my own thoughts. Especially if I want to get to know these girls.

If I want any shot at fitting in.

I give the foam blades a good spin. "Raleigh. I live downtown."

"Really?" Her eyes light up. "My mom went to NC State!"

"No way!" I love North Carolina State University, and if Mom didn't have such high expectations for my college career, she'd probably be happy with me going there. There's nothing more relaxing to me than spending afternoons wandering the massive campus, imagining myself weaving in and out of the dozens of redbrick buildings, or sprawled on the open lawns with a book for class, surrounded by new classmates who've never seen me before. "Did your parents meet there?"

Winnie's face falls a little. She clears her throat. "They did, though . . . my mom died, um . . . giving birth to me. It was her senior year."

Shit. Why did I assume? "Oh, Jesus, I'm so sorry—"

She waves a hand like she's used to this reaction. "Don't be. I brought her up. But yeah, Dad was only a sophomore at the time, and he ended up transferring to Duke. Closer to his parents, and good for me, since he brought me with him." That cute crooked smile returns. "I grew up playing quietly in the corner of psychology lectures and listening to academic audiobooks on the way home from day care. Now I'm a Duke legacy. Of all the tragic cosmic fates to befall a motherless child, it could have a worse ending, you know?"

A genuine laugh tumbles out of me, maybe my first happy laugh all day.

Winnie's smile widens. This close, I can see all the freckles on her eyelids. She gives my arm a playful nudge. "Any, uh . . . awkward family tragedies you want to randomly share within hour one of meeting me?"

"My dad gave up on my mom and me a few years ago," I hear myself admit. "He walked out. Barely speaks to us now. Does that count?"

"I'm sorry about that. Seriously. Fuck him. Fuck the fates, right? They can be cruel sometimes."

I've never quite met someone like Winnie before.

I'm startled by a sudden blur of brown and yellow. A giant moth whizzes past my ear and lands right on the window ledge beside my bed. The patterns on its enormous brown wings resemble eyes. Wide, yellow owl eyes. The wings flutter. My spray-bottle fan clatters to the wooden floor. I barely suppress a scream.

"Arlee?"

I realize that I'm shaking, that all my muscles have gone rigid and I'm gripping at the bedspread, breathing hard. My entire body recoiling from the moth. I can almost feel its little feet on me, its too-long antennae tickling at my cheeks. *Go away, God, please, make it go away.* I shut my eyes tight.

"Can you please make it leave?" I beg. I feel weak and pathetic, but my eyes are wet again, and the urge to scream at the top of my lungs is growing with every second. The tears I fought back return and spill down my cheeks.

"Oh . . . the moth?" Winnie sounds genuinely confused, but she does as I ask, or at least I trust that she does, because she scrambles about the cabin, opens and slams the screen door, and by the time I open my eyes again, it's gone.

I breathe a deep sigh of relief and shudder, rubbing my bare shoulders, which are now prickling with goose bumps. I feel dizzy, unsettled. It's usually the flies that get me more than anything else. I don't know what it was about that moth, but it was particularly horrifying. My hands still shaky, I reach for my water bottle and take a long swig.

"Are you okay, Arlee?" Winnie asks, her voice laced with concern. She sits back down beside me on the bed, this time a little closer.

I could lie. I could make something up about having terrible spasms or a tic that comes on at random, but with Winnie, it feels wrong, plus deeply offensive to people who *do* have tics and spasms. "I . . . I'm really afraid of bugs," I admit, cheeks flushing. "Flying ones, especially. They're *horrible*."

Winnie raises an eyebrow, and for a second I think she's decided then and there that I'm a complete fucking shitshow, but then she cracks a grin and chuckles. "Shit. This place must be your personal Dante's *Inferno*."

I snort and then we're both laughing. Some of the shakiness melts away. "Yeah, it's, uh, something I'm working on this summer. I've been reading about exposure therapy, you know?"

Winnie chuckles. "All too well. Dad's still a big fan of psychology audiobooks. Car rides with him are always educational, you know?"

For just a moment, there's a brief, beautiful stillness between us. A comfortable kind of silence you usually only feel with people you've known a long time. Outside, the birds chirp and other girls talk and laugh, and I realize that I could just stay here, on this bed with Winnie, in this stillness, all damn summer long.

Then the screen door opens again. This time it's Anna

peering in, a bored expression on her face. "You two are late. As predicted by past events. History is a circle, et cetera. Campfire circle. Now."

"Oh, shit!" Winnie springs to her feet. "Sorry, Anna Banana." She reaches out a hand for me, and I take it, electricity sparking between our fingertips.

Winnie rubs her thumb against my palm, making me shiver. "Let's go meet the wild girls of Unit Seven."

CHAPTER TWO

By the time Winnie and I make our way down the hill, everyone else in the unit is seated on the two long wooden benches that encircle the campfire.

Six counselors stand with clipboards in hand and serious looks on their faces. No one is chatting or laughing anymore. All eyes follow us like a magnet.

Winnie dashes to find a seat, but there's no room left on her bench, so I have to make do sitting next to a girl I don't know. I try to flash her a small smile, but her face remains stoic as she gives a cursory nod, like we're at a funeral or church sermon or something.

My eyes dart back and forth across the faces of the other girls, who look just as serious and emotionless. My throat goes bone dry. A hint of metal on my tongue.

Christ, Mom, you said this wasn't a Jesus camp.

It seems as though we're all waiting for something, because the seconds stretch to minutes and still no one says a word. The silence is jarring, and in that quiet I can fully hear the crickets, the cicadas, the birds calling and singing softly. The forest is never silent, even when we are.

I bristle at a sudden, hollow clang of what sounds like church bells. They chime a strange, bittersweet melody, something in a minor key that sounds neither happy nor sad. It sounds . . . off. I don't recognize it, not even from my years of practicing both simple and complex songs on the piano.

After the song completes, the bells clang one solid tone three long times, then finally cease.

Anna clears her throat and taps her pencil against her clipboard. She nods to the six other counselors standing at attention. "Shall we begin?"

They nod in return. A ghostly pale counselor with hair so blond it's nearly white stomps her feet three times. So does everyone else. Everyone except for me.

"Unit *Sev-en!*" she calls out like a drill sergeant.

"Unit Seven," the campers say in unison. "Unit Seven countdown."

The pale counselor points to a girl at random . . . the girl next to me. "One!" the girl calls out, then looks at me expectantly, as does everyone else when I don't say anything.

"*Two,*" she mutters under her breath. "*You're two.*"

"Oh. Okay. Um. Two!" My voice cracks as I try to speak up, but by then the girl to my right is shouting, "Three!" and the next girl, "Four!" and on and on it goes, spiraling out from the center of the circle until the last girl shouts, "Thirty!"

"Thirty in Unit Seven," they all chant in military unison.

The girls all clap three times.

What the fuck?

"Welcome to another Rockaway summer!" the pale counselor says with a smile, and everyone's shoulders and faces relax in turn. "I'm Bea, last year's head unit counselor, but this year—and God knows I've earned it, dealing with y'all—you can consider me more or less retired." Some of the girls giggle. "Still, I'll be helping out your new unit head, Chantal, and the rest of your counselors with day-to-day programming and making sure none of you fall off a cliff and die or anything. As a reminder, wake-up time is eight A.M.—absolutely *no* dawdling—then weekday breakfast starting at eighty thirty on the dot, and then you have daily test prep at nine thirty each morning, barring weekends." A few girls groan, though in a good-natured, *we're used to this* sort of way. "I *might* consider allowing sleeping in until ten or ten thirty on weekends, but everyone *must* attend all their test-prep sessions and electives and get there reasonably on time. Understood?"

"We got you, Bea!" one girl cries. Across the circle I spy Jane and Olive, heads bowed, caught up in some hushed private conversation. Every now and then, Olive glances at me, but looks away as soon as our eyes meet.

"We *do* have one new camper joining our unit this year," Anna says in voice so flat and monotone it's like she's being sarcastic. "We should all be sure to introduce ourselves and help make her feel welcome. Welcome, Arlee!"

She extends her arm toward me, and all the other girls do the same.

"Welcome, Arlee!" they echo.

It's so weird, almost like something out of a bad sorority movie. I try my best not to burst out laughing, to smile and nod and play along with these echo-y rituals, even if they make me feel itchy all over.

"We probably should've worn name tags, considering . . . ," I hear Anna grumble to the other counselors, cutting a sharp glance at me over her shoulder. "Whatever. It'll be fine."

Once more, I feel like an afterthought, but also like the spotlight is glaring in my eyes at the same time.

Chantal, our unit head, introduces herself next.

"You'll be signing up for this summer's elective courses through me," she says in a curt, tight voice.

She reminds me a little of Megan Fox, like something out of a teen boy (or girl)'s action-movie wet dream. High, arched eyebrows and sharp cheekbones. Long, wavy dark brown hair. Her red T-shirt stylishly tied and cinched at the waist. I don't know why, but she instantly intimidates me. She passes out red folders for each of us, complete with detailed information and forms on all the electives available. Listed are what look like cool outdoor courses associated with the things I saw on the map: archery, swimming, horseback riding (which we're all required to do at least four weeks of), along with theater arts, music lessons, challenge courses, and on and on. Even an in-line skating course, which makes sense, given the rink. We have to decide by tomorrow morning which electives we want to take for the first half of the summer, and I get a rush of excitement at the prospect of choosing my own schedule. Mom always had so much say in my extracurriculars. She even forced me to choose piano over guitar.

"Let's do a quick icebreaker for this one!" Anna announces. She points at me in a way that makes me want to dig a hole into the ground and hide. "Go around. Names. Hometown. Whatever."

The names and hometowns spill out of all twenty-nine girls, including Winnie and Jane, as well as the two girls I met earlier in our cabin whose names I failed to recall: *Uma and Porter. Uma and Porter.* I repeat them in my head, over and over like a chant, as the other girls say their names and where they're from so fast it makes me light-headed.

Finally, the circle ends with me and the girl who called the number one, whose name I think is Rachel. "Arlee," I say, and I hate how quiet it comes out. I clear my throat and try again. "Hi, I'm Arlee! I'm from Raleigh."

But by then, no one is listening.

"Cabin meetings before dinner tonight!" Chantal shouts over

the din of voices. She hovers by me and leans so close to my face I flinch. "I'm in your cabin, Arlee. So is Bea. Come see me if you need anything, all right?" She doesn't smile, doesn't move to hug me or shake my hand, just nods and stalks off to where the other counselors are hanging out. Bea doesn't approach, either.

As the girls of Unit Seven stand and brush the dirt off their shorts and rompers, Winnie, Jane, and Olive bound over to me. A few other girls and counselors say hi and wave, including one counselor with kind eyes and the cutest white denim shorts I've ever seen. She even shakes my hand and introduces herself, but I'm so anxious I forget her name on the spot. Most, though, seem wary of me, not bothering to really look my way. If they do smile, it's a pinched, brief one, or one that quickly fades into a flash of what looks like . . . suspicion.

They must be wondering the same thing Olive was earlier: *Who the hell is this girl? Where's Vidhya?*

Or maybe . . . is it something else? Something related to my mom? *The* Sam Gold? The thought makes me feel more than a little uneasy.

Or is it just something about me? That's what I've been dreading. That they'll take one look at me and see how off I am . . . how wrong everything about me is.

The church bells toll once more in that strange, melodious harmony that everyone else seems to understand the significance of, before ending in three long notes.

"Hey, Arles," Jane says with a grin, elbowing my arm. "Now we finally get to eat something more than Winnie's Swedish Fish."

o o o

I walk with Unit Seven down a steep hill that takes us even deeper into the forest. The moss-covered trees above us seem to grow longer and wider with each step we take, their branches swaying in the afternoon breeze. Squirrels skitter across their gnarled trunks, and birds trill pretty songs, blending with the rise and swell of the voices of the girls.

More of the camp whizzes past as we walk: brightly colored cabins that belong to other units. A gleaming wooden studio with glass-paned floor-to-ceiling windows, yoga mats, and exercise balls stacked against a corner inside. Is this a camp or a resort? At times it's hard to tell.

A flash of white catches my eye.

Not so far off the forest path, a *thing*—no, a human figure in a mask—stands still between the trees, and I swear to God, it's wearing a long-faced, white wooden mask of a . . .

Horse.

I hang back from the group and stare. It seems to stare back at me with its big, empty black eyes.

The thing raises a human hand in greeting. My blood turns to ice.

"Winnie!" I breathe. "Do you see—?"

By the time she turns in my direction, the thing is gone. As if it were never there at all.

My heart pumps blood into my ears. A rush of dizziness passes over me.

"See what?" she asks. "Arlee . . . ? What is it?"

I want to tell her, want to attempt to explain, but I'm tongue-tied and embarrassed all at once and I can't. I don't want her to think I'm totally bananas. Not yet.

"N-nothing. Just a weird-looking bird," I stutter, and she gives me this look like she doesn't believe me.

"Must've been one creeptastic bird. You sure you're okay?"

"Just hungry."

Winnie gives me a sort of half grin, half grimace, then nods and strides ahead to the other girls. Girls who are obviously way less weird and skittish than I am. I sigh. That's the second time I've freaked out in front of her, and it's barely been two hours.

Part of me wishes I would've just been honest like I was honest earlier with her in the cabin. I watch her laugh with Uma and Jane, and it's there on the tip of my tongue: *Winnie, I saw the scariest shit in the trees. What the hell is it? Have you seen it before?* But I can't make myself bold enough to form the words.

Especially when it's entirely possible that I imagined it. When it might not even be real.

I cringe as we pass through a massive swarm of gnats, trying not to think about all their tiny little wings and feet in my face. I realize that I've strayed to the very back of the group, and that no one else is behind me. At least, no one that I'm aware of.

I glance over my shoulder, but there's no one and nothing there. Still, I pick up my pace, name all the states in my head in alphabetical order, count down from one hundred, anything to take my mind off that *thing* and its eyes. . . .

You really need to stop this, Arlee. You have an overactive imagination and it doesn't help that you're already so wound up. Remember what that doctor said. He was dismissive, yes, but he was probably right.

It's all in your head.

○ ○ ○

We reach the dining hall minutes later. Lunch is, thankfully, a far less bizarre endeavor.

Dappled sunlight falls through the screens in the wide, high-ceilinged building. From the rafters hangs a massive golden light fixture shaped like a pinecone. White wooden picnic tables are lined against the walls, and in the center are serving tables full

of finger sandwiches, a salad bar, fruit bowls, bread, and gourmet entrées like grilled salmon served with saffron rice. There
are plates of artichokes stuffed with vegan cheese and walnuts.
Fresh waffles with berry compote and cream on the side. Stacks
of grilled cheeses with truffle oil and tomato. Everything is carefully labeled with little markers written in stylish cursive, including potential allergy alerts and detailed nutritional content. It's
like something out of a five-star-hotel buffet.

My mouth waters. This certainly isn't burgers and hot dogs on
paper plates.

I'm so hungry and ready to eat that I move to sit at one of the
first tables I see, but a girl from another unit glares at me like
I've broken some unspoken rule, so I follow Jane and Winnie to
the back room. I sit at the end of the table next to Winnie, along
with two girls from our unit and two boys who look about our age.
While everyone seems to be free to intermingle at mealtime, it's
clear there are unspoken pecking orders, cliques, and established
territories. One of them is apparently ours.

The two Unit Seven girls at my new table are Uma and
Porter—Uma, with a crisp British accent and stylishly short,
slicked-back black hair, and Porter, a tiny brunette swallowed
by an oversized T-shirt, and the only other camper I've seen so
far besides me who wears glasses. Her gaze wanders around the
room, studying people before she murmurs comments under her
breath to Uma. I can almost see the wheels in her head constantly spinning.

The boys, I piece together, are dating. Reyes and Gabe hold
hands under the table and keep sneaking in kisses and little
glances as everyone else chats and I sit and observe. Reyes moves
with energy and emotion, filling us in on the latest camp gossip
through sweeping hand gestures. Gabe waits every few minutes
to make a well-timed, sly interjection that makes me laugh. My

stomach growls as the waffles and sandwiches taunt me from just a few feet away.

The food surely isn't getting any warmer. "When do we eat?" I ask, interrupting Reyes and Jane's intense discussion of some TV show I've never heard of.

Everyone at the table stares at me like I've appeared out of nowhere. Reyes bursts out laughing. "Oh my God, you're *hilarious*. What was your name again?"

"This is Arlee," Jane says, putting a protective arm around me. My leg bounces restlessly under the table. It's already been tiring, all this attention on me so far today. I feel like the new kid on their first day at school . . . only it's the world's weirdest, most elite prep school in the universe, and we all sleep in the woods.

"Arlee's awesome," Winnie chimes in, flashing me a smile that melts my insides and gives my spirits a bit of a rise.

"Brill," Uma says dryly. Porter snickers at her.

"Well, if *you* like her, Winnie, *we* like her. Right, girls?" Reyes prompts. Uma and Porter just smile politely before going back to their own private murmurs.

I reach for the glass cork-topped bottle at the center of the table and fill my own glass with water, taking a nervous gulp. It's delicious. Definitely not from the tap.

The clanging, bright sound of another bell echoes throughout the dining hall. It rings and rings until everyone quiets down.

Caroline Rhinelander stands at the threshold between the hall's front and back rooms, a cowbell in one hand. She looks as pristine and graceful as she did earlier, in her lavender pumps and striking pantsuit. "My campers, welcome to another wonderful summer!" she declares. As Caroline speaks, it's like the room is hypnotized. All eyes on her, campers and counselors alike nodding and smiling, much like the parents watched her with admiration in the Welcome Center. "I'm so excited to have all of you back, and if this is your first summer here, we are all delighted to welcome you." She has this strange lilt to her voice, like she's an Old Hollywood starlet plucked straight from a black-and-white film. "As always, the first two tables at the front left of each room will serve themselves first, and when they've finished, the next two will, and on and on. I know, you're all hungry, but patience is a virtue, is it not?"

Some people laugh, though good-naturedly.

"That's our Caroline," Jane says with affection.

"Have a great lunch!" Caroline trills. She gives the cowbell another ring, and suddenly everyone is talking again. Campers stand and line up to file their plates with food. My stomach growls in anticipation as I watch them. Maybe that's why I've been so anxious, dizzy. *Seeing* things. I'm famished. I take another long drink of water and refill my glass to the brim. I should make sure I'm hydrated, at the very least. Mom is always telling me I don't drink nearly enough water. The thought of Mom calms me down. If she were here, she'd tell me I have no reason to worry. She did say I was going to fit in, after all. That this would be a summer to remember.

Someone in line bumps against our table, knocking my water glass over and into my lap.

"Shit!" I hiss.

"Oh, my *God*, I'm so, *so* sorry!" A girl with blueberry-black bangs bends down to help me wipe up the spill, though most of it has already soaked right through my shorts. Fantastic. The girl places a hand on my shoulder and flashes me a guilty look. "Seriously. I'm such a fucking screwup. I *can't* believe I did that!"

"It's okay," I reassure her, swallowing down my irritation. "Seriously, it's no big deal. It's just water."

"Lisha, she's good," Jane says darkly, a bit of bite in her tone. I feel Winnie shift uncomfortably beside me.

The girl just blinks at Jane with a blank expression, then gazes down at me like I'm the only person who exists in the room. The only one who matters. She steps to the side so a boy can pass her in line. "Are you new? I haven't seen you here before. I'm Lisha, like she said."

I think I hear Jane scoff.

"Arlee. Yeah, it's my first summer here."

Lisha cocks an eyebrow and smirks. "Bet you didn't expect to go swimming so quickly. Water sports are popular here, sure, but usually not at lunchtime."

I laugh, the breezy way she jokes lowering my defenses. She laughs, too, her eyes still locked on mine.

Winnie clears her throat loudly. "Arlee. It's our turn to get food." She and the rest of the table stand. I notice they're all wearing similar expressions, like there's something about Lisha that deeply annoys them. I even catch an eye roll from Uma.

"Well . . . how about those waffles?" Reyes asks. Gabe gives a low whistle, like, *Well, this is awkward.*

"Fuck me, carbs and sugar are *exactly* what I need right now," Uma says. She, Porter, Reyes, and Gabe shuffle away. Jane singsongs, *"Excuse you,"* to Lisha as she pushes past us to get in line. Winnie follows, though she does look over her shoulder and beckon for me to come.

I hesitate. Why are they all being so rude? I'm starving, but it feels awkward to leave Lisha like this, so I decide to hang back for a little. "Sorry, Lisha. I . . . don't know what that was about."

Lisha's face hardens for a split second as she stares after them, but relaxes again when she turns back to me. "They don't like me," she says matter-of-factly, like it's no big deal.

"Yo, Lisha!" a boy calls from across the room, and I see it's the pale, freckled boy from earlier. The blond one with the sunglasses who wouldn't stop staring at me. "Get your ass back in line and come eat!" His friends next to him chortle.

"Keep your panties on, dipshit!" Lisha yells back, though it's playful, maybe even weirdly flirty. "Sorry about him. Zach is . . . ugh." She shudders and smiles all at once. "Anyway, sorry again for drenching you on your very first day. Hopefully next time, it'll be during a water-balloon fight or something." We both laugh. "Let's get some food, yeah?"

Even though my tablemates don't seem to like Lisha, she is one of the first people to show genuine interest in me, and it's given me a new burst of energy. Confidence, maybe, though I'm not used to feeling confident. I load up my plate until it's full with a bizarre arrangement of grilled cheese, berry-compote waffles drenched in syrup and butter, fresh fruit, raw veggies, and a heaping serving of French fries that I drizzle with ketchup. Enough to feed a whole family on Thanksgiving. There's even a coffee and tea section with jugs of fresh-squeezed juice in all kinds of fancy flavors. I treat myself to a giant glass of iced mint tea.

Back at the table, the energy seems to have gone back to normal. Uma and Porter even open up to me, explaining they're both from the same area of Boston, while Reyes and Gabe feed each other strawberries in between kisses on the lips. They're pretty adorable, and I can't help but glance at Winnie. . . .

You just met her, Arlee. Chill.

My heart thumps and my palms begin to sweat. I clear my throat and chime in, if only to distract myself.

"So, what's the deal with Lisha?" I ask. "Why don't you guys like her?"

Reyes clicks his tongue and looks away. Uma and Porter exchange an uneasy glance.

"She's bad news," Jane says in between bites of her vegan

cheese–stuffed artichoke. "Plus she hangs out with asshole Zach, who was notoriously *awful* to Winnie at last year's Midsummer Concert."

"Really? What did she do, though? And Zach?"

Winnie stares down at her plate. I notice she hasn't touched a single thing, not even her waffles (which are *amazing*).

"She . . . they . . ." Winnie takes a deep breath before letting out a massive sigh. "Let's just talk about this later, okay? Arles, don't worry about it." That's the second time she's said that. It stings. Does she think I'm not smart enough to understand or something? "Anyway, what are you guys choosing for your electives? I was thinking yoga, archery . . ."

"Oh, *definitely* yoga!" Reyes says. "Or maybe soccer. I really need to tone my thighs this summer."

"Please do," Gabe says.

I feel myself shrinking inward again. Sometimes these kinds of social interactions overwhelm me to the point where I just need to zone out and be alone with my thoughts. The conversation continues as I eat and sip my iced tea in silence, trying my best to just enjoy my food.

Now and then, I glance over at the table where Lisha and the alleged asshole named Zach are sitting. And now and then, I think I see Lisha wink at me.

∘ ∘ ∘

After lunch we do our count-off outside the dining hall. This time, I don't miss my cue. While the other Unit Seven girls gossip and joke, I walk alone, taking in the peacefulness of the forest path, the way the air smells so fresh and clean here. There's no honking cars or blaring sirens. No noisy neighbors blasting music and throwing parties late into the night.

Olive strolls over, matching my pace. "Hey, Arlee." She gives a sheepish, shy kind of grin. "Sorry I was weird earlier. I just thought you were . . ."

"Vidhya?"

She winces. "I was hoping it was her. Sorry. No offense. I like you! I'm glad you're here. It's just that—"

"It's okay," I assure her. I'm oddly soothed seeing someone act as frazzled as I've been feeling. "You don't have to explain if you don't want to."

She leans closer to me and murmurs, "Yeah, she, um, she was kind of my girlfriend."

"Oh, wow. Shit. I'm so . . . sorry. She didn't tell you she wouldn't be here this summer?"

Olive bites her lip. "Not exactly. We texted and FaceTimed all school year, but then she went silent right before camp started. I figured I'd see her here, but . . . I guess she didn't want to come back. She and Jane go the same prep school, and Jane did tell me today she'd decided to drop, and I get that they're close, but why didn't Vidhya tell *me*?" Her voice breaks over the pain in her words. "Jane didn't know why, either. Maybe it was me, I don't know. Or maybe it was . . . something about this place."

I feel a strange prickle of dread and my heart picks up speed again. I think of the strange terror I felt in the parking lot, the way Anna looked for a moment as though she'd sprouted fangs. The inexplicable buzzing energy in the air. The human *thing* in the forest wearing the long white face of a horse. "What about this place?" I ask.

"I . . . I don't know how to say it without sounding completely . . ."

"Bananas?" I offer. I've always hated using the term "crazy," even in jest.

She chuckles and so do I. "So, you get what I mean, then? I

mean, it's beautiful here. It's . . . almost like paradise. But there's something off, too. You know? Though I guess you wouldn't since you just got here." Her face crumples and her voice lowers to a near whisper, like she's about to tell me a secret. "I've felt that way since my first summer. I remember being so excited, that this place was so *cool*, and these people were so *awesome* . . . but then . . . things change you. Things I think you can only understand once you've spent time here."

My mouth goes dry. "What kind of things?"

We're at the rear of the group, trailing far behind the other girls. The air smells like honeysuckle and lavender. Lavender. The color of Caroline's pumps. There's a richness to every texture of this place, from the clothes the campers wear to the polished gleam of the glazed wood that makes up everything from benches and chairs to tables and buildings. The sun is high in the sky, but we're kept cool and shaded by towering trees. *Paradise.* I could see that. It could be like that here, and yet . . .

Olive stops walking, so I do, too. "Arlee . . . you talked to Lisha today at lunch, right?"

I blink in surprise. "How did you know that?"

"I saw you both and . . . well, I'm risking a lot, saying this to you now." The other girls are far ahead, and for the first time, even with Olive by my side, I feel strangely alone in these woods, on this dirt path. The once-friendly sounds of the birds and woodpeckers now seem oddly menacing.

Olive looks over her shoulder several times. When she meets my eyes, I see uneasiness in them. "There are secrets here. Deep secrets. This place has a lot of history, you could say." She starts to walk again, though slowly, so we can still remain relatively alone and unheard. "It goes back generations. What happens in these woods, and by the river . . . you wouldn't believe me if I told you."

The image of the horse-faced figure flashes through my mind, and suddenly it's difficult to breathe.

"I do believe you. I saw something. In the trees before lunch. A thing. A person wearing—"

"A mask?"

My mouth flops open. "You know about that?"

She nods gravely. "A few of us do. Most don't. They're watching you, Arlee."

I force a laugh that comes out all frantic, panicky. "You're not fucking with me, right? Because if so, *bravo*, this is a pretty great prank on the new girl."

Olive shakes her head, and I can see it in her face that she's not lying to me. "I'm not fucking with you. Don't be scared, okay? Just be aware. I can't"—she looks around again, like a mouse searching for an owl hiding in the trees—"I can't tell you who they are. Not yet. But just . . . be ready, okay?"

Then she sprints ahead to catch up the with group, like she's terrified to say anything more, and I'm left by myself, trailing far behind the others, mind whirring, breath shallow, looking over my shoulder every other step for the thing with the long white wooden horse face and its black, beady, unseeing eyes.

They're watching you.

CHAPTER THREE

I need to forget what I saw.

My bunkmates are singing pop songs at the top of their lungs. They're devouring candy, trying on each other's new summer clothes, catching up on all the details of an entire school year spent apart. They're careless. Buoyant. They've piled blankets and beach towels on the floor and added pillows for a kind of makeshift cabin living room. Jane's even tossed her huge stuffed elephant into the mix. Porter sits in Uma's lap, letting Uma twist her hair into French braids. Jane lies on her stomach just inches from them, feet propped in the air. Winnie is on a top bunk with Ginger—the only girl I haven't gotten to know yet—weaving lanyard bracelets out of something they call gimp.

I sit on my bed and pretend to flip through the magazine Mom bought me at the gas station on the way here.

Watching the girls, I think I understand. This is their element. Their home, away from the normal judgment of parents and peers, the typical stressors of school and teenage ennui. A family exists here, something deep-rooted and tangible.

I want so badly to be part of it.

To do that, I know that I need to forget what I saw and what I heard Olive say on the path. I know this instinctually, somehow, even though I can't exactly rationalize why.

It would probably be wise to go to a counselor, report what I heard from Olive, the masked figure I spotted in the trees. Speak up to an adult about my fears. But Chantal, Bea, Anna, and most of the other counselors seem too busy smoking cigarettes and downing beers in the vacant cabin next to the bathrooms, a hangout spot they call the "no-kids zone." They don't seem to give a shit what we do, so long as we more or less follow the rules and don't wander off the premises or, as Bea so kindly mentioned, fall off a cliff and *die*. Chantal came in briefly to divvy up our cabin chores for the week. She did a quick head count and reminded us to fill out our elective forms for tomorrow, and then she was off again, slamming the screen door behind her like she couldn't be bothered.

I know my parents are paying for state-of-the-art facilities and gourmet food, but they're certainly not getting their money's worth with these counselors' salaries.

"Ladies, I want to play something," Ginger announces. "I've had it in my head all day. Jane, can you grab my baby?"

The "baby" is Ginger's acoustic guitar, a gorgeous Taylor GS Mini. It's the kind of guitar I always wanted to own, the one I'd fantasize about tuning in the band room after school instead of the run-down public school ones I'd play before Mom drove me to piano lessons five times a week. Ginger props it on her lap and strums a few chords, tuning the strings and bobbing her head. My fingers itch to hold it.

"Arlee, quit hiding and get up here with us!" Winnie calls. "You'll have a front-row seat to the concert."

I happily abandon my magazine and my racing thoughts.

Climbing up Ginger and Jane's bunk bed is almost as hard as

scaling mine was, and I knock over a few things on the way up and apologize profusely, but Winnie tells me to quit it.

"Relax, Arles," she says. "Camp is supposed to be messy." She scooches over so I can sit beside her. Our knees touch, as do the hairs on our arms.

Ginger plays the first verse of a haunting little country-folk song. Her voice is sweet, somber, with a bit of rasp to it as she sings:

> *Fields of white and wild and green*
> *No one ever heard me scream*
> *Standing alone, daring to dream*
> *I tried so damn hard to be a good girl*
>
> *Summer sunshine in my eyes*
> *Bright as hell, those blinding skies*
> *They say this is where good girls go to die*
> *Too bad I've never been a good girl*

We listen, enraptured, Winnie so close to me I can feel the movement of her belly as she breathes. Our fingers inch just slightly closer, a surge of electricity sparking between them.

Then Ginger plays a sour note, throws back her wavy dirty-blond hair, and laughs. "That's all I got for now!"

We burst into applause and cheers. Winnie, I've noticed, has leaned a little closer to me.

"Bang on!" says Uma.

"Seriously, Ginger, that was *amazing*," Porter gushes.

"Juilliard is next!" Jane declares in between bites of her candy bar.

Ginger shrugs and plucks at a few strings. "Maybe. New York would probably be the best place for me, all things considered. Juilliard, or maybe Berklee in Boston."

"Where are you from?" I ask.

Their heads all swivel to me, like they're surprised I'm finally speaking.

"Texas," Ginger says. "The Dallas area. My family is awesome and everything but . . . I can't do it anymore. The general culture, the attitudes. It's too dangerous for trans girls. Especially now." She strums a minor chord.

"People are fucking sick," Winnie laments.

"The *worst*," Jane agrees. "Racist. Sexist. Transphobic. Homophobic."

"Launch them all into the sun!" Uma says with a wave of her hand. Porter laughs, still nestled in Uma's lap, even though Uma's long since finished braiding her hair.

"Thank God I have you all," Jane says with a sigh. "Thank God we have *this*." She gestures around the cabin, and I do feel it, especially now: that safe, warm energy. That sacredness that maybe I can be a part of.

"I'm so glad I got assigned here," I admit to them, letting my shoulders fall. "Seriously. I was so nervous coming in, and I still am, but you guys have made me feel so welcome . . . overall."

"*We're* so glad you're here," Winnie says, and the other girls nod. She gives my hand a gentle squeeze and my stomach does about forty-five somersaults.

We. I'm really doing it. Fitting in. Acting normal. Making friends. Finding my place.

Mom was right.

Mom would be proud.

Maybe it's awkward, and maybe it's the wrong time, but I feel bold enough to ask it. "So, why don't you guys like Lisha?"

Jane's mouth forms a wide O of surprise. Porter squeaks. Uma chuckles to herself, even though it's clearly not the least bit funny.

Winnie looks like she's maybe about to say something when the door creaks open.

Chantal pokes her head in. "Girls, unit meeting in thirty minutes." Once again, she points in my direction, but this time, she beckons with one long, slender finger. "Arlee. You're coming with me."

○ ○ ○

The vacant cabin smells like cheap beer and stale cigarettes.

Welcome to the "no-kids zone," I guess.

Beanbag chairs and bookshelves covered in scribbles and graffiti line the screened walls. From one corner, a portable speaker plays soft indie rock. In another is a humming minifridge. Must be where they keep the beers. We have electricity for the lights in our cabin, but nothing this fancy. Electronics aren't allowed for campers.

Anna is in one of the beanbag chairs, her feet propped up on a scratched-up old coffee table. She clutches a bottle of yellow nail polish, her toes and fingernails freshly painted the same cheery lemon color. Bea is in the beanbag next to her, legs tucked beneath her, openly sipping from a can of Corona Light.

"Hey, Arlee," she says, in a voice that doesn't quite sound inviting.

"Have a seat," says Chantal, plopping herself into a beanbag, leaving the only empty one left for me. The one right in the center of them all.

When I sink into the beanbag it's like I'm sinking right into the floor.

This close, I can finally study each of them. Anna's ponytail is down, her wavy blond hair long and loose down past her shoulders. Without that chirpy voice she used on me and Mom, there's something unsettling about her hardened expression, her thin lips pressed together, too-blue eyes considering me like some kind of predator.

I guess my first instincts were right.

Bea's startling pale hair is now pulled back into a bun with a purple bandanna. Her eyebrows are just as light, a contrast to her deeply sun-tanned skin. Or maybe she has a spray tan, it's hard to tell. All three of them wear the red Camp Rockaway T-shirts and jean shorts, but I notice other details: designer sneakers. A thick gold anklet on Bea that looks real. A silver nose ring on Anna that she didn't have on earlier.

Then there's Chantal. Megan Fox eyebrows. Full, beautiful lips, maybe plumped with fillers. High cheekbones and a perfect nose. This girl needs no makeup to look like a walking Instagram filter.

She carries herself differently than the others do, too. Guarded, yes, strangely wary of me, but confident and dignified. She's hard not to look away from, but I avert my gaze when she notices me staring. One of her sharp eyebrows rises like a question mark.

Chantal steeples her hands and assesses me. "Arlee Gold. How's Camp Rockaway been treating you so far?"

Anna and Bea watch me closely. I'm starting to sweat, even though it's pretty cool in here, with a giant room fan blasting. Bea clicks her long, pink nails against her beer can. *Click-click-click.* I don't know where the other counselors are, or why it's just the four of us in here.

What the fuck is this, some kind of mafia meeting?

I choose my words carefully. "Okay. Good, actually. Everyone has been really nice and welcoming so far." *Sort of. Except you three.* "I'm a little nervous but . . . I'm also excited to be here." I give an awkward laugh, but none of them laugh along with me or even crack a smile.

Anna presses her lips together. "We know your mom was *popular* here, back in her day." She says "popular" like it's a curse word.

What?

Chantal shoots her a warning look. "I'm *sure* she was, but we're here to discuss Arlee. She's not her mom."

Anna shrugs and pulls a pack of cigarettes from her shorts pocket, lighting one. It immediately starts to stink up the place anew. "Hopefully not, if the rumors are true."

"What rumors?" I ask. My palms start to itch.

Anna snorts. "Oh, I don't know, maybe the ones about her being a complete nightmare to her bunkmates and—"

"Enough!" Chantal snaps.

Mom, a *nightmare*? There's no way that's true . . . even though the thought of her being a bully did cross my mind earlier. The possibility, at least. Whatever, it's just a rumor. *Nightmare* is subjective. She was a teenage girl, after all. *Don't let it bother you,* I tell myself, though my face is growing warmer by the second. Still, this insistent thought prickles in the back of my brain, one I can't make go away: *You know why they're saying this, Arlee.*

Chantal turns her attention back to me and frowns. "This is your first summer here, yeah, Arlee? What made you decide to start now? Most of the campers begin as rising freshmen. You're the first Unit Seven girl we've had in years that started in the middle."

The middle?

"Uh . . . I didn't know that," I admit. "What do you mean, the middle? I thought this was like a camp that anyone could do a summer at . . . at any time?"

Chantal seems almost amused by me and my confusion. "So, your mom *didn't* tell you how things are here. That's certainly interesting." She glances at Anna, who nods in agreement, looking smug. "Regardless, we just want to make sure you're getting along with your bunkmates so far. Adjusting well. As you're new, we also want you to understand some ground rules."

Bea clicks her pink nails against her beer can again and takes a swig. "Don't look so nervous, Arlee. We're only here to get to know you. You want a beer to loosen you up?"

"Jesus, Bea, she's fine!" Chantal snaps. "You're fine, right, Arlee? Do you even drink?"

What the actual fuck is going on? I elect not to answer.

"Because while we've been known to let campers break a few rules now and again, we have a strict no-drinking policy here at camp. Did you know that, Arlee?"

"Unless I offer you one," Bea says, toasting her beer to me with a wink. "Our little secret, of course."

Chantal huffs in irritation. "*Beatrice.* Not the time."

Bea shrinks back into her beanbag chair and pouts.

"We also have a rule about staying in your cabin after lights-out," Chantal continues. "During the day, if given permission by another counselor, you can go somewhere else if you bring a buddy with you. At night you may use the bathroom, of course, but you aren't to leave the unit grounds. No matter who tells you what or what any of your unit sisters might say, *don't* listen to them. Come to me, because whatever you hear is probably bullshit. We absolutely need to know where all of you are at all times. Make sense, Arlee?"

I nod, even though that somehow feels like the wrong answer. Like no matter what I say or do, it'll be wrong to Chantal. She reminds me a bit of my old piano teacher: prickly, no-nonsense, and a little scary.

But I refuse to let her scare me. The way she's talking down to me, it's churning something deep inside me. A familiar old, simmering rage I've been swallowing down again and again . . . ever since what happened in the woods.

"What I said earlier, about attending test-prep sessions barring weekends. That's *also* nonnegotiable, Arlee." How many damn times is she going to repeat my name? Another wave of anger burns in my throat. "While we bend the rules around here on occasion and want you all to enjoy your summer, socialize, have fun . . . whatever, we also have policies we need to abide by, and that includes strict academic requirements. You are here, first and foremost, to improve your test-taking skills, are you not? Based on the practice test you applied with, I'd say for sure you need to—"

"Are you in college?" I interrupt her.

Anna and Bea's eyes grow wide, and it gives me this delicious, familiar feeling of satisfaction, like running into an old friend. Chantal's eyes narrow as she stares me down, back arched like a cat ready to pounce. Anna, on the other hand, maybe looks a little impressed. She shakes her bottle of lemon-yellow nail polish and begins to do her toenails. I sit up straighter and lean forward, facing Chantal head-on.

Not only does she *not* scare me, I realize, her provocations are fueling me. This burning something, whatever it is.

"Because you can't be much older than me, right?" I continue. "What, like, early twenties? I get it. I know kids here probably drink as much as you do. They probably party at night, too. You guys have a boss, things you need to do to keep her happy." I scoff. "I may be new here, but I'm hardly some naive homeschooled kid. Yes, I do drink sometimes. I do party on occasion. That doesn't mean I'm going to fail here or fail to attend test prep. I may not have the best SAT practice score, but I am fairly good at reading people. I know you're trying to intimidate me, *Chantal*, but I just can't figure out why. Or why anyone has such a problem with my mom."

For a long moment, none of them speak. I don't blame them.

This is a part of me that rarely emerges, and when it does, it shocks me, too.

Bea gapes between me and Chantal, waiting for her reaction, but when none comes, she bursts out laughing. "Jesus, Chantal. I don't think I've ever seen you speechless."

Chantal grits her teeth. Her cheeks are flushed. She doesn't bother to chastise Bea, not this time. All her attention is focused on me. There's something there, though, in her eyes. A spark of fear, maybe? Intimidation?

"Get out of here," she says darkly. "Don't make me bring you in here again."

Anna studies her newly yellow toenails. I think I see her smile to herself.

"Gladly," I say. I stand, steal a beer that I knew would be there from the minifridge, slam it shut, then walk right out of the vacant cabin and back toward mine. There is no greater rush than what I feel now. A surge of energy like a wave before the inevitable crash back down to earth, when I realize what I've done, the shit I've gotten myself into. The bridges I've no doubt burned already, and it hasn't even been a full day yet.

I crack open the beer and take a swig. It revs my engine a little longer.

They're shocked, I know. Most people are when this side of me comes out. It's like a vise or a trap, waiting out in the open, ready to snap the foot off whoever makes the mistake of taking the wrong step.

I know when people see me, they see timid, anxious. Insecure. For the most part, they're right. Most of the time, that side seems to win.

But they have no idea the kind of girl that Arlee Gold can be.

CHAPTER FOUR

I always assumed that my piano teacher hated me.

Not just moderately disliked, or found me annoying and willful.

Hated.

Miss Teresa never smiled. She rarely gave out compliments or praise, even when I played my scales perfectly for her, over and over. Even when I hit every note at just the right length during my recitals, my legs itching from the stockings Mom made me wear, and Mom and her friends would cheer and clap from the audience as though I was the incarnation of Beethoven himself.

For years, every day after school, while other kids raced home to play outside or go do some fun activity, Mom drove me down the long, bumpy road that led to Miss Teresa's house.

For years and years, I wanted nothing but to quit. When I first started going, I begged Mom to let me stop. Pleaded. Threw tantrums. One morning I even refused to get out of bed.

But Mom always won in the end, and so I went every time, even if I cried on the way there and all the way home.

"Stop that, Arlee," she lectured me the time I threw a toy car across my room so hard it broke. Her voice was ice-cold, her face pinched with fury. I'll never forget that look she gave me, like

I was bad and wrong. Like I was some defective child. "You're going. It's good for you. You'll learn to like it."

"I hate it!" I screamed. "I hate you!"

She flinched at that.

I raced outside and tore apart a neat pile of autumn leaves she'd spent the morning raking. Dad watched from the porch and said nothing. He did nothing. It's funny, how I'll never forget that, his lack of action.

Mom came outside, the front door slamming behind her, her voice growing meaner. "Arlee Samantha," she warned.

A plump little squirrel was scuttling across the base of the big oak tree in front of our house. The one that always shed so many red and yellow leaves.

I picked up a sharp rock, screamed, and threw it at the squirrel with all the might a seven-year-old can muster. The squirrel got away, but only by a hair.

Mom grabbed my arm and pulled me back. She kneeled down and made me look her in the eyes. "When you act like that," she said, her voice brittle, "you're no better than a *wild animal*. Do you understand me?"

I went quiet. The tears all gathered up inside me, stuck in my chest and my throat.

That's when the shame hit me. The horror at what I'd tried to do.

Hurt an innocent animal.

Mom's face shifted when she saw me give in. She smoothed out my hair, wiped away my tears, and promised me it would get better.

That I'd learn to love piano as much as she did.

I learned to stop fighting. I realized it was inevitable.

Miss Teresa's house was small and quaint, more of a cottage than anything else. What I remember most is how it smelled inside: mothballs. The faintest hint of licorice. A strange tangy scent she used for cleaning, and of course, her personal, distinctive scent: sandalwood and apple blossoms.

There are striking images that go along with the memories of smell: yellowing catalogues with clipped coupons littering her antique coffee table. The turquoise eyeshadow she always wore that would crinkle and crease as she scowled at me. An antacid tab dissolving in a tall glass of water before the start of each lesson, as if the anticipation of working with me was enough to turn her stomach.

"*Play*, Arlee," she would instruct, her voice harsh. "Play it like you mean it, and play it *well*."

She taught me everything I needed to know: scales, chords, fingering, the most efficient way to read sheet music for both hands. Learning to read the music was always the hardest part.

It was hours and hours of practice. I played until my hands ached, until my wrists felt numb, and then at home Mom would have me sit in front of our grand piano and practice more and more.

"You're a genius, Arlee," she'd say, her voice choking up with tears. "A musical prodigy. Keep playing, my love. One day you'll play for a symphony. Don't you believe me?"

"Yes," I said. I always said yes.

I remembered the way she stared at me. I swallowed down my feelings, pushed my thoughts to the back of my mind.

I kept playing. For her.

Because it felt good when she showered me with praise, even though I had to grit my teeth to get through every lesson, every recital, every second of practice. It felt affirming.

I craved Mom's validation. I became addicted to it.

Recitals took place in a cavernous auditorium downtown, the plush red seats filled with over a hundred people from all across the county, including Mom and her smiling, waving, misty-eyed friends. They were special recitals, Mom told me, for the top performers under seventeen.

Sometimes there were judges there to give advice or critique, though my mind would always go fuzzy and full of white noise when they said anything to me. All that mattered, all I could think about, as I sat onstage at the piano bench and hammered out my notes, was what Miss Teresa would think of me this time. If she would, finally, be satisfied. My stomach would roil and I'd sweat and flush hot and then cold until I played the final note.

I would take my bow to glorious applause, to the tears and proud smiles of Mom's friends, and Miss Teresa would be sitting backstage in the shadows of the wings, hands folded, face solemn.

She'd asked me things like, "Did you not notice the last two notes in that stanza were not staccato?" Things like, "So much repetition in this piece, and yet you always remain so inflexible with the tempo."

I'd always say, "I'm sorry, Miss Teresa."

And then one night after a particularly dizzying concerto I'd thought I mastered, I apologized once more. She turned her cold gaze on me, a gaze that could crush any heart like a wild, bleeding thing, and said, "Don't be sorry. Don't be good. Be *great*. Arlee Gold, you will never be great unless you listen to me. You aren't listening."

"I . . . I am, Miss Teresa."

"You are *not!*" she snapped, her voice like a slap to the face. "You want to me to tell you 'Good job?' You want me to tell you 'You did great'? I won't lie to you. I'll never lie to you. The worst thing I could ever do would be to tell you what your ego wants to hear."

I thought about telling Mom what she'd said, but then thought better of it.

No better than a wild animal.

I stuffed the bad feelings deep down inside, but it didn't stop the swelling anger from growing. Some days, I thought about breaking every plate in the house, every piece of fine china. So often, over and over, I thought about breaking every piece of my mother's heart.

Even though I loved her fiercely.

I kept playing the goddamned piano.

o o o

When I get back to the cabin, I'm a little surprised that I don't immediately collapse into a ball of anxiety. Surprised that I don't run to my bed and curl up and sob, racking my brain over what compelled me to speak like that to the head counselor of Unit Seven. Whom I share *sleeping quarters* with. Who could very easily cut off all my hair in the middle of the night, or throw my clothes into the darkness of the woods.

Strangely, instead, I feel weirdly calm, much calmer than I've felt for days. I hang out with my bunkmates, basking in the glow their presence emits, and open the folder Chantal gave me. It even includes a fancy red Camp Rockaway pen, my name engraved on the side of it.

After speaking with Winnie and Jane about their choices, I fill in my electives (riding, swimming, archery, yoga), satisfied with my decisions, even though I'm not normally so decisive or quick to make them.

I could ask them again about Lisha, but I don't want to break the peacefulness I've been feeling. This odd, lucid tranquility.

I take a shower and scrub my filthy sneakers as clean as I can in the sink.

Act normal.

Fit in.

That evening, I sit with my unit at the campfire circle once more. Chantal avoids me. Anna flat out ignores me.

I love that it doesn't bother me. As if I'm numb to it. At least, for now.

We sing camp songs, are assigned the horses we'll be riding for the summer, and drool as the delicious smell of hot dogs and burgers grilling fills the air. There are, of course, bean burgers, too, and Anna even brings out several veggie plates with hummus. The counselors make the meal, and our campfire roars, crackling and warming us. I'm not on my phone like I normally would be at this hour, or glued to the glare of my laptop screen. There are no distractions, nothing to keep me from savoring every single moment.

And with the campfire roaring, the bugs keep far away.

We eat and drink from our water bottles and enjoy the homemade lemonade Chantal set out for us on one of our picnic tables, and soon I'm singing the new campfire songs as if I've known them by heart forever. Roasting marshmallows on sticks and joining in on a game of charades, which Winnie has to remind me the rules of, since it's been a while since I've had friends.

I definitely don't mind her reminding me, either, because she keeps brushing past me in what doesn't quite feel like an accident as she demonstrates the game's many hand gestures. Olive and Ginger join in, and soon we're all bursting with laughter until our sides hurt. The flames from the fire lick my skin and for five luxurious minutes, Winnie sits next to me and leans her head against my arm as we watch Ginger desperately try to act out "motorcycle." Winnie sighs contentedly, and I practically melt.

The campfire fades away, as do the other voices and the chatter. My heart hammers against my chest and climbs up my throat, and when no one seems to be looking at either of us, I lean my head against her arm, too. It leaves my head feeling woozy and my body full of tingles that reach down to my toes.

We stay like that for quite a while until Jane pulls her away for a moment—something about a missing diamond earring she dropped in the dirt—but I can barely hear them because I'm buzzing like a bumblebee, the feel of Winnie's phantom hands and fingers still on my skin.

All night long, Winnie continues to giggle at all my jokes and lock eyes with me a little too long. She helps me learn the new songs and navigate the cookout. When one of my marshmallows falls into the fire, she grabs me another one and places it into my palm, letting her hand linger in mine.

It's beyond exhilarating.

As we wind down for the night, I brush my teeth to the symphony of crickets and owls and the low murmur of happy voices. I wash my face as quickly as I can, so I can get out and away from the horrifying wings of the bugs attracted to the bathroom lights.

Back in my cabin, my bunkmates and I play round after round of crazy eights, stuffed with roasted marshmallows, burgers, and candy. We're all laughing until it's hard to breathe, feeling as light as air. We're cozy and dressed in our sleep clothes, and the night breeze is blissfully cool through the screens.

Chantal and Bea's bunk bed remains empty. They must be out partying somewhere deeper into the belly of the camp, or maybe by the river at the big counselor welcome-back party, as some of the girls have gossiped.

Good riddance, I think. Bea has been nice enough to me, but Chantal . . . She seems to hate me, and I have no idea why.

Maybe I gave her a real reason to in that vacant cabin.

For now, though, my body feels connected to the dusty wooden floorboards and the blankets we sit on in our makeshift cabin living room, my head spinning with happiness. It's like I'm being rooted to this place. To these girls surrounding me.

Sister, I think, like Mom said this morning about Caroline Rhinelander. Maybe now I'll learn why. Maybe I'll learn what it feels like to have a sister.

Mom was right. There is something rare and magical here. Strange and eerie as it's been today, it's like Camp Rockaway is already beginning to claim me.

CHAPTER FIVE

I wake to the sound of a militant bugle call. I check my watch. Eight A.M.

Jane groans in protest, her huge stuffed elephant toppling off her bed and to the floor. Above me, Winnie rolls over and mutters a curse. Ginger sits up slowly in bed and rubs at her eyes. Uma is still snoring away.

Porter has been up for some time now. She lies on her made bed, fully dressed, reading a book.

I, too, feel wide awake. Startlingly so, considering how late we stayed up. Like I could run a whole lap around the camp and then swim thirty laps in the pool. I pop my glasses out of their case and slip them on, the world sharpening into focus.

It's cloudy this morning, with a touch of humidity in the air. We go to the bathroom to brush our teeth and wash our faces. Some girls shower, but I prefer to do it later in the day so I'm not as gross and sweaty when I finally get into bed.

"Lord, grant me coffee," Jane whines, banging her head against Winnie's arm. "No one talk to me until I get it." She's bleary-eyed and can't stop yawning.

"I'll ask my dad to send me some cold brews," Ginger promises through a mouthful of toothpaste. "They won't *stay* cold but, they'll be good for wake-up."

"Bless you, Ginger," Winnie says.

I run my toothbrush under the tap and add an oversized glob of toothpaste. "The counselors have a minifridge in the vacant cabin," I say, and the girls in the bathroom stare at me. "It's where they keep the beers, and other liquor, I'm sure."

In spite of her moodiness, Jane chuckles. Winnie grins. She faces the mirror and pops in her contact lenses. "Well, damn, thanks, Arlee. Thank God you're here."

Back in the cabin we get dressed, and I notice Bea and Chantal are still missing, their beds un–slept in.

Weird as it is, I'm relieved. I'm starting to feel embarrassed about my outburst yesterday, shame and anxiety creeping in where that weird peacefulness was temporarily. . . .

Don't think about it. Act normal.

I will. I vow to make today a good day. A better day.

From my footlocker, I choose a comfy sports bra and matching underwear, douse myself in a layer of spray-on sunscreen and bug spray, then consider the rest of my options. Yesterday I wasn't super into my outfit, and felt weirdly underdressed compared to the rest of the campers here. Today, I try something new: a sky-blue T-shirt that's soft to the touch and loose-fitting, paired with high-waisted black cotton shorts. Nothing in my wardrobe is as fancy as what these kids wear, but I can at least make an effort. I slip my compact mirror out of my shower caddy and inspect myself, then tie a knot at the end of my T-shirt so it cinches at the waist. Instead of a ponytail or a bun, I leave my hair down and long, and smile at my reflection in the tiny mirror.

I look cute. Really good. Pretty, even. Mom always said you should dress for the role in life you want to play, and for me, that's the girl who effortlessly fits in here. When I turn around, Winnie is pulling on dip-dye shorts that accentuate her waist. My face reddens as I catch a glimpse of her Calvin Klein sports bra before she slips into a slinky black tank top. She combs the ends of her thick black hair, long enough she can pull it back in a tiny bun, but short enough it only hits halfway down her neck. When she turns around, she most definitely notices me staring.

My breath catches in my throat. I want to look away, but that would feel creepy somehow, so I smile at her, and she grins again at me in that crooked way she does. My heart soars out of my chest and up to the wooden ceiling rafters. Winnie doesn't break eye contact for several seconds.

Is she being flirty, like she was last night?

No, it can't be. I'm just crushing too hard, too fast, and seeing what I want to see. Mistaking friendliness for romantic interest.

Right?

We sit at the campfire circle and wait again in silence for that strange melody of the bells that end in three final long, somber notes. I'm not quite sure if it's their hollow sound or the bite of chill in the morning air that makes me shiver.

"Unit *Sev-en!*" calls out a counselor whose name I don't remember. She definitely did not say hi to me yesterday.

"Unit Seven," the campers say in unison. "Unit Seven countdown."

As we do our count-off, Chantal and Bea are still nowhere to be seen. This time, as we go down the line, I shout, "Two!" with gusto, like I've been doing this all my life.

The path to the dining hall is blessedly free of masked figures and general paranoia. Olive walks with Jane at the front of the group, while I hover in the middle with Ginger and Winnie. The air is refreshing, dewdrops clinging to blades of grass and vibrant green leaves.

I intend to sit with the same group I did yesterday, as the pecking orders here seem well established, but when I enter the dining hall, someone bumps me gently and nearly knocks me off-balance.

"Hey, girl!" It's Lisha, beaming at me. She wraps me in a big hug, like we haven't seen each other in weeks. "You're joining *us*, yeah?"

My gaze flitters back and forth between my group and Lisha's table, where the freckled white boy sits, along with two of his bunkmates and . . . Anna.

A question floats through my mind: *Is this even allowed?*

"Um . . . I was going to—"

Lisha places her hand on the small of my back and gently steers me in the direction of her table. "My friends are *so* excited to meet you, though, of course, you know Anna, *duh*. She's the coolest, isn't she?"

I glance back at my group and mouth, *I'm sorry* to Winnie, who I think looks a little sad. Jane's eyes narrow and I see her whisper something to Uma. Porter shakes her head and sighs. Reyes and Gabe arrive seconds later, but I guess they're too loved-up to notice my absence.

"Come, sit!" Lisha squeezes in next to one of the boys, then pats the spot beside her at the end of the bench. "God, I'm *famished*. I was on this Whole30 diet all spring and I am so fucking glad to be breaking the fast, so to speak. I'm about to go to town on that French toast." She laughs in this bubbly way. "Oh, guys, this is Arlee Gold. Unit Seven. It's her first summer here. We like her. A *lot*."

I can't help but tingle with glee at so many people accepting me so quickly. Well, save for a handful of my counselors . . . and everyone in Unit Seven who isn't my cabinmate, who still seem largely suspicious of me, though I suppose that's normal with me being new, right? Anna doesn't seem particularly happy that I'm sitting at her table, but she hasn't told me to fuck off yet, either. Points for that?

Instead she shoots me a sarcastic smile that quickly dissolves into her usual stoic expression, while the boys introduce themselves. I forget their names as soon as they tell me, though I think one is maybe Mike or Michael. All I can focus on is Zach.

The alleged asshole who was awful to Winnie at last year's Midsummer Concert.

I want to hate him automatically for that, but part of me really wants to give him a chance . . . just like I've been giving one to Lisha. She's been nothing but kind to me so far, after all.

I can almost hear Mom's voice in my head. "Not everyone gets along, Arlee Samantha."

Zach's big brown eyes seem to cut into me, slicing me into little pieces, though not in a bad way, per se. He's handsome—very handsome—with high cheekbones and pouty lips, much like Chantal's. He wears a backward baseball cap, his floppy brown hair peeking through. He leans forward against the table on his elbows, muscular, freckled arms revealed by a green Boston Celtics jersey. The kind of guy to wear athleisure with cologne at camp, and it smells expensive.

The freckles cover nearly every inch of him.

When he speaks, his voice is deep, deeper than most teen boys, and rich and warm as dark roast coffee. "That shirt looks really good on you, Arlee," he says, eyes cascading down my face and landing on my chest. They stay there for a moment before he looks back into my eyes, leaning forward a little more. "Where you from?"

"Raleigh."

His guy friends make some general comments of approval about the college-sports scene there. They, too, wear professional basketball jerseys, though clearly the kind for fans, not professional players.

Zach takes a sip from his water glass, then lets out a long, refreshed *"ahhh"* before following with, "Thinking about NC State? Though to be honest, you look like the kind of girl who'd get into Duke no problem. Chapel Hill is great and all, but you can't beat Duke. You play sports?"

I've never heard someone tell me I look like the kind of girl who could get in anywhere, and it disarms me. On one hand, it feels like a compliment, but on the other . . .

"What about me looks like the kind of girl who'd get into Duke?" I ask with a smirk.

Anna's eyebrows shoot up to the sky. Lisha tilts her head, as if considering me in a new way.

Zach flashes me a wolfish smile. He leans in even closer, so close I feel his breath (which smells like spearmint) on my cheek. "The kind of beautiful girl who has brains and the appropriate amount of balls." Then he leans back, satisfied with his retort, winks, and starts chatting it up with the guys.

It takes me a second to gather that my heart is racing, my cheeks burning. I feel tingly again, only for a different reason.

No, I don't play sports, but something about Zach might make me interested . . . even if he is an asshole.

Or *was*. That was last summer, after all. Maybe he's changed.

Caroline Rhinelander rings her weird little cowbell and welcomes us to our first Camp Rockaway breakfast.

"Remember to be *on time* for your test prep this morning," she announces, "as being *on time* and orderly ensures you may enjoy all the things you really came to do here!" That gets a few laughs and a loud scoff from Anna.

"Be more theatrical, Mom," she murmurs.

The spread this morning isn't quite as fancy as it was yesterday at lunch or brunch or whatever kind of gourmet meal that was. Still, it looks incredible. When it's our turn to get food, I load up my plate with scrambled eggs, hash browns, fresh fruit, and toast. Something about this dining hall, the way it smells like fresh cedar and sizzling bacon, sets off that same ravenous feeling in my stomach.

I set my plate down at the table and head to the drinks station, deciding to treat myself to a steaming mug of Colombian coffee. Olive is in the middle of pouring herself a glass of orange juice. She waves when she sees me.

Once again, she's effortlessly stylish in a slouchy maroon tank top, frayed denim shorts, and a silver horse necklace. A pair of designer sunglasses is perched atop her head. I praise myself for putting a little more effort into looking good this morning. Though I can never look as good as anyone here.

"Excited for a rousing test-prep session?" she asks with a playful roll of her eyes.

"Oh, it's truly the one thing I've been looking forward to most about being here."

She laughs. "Well, see you in our special daily hell, then." As she moves past me, she slips something into my hand. Something that feels like paper.

At first, I think maybe it was a mistake, that she didn't mean to give me something. I open my mouth to call to her, but she's already back at her table, chatting with Ginger and other girls from our unit.

I glance over my shoulder a few times, then open my palm.

It's a small golden envelope with beveled edges. A message is scrawled on the front in neat cursive: *Open when you are completely alone. Mention this to no one. If you do, we'll know.* I flip it over. There's a maroon wax seal on the back with the insignia of a horse.

The same horse dangling from Olive's necklace.

Goose pimples prickle on the back of my neck, and though it's warm in the dining hall, a chill goes through me. I slip the envelope into my pocket and resolve to deal with it later. But my hands start to shake as I add sugar and milk to my coffee and stir, and keep shaking when I sit with my table.

Zach's plate is absolutely piled with pancakes drenched in syrup, bacon, sausage, ham, the works. He shovels the food down his throat like it's his last meal on earth. "God*damn*, this is good," he gushes. "My mom is the worst fucking cook. It's nice to eat a real meal again."

Okay, so, he's hot but . . . kind of sexist. Noted.

Maybe he didn't change.

Lisha nudges me with her elbow. "You okay, Arlee? You look like you've seen a ghost."

I force a smile and nod, willing my hands to stop shaking. I'm hungry, that's all it is. I take a few bites of eggs, then put my fork back down. They're delicious, but my stomach suddenly hurts again.

"So, you coming to the barn parties, Arlee?" Zach asks. Syrup drips down his chin. I spot Anna give him a swift kick under the table, but he doesn't react. "You'd like it. Camp's fun and shit, but the barn parties—"

"Oh, I just *know* I didn't hear that," Anna warns, glaring at him. Zach's face flushes for a moment.

When her back is turned and she's caught up in conversation with someone at the table behind us, he leans in close to me and whispers, "Every Saturday after lights-out. You should come by sometime, Arlee."

"Yeah," one of his friends whispers in agreement. "The barn parties are dope."

"Sick," echoes the other.

Lisha tears at the ends of her paper napkin and stares into her bowl of corn flakes.

I can't focus on this. My leg won't stop jiggling. My heart won't stop pounding. I need to know what's inside the envelope, and *now*.

"Cool. Awesome. Where's the bathroom?" I ask, then make a beeline for it when one of them points the way.

Once inside, I lock myself in a stall and pull the golden envelope from my pocket. I have this sudden urge to tear it open, but something about its delicate nature compels me to be careful.

Inside is another note on a sheet of thick paper. Written once more in cursive is the message:

You have been invited to join a secret camp sisterhood. If you wish to proceed, initial the bottom of this note and hand it back to the sister who passed it to you before sunset tonight. If not, destroy it and let no one see it or hear of its existence. (We'll know if you did.)

My mind whirls. A sisterhood. A *secret* sisterhood. At a summer camp? Was Mom part of it? Was that why she referred to Caroline as her sister?

It would make sense. *The* Sam Gold. Mom was kind of a legend, maybe.

Olive's horse necklace, the horse-masked figure I saw on the path . . . they have to be connected. Why a horse? What would it symbolize? What could it all mean?

It's all I can think about during the rest of the meal, while Zach brags to the guys about how he's going to win every one of his soccer intramural games this summer, and Anna and Lisha discuss something in low voices. I chew my food without tasting it and gulp down my coffee.

Should I do it? Say yes to the invite? I only have until sunset to decide, and that's what, in, like, ten hours? I told myself I wanted to fit in here more than anything, and this could be my chance. I don't know any details, like who is in the sisterhood, or what it entails to become a member. I'm still not entirely sure it's not some cruel prank. But Olive wouldn't do that to me . . . right? In each of our interactions so far, she seemed sincere. Like she was willing to share things with me . . . willing to trust me.

Though she warned me this place could be dangerous. Unless she's an amazing actress, there's no way she was making that up, right? I think of the masked figure staring me down with its empty gaze, and shiver.

Maybe I shouldn't.

The invitation is all I can focus on as we head back outside. Bea leads our unit count-off. Chantal stands close beside her, watching us call out our numbers and nodding in approval like a proud drill sergeant. Then Chantal gives a big yawn. Both she and Bea have deep bags under their eyes, like they haven't slept a wink. Like they were out doing anything but sleeping.

"*Party animals*," I hear one girl murmur. "How come they get all the fun?"

"Saturday, Emily," her friend whispers back. "Just wait till Saturday. . . ."

Was that where they were? Partying? It could be, but maybe that's what they want us to think. . . .

"It smells like rain," Winnie says, joining me in step as our unit heads to our very first test-prep session of the summer. "I hope it doesn't rain today, because I'm dying to get a bow in my hands."

Her smile is friendly, warm, and inviting, but it doesn't draw me in like it normally does. With each step, the golden envelope weighs heavier in my pocket. I can hear my watch ticking down the seconds—

"Arlee? Did you hear what I said?"

"Huh? Sorry. What?"

"I said, you're doing archery, too, right?" Winnie asks patiently. "Are you okay? Is something on your mind?"

"Yeah, yeah, sure." I hear her, but it's like her words don't fully connect to my brain. She frowns at me in confusion. "I mean, yes, I'm doing archery, and yes, there is something on my mind, actually." I lower my voice and sidestep us away from the main group. "Do you know where Chantal and Bea went last night?" I can't ask anyone directly about the secret sisterhood, so maybe I can get information covertly.

Winnie's frown of confusion deepens. "No? They . . . do go off by themselves sometimes and do their own thing, but all the counselors do that. We all have a lot more freedom here than at most camps, I guess you could say. What did they want to talk to you about yesterday, anyway? You didn't tell us, so I figured it wasn't a big deal, but I'm wondering if maybe it was?"

I flinch at the memory of me exploding in Chantal's face, lashing out at the head of Unit Seven on my very first day as a new camper. It feels like a fuzzy dream I had, like it didn't even happen. "It wasn't," I lie, kicking at a stray pinecone in my path. "They just wanted to welcome me and make sure I was adjusting well and stuff."

"Oh, good!" Winnie's face brightens again. "You are, right? I really do hope so, because we're all really glad you're here, Arlee."

The way she says it and the way she's looking at me now make my nerves start to settle, makes my body and brain feel pulled back down to the earth. Back to the same rooted sensation I had last night, when all of us were laughing and alive and on fire with love.

She extends her arm, and I link mine through it. A warm, honey-drizzled feeling courses through me all the way to the

Little Amphitheater. It's where Unit Seven will be doing test prep every weekday morning.

We sit on the wooden seats, carved with owls and deer and horses, passing around a coffee tin filled with different-colored pens and pencils. Each of us receives a spiral notebook with CAMP ROCKAWAY written on the front in golden lettering.

During the beginning, I mostly I tune out. I let my mind wander as our instructor—a soft-spoken Unit Seven counselor named Ruth, one of the few to actually acknowledge me yesterday—writes out a number of target test scores on the chalkboard. Scores needed to get into the most elite, competitive schools. The smell of rain grows stronger and the clouds darken, but in the Little Amphitheater, we're covered by a massive wooden canopy.

Ruth asks us to take five minutes to ourselves and write down a list of expectations we have for this summer. The other Unit Seven girls hunch over their notebooks and dutifully write out long, detailed lists, while I doodle little horse faces in each corner of the first empty page.

Ruth asks us next to list ten things we're most worried about when it comes to the ACT and SAT.

I think about the envelope.

The masked figure I saw on the path. The sightless stare of the horse face.

I begin sketching an open grassy field full of grazing horses. I imagine what it will feel like to ride one along a forest trail. If I close my eyes, I can almost feel the horse's muscular back beneath me, its coarse mane wrapped between my fingers. . . .

This always happened to me in school. The teachers spoke, and though I heard it, my brain turned everything to white noise. People in class nodded and took notes while I found hidden patterns in the brick classroom walls.

Mom said she thought maybe being outside in the fresh air as opposed to a stuffy room would help me concentrate, but that doesn't seem to be happening. How can I possibly focus on tests and numbers when there's so much to hear in the forest? Rustling leaves, songbirds, woodpeckers. Creatures scuttling through the dirt. A symphony of sounds.

How can I be expected to think about things like tests and colleges when the summer is laid out before me like a tapestry of possibilities? When I've been offered this strange, rare chance to join a secret sisterhood?

When I only have hours left to decide?

Winnie elbows me.

"Your turn," she whispers.

I look up from my new sketch pad. Everyone is staring, waiting for me to speak. Ruth's eyebrows are practically raised to the rafters of the canopy.

My mouth flops open but I can't find the words. I don't know the question, and so I don't know the answer. I glance at Winnie for help, and she softly murmurs, "One thing you're worried about when taking the test."

"Thanks," I whisper back, and she nods but gives me this funny look, her eyes flickering over my drawing of a horse field. Cheeks burning, I close my notebook and clear my throat.

"Concentrating," I say. A few girls snicker, though if it's at me or with me, I can't tell. "I'm worried I won't be able to stay focused the whole time."

Ruth's face relaxes. She asks the rest of the girls to raise their hands if they're worried about that, too, then launches into a quick spiel full of advice on how to stay focused. Her words grow wings and flap right through my ears and back out into the darkening sky. There's a faint sound of thunder in the distance, but still, it doesn't rain.

This is how every test prep for the rest of the summer will go for me. I can feel it. Mom is wasting her time and money sending me here. I shut my eyes and cradle myself in my arms, trying to forget where I am. After a while someone gently taps me. I look up to see Ruth standing over me.

The rest of my unit is gathered by the amphitheater entrance. I hadn't even noticed the session end or anyone get up. Not even Winnie gave me a heads-up, though now she watches me expectantly.

Jesus Christ. How long have I been sitting here?

"Hi, Arlee," Ruth says. Unlike most of the other campers and counselors, she's dressed simply, in a striped linen pullover and denim shorts, her brown hair pulled back into a functional ponytail. She kneels down until she's at my level and offers a smile. The teachers at school used to look at me like this, too, eyes full of pity. *Poor Arlee. We should help her. Why won't she let us help her?*

"Listen," she goes on, voice soft as raindrops. "I know this all can be really overwhelming, especially when you're new, but just know that I'm in the main office every day from three to five, if you'd like to skip an elective and get some extra help." The teachers used this same tone with me, too, like I was so delicate their words might break me. I spot Chantal at the head of where the group gathered, shooting me an icy glare. Some of the girls turn to look at me, too, including Jane and Ginger.

Everyone is waiting. They *have* been waiting. I'm holding them up for who knows how long. *Oh God, Oh God.*

My heart pounds so hard I can feel it throbbing in my ears. Shit. Shit. *They know I'm a freak and I ruined it and I need to stop it RIGHT NOW and act normal and—*

I stand so quickly I trip over my seat, my notebook and pencil scattering to the floor. Ruth reaches out to help me, but I shrug her off. "I'm fine, thanks," I mumble. "I'll think about it." I grab my stuff and hurry to where the rest of the group is, face on fire and stomach roaring, utterly horrified. I wade into the sea of girls and do my best to blend into the center as Chantal calls for a count-off. I squeeze my notebook to my chest and try to breathe.

"One!"

My voice cracks as I yell, "Two!"

I was doing so well so far, fitting in. Not being weird. Not making waves. Except I did snap at Chantal in front of Bea and Anna, and I *did* act pretty awkward at breakfast this morning, and now I've gone full space cadet and made a fool of myself in front of everyone in my unit and—

Get it together, Arlee.

No, no. This isn't me. I left that girl behind in Raleigh. The first two years of high school are over. I'm not that Arlee anymore. I promised myself I wouldn't be.

But I can feel her all the same, as we walk back to our cabin to get ready for our next activity, and Ginger starts up some small talk with me about instruments. She must feel sorry for me. That must be why she's talking to me, after I drifted off and spaced out and made myself look so foolish.

I thought this summer would be different.

I thought . . . and yet.

"You good, Arles?" Jane asks. She wraps her arms around me from behind. "You awake after your midmorning nap?"

"God, that was so *boring*," Ginger whines. "I don't blame you for spacing out. I usually do, too."

Uma yawns dramatically. "Every fucking morning. Can you believe we have to sit through that every fucking morning?"

"Excluding weekends." Porter adjusts her glasses as she reminds Uma. "I don't know, I found it pretty informative."

My heartbeat starts to slow. The fire burning in my face fades to embers.

They don't think I'm a freak at all. They didn't see what I thought they saw.

"Ruth's voice is so soft it's like a damn lullaby," I say, and they all laugh in agreement.

"Puts me right to sleep," Uma agrees.

"So dreamy," echoes Porter.

Oxygen floods my lungs. I smile at them, and once more, I feel rooted. Calmed. Like nothing weird just happened, like that's all I was doing . . . just spacing out.

Except . . . Winnie keeps giving me that same funny look from earlier, when I was daydreaming and doodling all kinds of nonsense in my notebook.

Chantal appears beside me and says, "Everything all right, *Arlee Gold*?" It doesn't exactly sound like she's all too concerned about my well-being.

"I'm fine," I mutter. I wish I had the guts to ask, *Are you still mad at me for blowing up at you? Do you hate me? Actually, should I hate you? I mean, why are you such a bitch?*

She stares at me for a long moment, as if searching my face for the real answer, then nods and strides ahead, matching her pace with Anna and Bea.

On whether or not she hates me, and why, I guess I'll have to wait and see.

o o o

My first elective is horseback riding. Back at the cabin, I bounce around until I can yank my jeans on, then lace my boots and grab my helmet and refill my water bottle at the pump outside. I tuck the golden envelope under my pillow and whisper to it, "I'll figure you out later."

I can almost hear it whisper back, *I'll be waiting. Nine more hours.*

I spend the rest of the morning getting to know my new horse, Velvet. She's a sleek black Friesian, gorgeous and a little feisty. I'm in a beginner class along with Olive. I rode for a few years as a kid, but I definitely could use the refresher. Most of the other campers in this class are rising freshmen, including a nervous-looking boy who jumps every time his horse stamps its feet or our instructor, Cara, snaps at us to "mind their backsides" and never walk where the horses can kick us in the head.

We learn to put on their bridles and blankets and saddles, how to mount them and get comfortable sitting on the backs of these magnificent beasts. Cara reminds us of the correct way to hold their reins as we steer them toward the ring we'll be practicing in, and as I mount Velvet, I give her a pat on the neck, running some of her coarse mane through my fingers.

"We'll be friends, I can tell," I whisper to her.

The only problem is the flies. Though we spray our horses down with special bug repellent, the horseflies come all the same. The flies land on the poor horses' legs, knees, rumps, and even their eyelashes. Velvet's body twitches and shivers in the spots where the flies invade. She stomps her feet, shakes her head, rubs at her legs with her bridled mouth. They buzz away and come right back. I swallow down a familiar scream.

Thankful for my long pants, I focus on how, sitting on Velvet—my helmet buckled under my chin, sweating in my leather boots and jeans in the summer heat—I feel regal. Calm and focused.

Even with all the disgusting flies.

We practice riding in circles around the ring, and Cara lets us try trotting, though the nervous boy nearly slips out of his saddle and declares he's done for the day. I sit atop my horse, fighting back the urge to kick her into a canter and run us the fuck out of there.

Olive gives me no sign. No signal. If she's anxiously waiting for my reply, she sure isn't showing it.

Next is aquatics. I change into my blue one-piece in the pool bathroom, extremely conscious of the way I feel wearing a bathing suit. Especially around so many boys.

But the chlorinated water feels amazing after so much sweating in the ring. Our instructor, Eric, demonstrates the backstroke, the breaststroke (which gets laughs from some of the boys), and the butterfly stroke. I tune out his whistle and his voice and pretend that I'm a butterfly, weightless in the air instead of the water.

Even though the envelope is back in my bed in the cabin, it still weighs heavily on my mind.

Could it be dangerous to accept the invitation? Here in the sunshine, in the huge swimming pool with so many impossibly beautiful people surrounding me, that doesn't feel remotely possible. No one else here seems nervous or scared in the slightest. Even the youngest campers appear calm and focused on the day-to-day. If they're homesick, they don't show it. It's like they all know deep in their bones that they fit in and belong here. Even though it's their first summer, and presumably their first summer away from home.

It definitely is mine. I've never been away from Mom for more than a few days at a time. Even that time Dad came crawling back and convinced me to come with him to his scummy apartment fifty miles away, I called Mom to pick me up and take me home not even an hour into my visit.

A younger boy in bright blue swim trunks does a cannonball into the pool, splashing an equally young girl in a yellow bikini who just finished toweling herself dry. Rising freshmen. She shrieks and flips him off. "Douchebag!"

He smirks and spits water at her between his teeth before he growls, "*Bitch!*"

She looks as though he's slapped her right in the face with that word alone.

Eric blows his whistle and gives the time-out hand signal. "That's enough! Jonathan, no cannonballs, this isn't free swim! Melody, why are you out of the pool? Are you okay?"

Blue Trunks Boy's smirk grows even wider. He says it in a low enough voice so Eric can't hear, but his friends behind him sure can. "She has her period and she forgot her tampon. If she gets back in, it'll be shark week." They cackle and hoot.

I think of how it would feel to punch them in the nose.

"Melody?" Eric repeats loudly. Everyone in the pool who was just working on their backstroke turns to watch her.

"I got water in my ears," she murmurs to the wet concrete. "I'm going to the nurse." The boy and his friends pretend to do the backstroke but somehow manage to keep splashing her.

Eric seems to hear *her*, at least. "Take a buddy with you, then!"

I can't stand it anymore. The hurt and embarrassment she radiates, the leers of the boys. "I'll go!" I say. I clamber out of the pool and grab my own towel, but Melody makes a face at me.

"No!" she says quickly, something like terror flashing in her brown eyes. It's a terror I recognize, mixed with disgust. Distrust. It's the same look Chantal gave me yesterday in the vacant cabin, when she talked down to me as if I were a dead fly stuck to the bottom of her flip-flop. "I mean, um, thanks, but, my other friend will." Melody looks across the pool desperately, as if her other friend is hidden among us, but no one volunteers.

"*What friends?*" I hear one of the boys snicker.

Now all the attention is on me. Me, dripping wet in my bathing suit, clutching the towel Mom gave me, feeling as though someone just shone a giant spotlight over every bit of me. I can feel the eyes of the younger boys on every inch of my exposed skin. I cover myself quickly with the towel.

Eric sighs impatiently. He's tall and lean, maybe in his early to midtwenties, with muscular arms he must've gotten from swimming long, hard laps day after day. He's past high school, definitely past college. He has no time or patience for the fluctu-ating whims and moods of rowdy teenagers. "Just go with her, Melody. We only have ten minutes left and we've got a lot to cover."

Melody shrugs and walks ahead, and I follow her out of the gated pool area. As we enter the damp locker room where our stuff is stored, I can hear one of the boys say, *"Stupid bitches."*

Everything in the locker room is painted a melancholy ma-roon. Melody and I slip our T-shirts and shorts over our wet swim-suits in silence as a light bulb above us flickers on and off, buzzing and humming.

She continues to ignore me as we walk the path that leads to the nurse's station until I blurt out, "Why are you being so rude to me?"

Melody stops in her tracks. When she turns to face me and finally acknowledge my existence, I think I see her shudder, if only a little.

"You're Sam Gold's daughter, right?" she asks.

"Yeah. So what? People keep asking me about that. What's the big—"

"I don't want any trouble."

"Huh?"

Melody's body tenses as if I'm a giant moth approaching her. "I may be new, but I'm not stupid," she spits. "Just stay away from me, okay? Go back to your unit!"

"Seriously, I have no idea what you're—"

"Leave me alone!" she shrieks, louder than she did at the pool when the boy in the blue swim trunks splashed her. Her voice ricochets off the winding branches of the mossy trees and their gnarled trunks. It seems to vibrate and carry into the depth of the woods. Before I can say anything more, Melody sprints away down the path, flip-flops slapping against the ground.

A chorus of cicadas buzzes around me. I can almost hear them as they say, *Eight more hours.*

○ ○ ○

I shower in the Unit Seven bathroom, trying to wash off the sickening anxiety along with all the chlorine that's stunk up my skin. I do my best to ignore the teeny tiny red bugs I see crawling between the wooden slats in the shower stall. I focus on my breathing, the way the shampoo smells, how the warm water feels on my body.

Clearly, for whatever reason, Mom has a horrific reputation here, and it's going to follow me around like a shadow no matter what I do or say. Maybe she was a nightmare to her bunkmates, like Anna suggested, or maybe it was something else.

Something worse.

Nightmares vary in intensity, after all.

Even if the girls in my cabin seem to like me, and even if not everyone knows who I am, it's clear: I'm branded. This isn't the fresh start I thought it would be.

I need to figure out why. What Mom supposedly did or said that has every other person I meet running scared from me like I'm some terrifying clown.

Then I hear Olive's voice echoing through the Unit Seven bathroom, "I *better* not get paired with fucking *David* again."

And another girl's, "Oh my God, *I know*. He *never* says yes."

"Never. It's the first fucking rule of improv, David Bower! I swear I could tell him the sky is blue onstage and he'd go, 'Oh, uh, I don't think so, actually' just to piss me off."

Improv. I remember seeing the elective in the packet Chantal gave us. So Olive *is* an actor. It makes sense, with her movie-star good looks and impeccable style, that she'd want to pursue a career on the stage or in film. All of that on the path with her threats of danger and the strange masked figure . . . it was just a gimmick meant to scare me. Entice me.

It worked, too. Damn she's good.

It was all an act. There's no danger here. I hold myself, letting the water trickle down my neck and back and loosen my tense muscles. The little red ants march on and on, and I can almost hear them whisper, *Do it, Arlee. Do it.*

Stop the countdown clock.

Join the sisterhood.

Maybe it'll get me closer to the truth about Mom. Maybe they'll understand what I'm going through, and they won't judge me or look at me like I've got three heads. Tell me to get the fuck away from them, like I'm a slimy bug. A moth. A fly.

In this moment, the marching red ants do not frighten me.

I dry myself off, then slip into my fuzzy pink robe and flip-flops. I grab my shower caddy and make my way back into the warmth of the day. The sunshine hits my eyes and warms me down to my bones. I inhale the sweet, fresh air and do my best to let go of all the anxiety I've been holding onto so tightly for the past day and a half, willing the fear to melt off me like snow beneath the summer sun.

I smile to myself, thinking of Mom and what she told me in the car. "*It's going to be good. So good. Things are coming that you can't even see yet. Believe me?*"

"I believe you, Mom," I whisper, then make my way back up the hill to the cabin I call home, the one that looks like a bird-house or a little wooden mailbox. Or maybe, some kind of magical treasure chest, full of riches and wonders I'm only beginning to feel.

Or perhaps, a little voice tells me in the back of my mind, a Pandora's box.

Right before we walk to lunch, I wait until everyone else has filed out of our cabin. I reach under my pillow and fish out the golden envelope, then initial it with my fancy Camp Rockaway pen.

No more hours until sunset. This is it. I'm doing it.

It's time.

CHAPTER SIX

In the dining hall, I sit with my original group. Lisha keeps glancing over at me from across the room, like she's waiting for me to sit with her. I shoot her a guilty look and then do my best to ignore her.

It's funny, I'm so in demand, yet so ostracized at the same time.

I catch Olive once again at the drinks station. When I approach, her smile glows like the shiny silver horse on her necklace.

Without a word, I slip the envelope back into her hand, and she nods at me before returning to her table, the envelope now in the back pocket of her own shorts. I'm unsettlingly giddy now, like I'm walking on marshmallow clouds and the air is made of candy and rainbows.

I can barely contain my smile as I sit back down. I can feel Lisha's eyes on me as I slurp my cucumber soup. Delicious, just like everything else here. Soft beams of light stretch through the screens and fall across the back room of the dining hall. Silverware clinks and voices rise and fall. It's *happening*. I'm going to be part of something, something big and important. I can feel it. Something that will change everything for me, just like Mom said.

"What're you in such a tizzy about?" Porter asks me.

"Nothing," I say quickly, taking a rushed bite of my grilled cheese. I accidentally bite the inside of my cheek, tasting metal. Blood.

"Well, *I'm* in a tizzy because my pottery instructor this summer is honestly *delicious*, and dare I say, *Daddy as fuck*," Reyes gushes in between bites of his summer corn chowder.

"You're such a horndog," Uma scoffs. "Doesn't this bother you, Gabe? Doesn't this qualify as emotional cheating or something?"

Gabe grins and shrugs. "I don't care. I'm attracted to other guys, too."

"Yeah, Uma, we always talk about it," Reyes shoots back. "Unlike in *some* utterly dull heterosexual relationships, we actually communicate with each other. I know that's a foreign concept in the straight world, but—"

Jane points her spoon at both of them. "Both of you, please put this rousing argument on hold. I already have a major sun headache."

"You know I have a whole stash of Excedrin, Jane," Uma says. Medication, I've learned, is typically doled out here after lunch to the kids who need it; it's highly controlled.

"Yes, please," Uma says dryly. "Let's talk about something else. Normally I'd munch my popcorn while you two bicker, but alas, they aren't serving any today."

"Fine, then," Reyes huffs. He sighs deeply and stirs his soup. "Winnie, what are you reading lately? You're always reading something good."

Winnie brightens and sits up straighter. "I'm actually reading Carl Jung."

Porter peels her hard-boiled egg. "Who's that? He sounds familiar."

"He was a Swiss psychiatrist and psychoanalyst," Winnie explains in between bites of her chicken salad sandwich. I can tell Gabe is already tuning this out, and Jane keeps rubbing at her temples, but Reyes and Porter perk up, as do I. "You know those online tests, like, are you an extrovert or introvert?" Porter nods. "He came up with that whole concept. Extraversion and introversion. People tend to think they're one or the other, but Jung argued that everyone has an extraverted and introverted side, though he did define them a bit differently than we do today. But yeah, that's what I'm reading about. Carl Jung and his many concepts. It's fascinating."

Reyes gets this misty look of pride. "'Where there is light, there must also be shadow.' God, I'm so glad I eat with you, Winona."

"What does that mean?" It's the first time I've spoken so far during the meal. Everyone turns to look at me. I feel my tongue grow heavy and begin to stutter a little. "I—I mean, I get what it means on the surface. It's kind of like yin and yang, right? Where there is good, there's also bad?" God, they must think I sound so ridiculous and uneducated.

Winnie gives me a crooked smile. "That's more or less it, Arles. Reyes is quoting Jung's definition of the shadow self. He believed we all have a shadow self, or a darker side to our psyches. It's like the parts of ourselves we don't like, or want to repress or ignore. Some of it is conscious and some of it uncon-scious. We present this, like, persona to the world, while we keep other traits hidden. The . . . let's say, undesirable traits."

Reyes nods. "Are we really good people, or are we hiding a monster within ourselves that might someday awaken? *Ooh*, spooky." He wiggles his fingers and Gabe laughs.

"Wait, that's fucking creepy," Gabe says.

"'No tree can grow to heaven unless its roots reach down to hell,'" quotes Reyes. "Yeah, he was kind of a creepy guy, Gabe.

Brilliant, though. The Germans called it *hintergedanke,* or deeply repressed thoughts that we know but can't admit to ourselves."

"And," Winnie continues, "the more you ignore your shadow self, Jung argued, the worse it grows. Or, at least that's how I've been interpreting it. We all have a capacity for evil. People like to blame external circumstances for the way we behave, but really, it's the work of our dark sides."

"Okay," Jane groans. "As much as I want to learn German psychology theories today, can we all be quiet for a little while? My head is killing me."

"You don't look so good," Porter observes. "Maybe you should go see the nurse."

"I'm fine," Jane grumps, though I'm not sure if I believe her, the way she's cradling her head in her hands.

Winnie turns to me, like she's trying to brighten the mood of the table. She nudges my knee gently with hers. "How was your first full camp day so far, Arlee?"

"Oh, um, it wasn't bad. It was pretty fun, though this is way more exercise than I'm used to in a day. I'm kind of tired already?" I laugh awkwardly and begin to tear the crusts off my grilled cheese. "And I still have archery and yoga after this, so—"

"Oh, right, we're in archery together!" Winnie squeezes my arm and I look away to hide my blush, though I'm pretty sure everyone at the table notices.

"I've never shot a bow and arrow before. Is it hard?"

She smirks and leans in closer to me, her elbow against my arm. She smells like fresh air and fresh-cut grass. My palms itch and my skin tingles at her touch. "You just need a good eye and good aim."

"Oh yeah?" I ask.

"Don't worry, I'll show you when we're out there." Her eyes stay glued to mine. "You straighten your back and hold your arms out like . . ." She gently lifts my arms and arranges them in an archer's stance. "Like this." I feel her breath on my cheek. I like this, her closeness to me, the way it sets off fireworks inside my stomach. My heart is pounding so loud I swear they can all hear it. Sweat prickles on the back of my neck.

I can feel everyone at the table staring at me—at *us*. Even Jane dealing with her painful headache. My stomach flashes hot and cold. All the voices and clinking of plates and silverware in the dining hall lower like static beneath a radio song. Oh God, it's happening. The glitch in my mind. It's happening again.

Without thinking, I jerk away from Winnie and shake out my arms, shuddering as if I've swatted off a giant grasshopper that's landed on my skin. Her mouth falls open in surprise.

"You okay, Arlee?" Gabe asks.

"Fine," I say sharply to the crusts I ripped off my sandwich, though I don't sound fine. Not at all. My voice is breathy and high. I realize my breathing has gotten faster. It must be because the floor is tilting, slowly, to the side. My stomach heaves like I'm on a roller-coaster ride. "I feel kind of sick. I just need to—"

I get up and race to the bathroom, lock myself in a stall, and lean over the toilet. I retch and retch but nothing comes out or up. I can't stop panting.

I slap my own face, hard. "Stop it, Arlee! *Stop it!*" I hiss. "It's only day *two*. Nothing's even happened to you! What is your problem?" I go to the sink and run the faucet until the water is so hot it burns, then hold my wrists underneath it. *One, two, three*, I count. The searing pain causes my breathing to slow, bit my bit. The room stops tilting. My stomach settles. I turn off the faucet and stare down at my bright pink wrists.

Damn.

In the mirror I see my cheek is turning red from where I hit myself. I grab at the edges of the sink and fight back tears.

"You have to calm down," I plead with myself, this time using a calmer, gentler tone. The door swings open and I straighten myself quickly as another girl walks in.

On the way back to my table, I pour myself a steaming mug of chamomile tea.

I ignore their worried questions and lie about sudden period cramps. I do my best to pretend that I'm absolutely fine.

Think of the rest of the activities you have today, and this week, and the secret sisterhood you've decided to join, I tell myself. *That'll be so fun, won't it?*

Winnie doesn't look at me for the rest of the meal. Not once. She eats her lunch and stares into the bowl of summer corn chowder sprinkled with oyster crackers she's now working on, swirling the spoon around and around. I want to apologize, to tell her she did nothing wrong, that it wasn't her fault I freaked . . . but I realize that I'm afraid. Afraid of what she thinks of me. What everyone here else thinks of me. That if I draw more attention to it, the conversation will start up again and I'll start to sweat and then have another glitch. That if Winnie responds in a dismissive way, it'll break my heart.

My heart.

I've barely known Winnie a day and a half, but here at camp, time feels longer somehow. It operates in a different way. At school I'd see my friends, back when I had them, a couple hours a day at most, in between and during classes. After school. Maybe during occasional sleepovers. But I wouldn't share a cabin with them. I wouldn't eat every meal by their side.

They weren't sleeping in the bunk above me.

As she and Reyes continue their conversation about Carl Jung and his shadow, I pay close attention to the freckles that dot not only her eyelids, but travel down her cheek and throat. There are freckles on her neck, her sternum. Some dark, some light. When she's thinking of a way to respond, she presses her teeth over her lip. When she's really listening, she nods a lot. She really listens.

I don't think I've ever met a girl as beautiful as Winnie, even if she may not be a supermodel or something the bro assholes at my school would call the "world's most bangable chick." But she's beautiful to me. There's something beneath the surface of her physical beauty that is good and pure, warm and nourishing. I can sense it. I inch a little closer to her, offer her one of the chocolate-covered strawberries I snagged on the way back to the table, and she accepts it with a small smile.

Maybe things will be okay between us. Maybe gestures and offers are like words unspoken.

o o o

We walk together to our elective, accidentally bumping into each other as we go. The hairs on our arms brush now and then, sparking once again with electricity.

I'm surprised to see Zach here in the archery field. He carries himself with the same cocky, arrogant swagger that he radiated in the dining hall, but this time, he doesn't pay me any mind. Doesn't even nod at me or glance my way. Too busy horsing around with his guy friends, including Michael, who I sort of met at breakfast.

Guess I'm no longer on his radar.

I feel shame in thinking it, but it makes me feel as though I did or said something wrong. I try my best to shake that thought away. It doesn't matter. Why should I care, anyway?

He was awful to Winnie. Fuck him.

By now I've shaken off my earlier glitchy attack, revived by a good meal and the afternoon sunlight. I don't need to focus on Zach. I don't need to care about what anyone else is doing.

Our instructor is a counselor named Heather, an enthusiastic local archery star that some of the others whisper is on her way to the Olympics. She unlocks the shed and shows us newbies how to pick the right bow for each of us.

"They're simple practice bows, nothing too fussy," she says, smiling down at her own fancy one with the fondness a mother might bestow upon her child. "But the best archers can make good use of anything."

"I heard she fucks that bow every night," someone murmurs, and a few boys start snickering. I turn and see the comment came from Zach's group. When our eyes meet, he winks at me.

Despite the heat of the day, I feel a chill run through me. I turn away.

Winnie is a natural with her bow, which she grabs right from the toolshed, not needing any of Heather's detailed directions. She knows right away what will work for her body—what will, as Heather explains, yield a smooth draw and deliver the best shock.

As Heather shows us newbies how to hold the bow and aim the arrow, the more seasoned archers line up to take practice shots. Winnie lands bullseye after bullseye, grinning each time she hits her mark.

"Not bad, De León!" Zach says with a smirk. "Bet I can best you in a round."

"You can die trying," she shoots back before landing another bullseye.

He laughs and sidles up closer to her so they're sharing one target. "Let's say we go five times each. Ladies first, Winona."

She makes a face of pure disgust and moves several steps away from him. There's this look in her eye for just a moment, like she wants to aim her bow at him and fire. . . .

Yet still, as rigid as she is around him, she grudgingly accepts his challenge. I don't like the way he keeps trying to lean into her, whispering things close to her ear like he's trying to trip her up. She flinches every time. I stand and watch her carefully aim until Heather hollers, "Arlee, eyes on your own target!"

Winnie and Zach might be amazing, but I'm awkward and shaky. The bow feels unreasonably heavy in my arms. I can't seem to hold my hands still enough to aim. Heather tries to show me how to get into a proper archer's stance. She helps hold out my arms, then gently kicks at my legs to straighten them out. Her touch is perfunctory and businesslike, nothing at all like the touches Winnie gave me back in the dining hall.

Winnie and Zach tie. He demands a redraw.

When I try again and shoot, the arrow lands in the grass a few feet from me. I swear under my breath.

"Don't get frustrated, Arlee!" Heather says. "You'll get the hang of it!"

This is not as easy as it looks in the movies.

Winnie and Zach tie again. Zach's a wizard with the bow and arrow, like he's been doing this all his life. As it turns out, he has. A group of younger girls and one boy whisper and giggle about what a pro he is, how his parents hired a private coach to train him for tournaments. As they shoot and mostly miss, they dare each other to go and talk to him. I try my best to ignore their voices, which buzz in and out of my ears like insects. It's bad enough there's a swarm of gnats in this field, too, hovering and humming. Disgustingly close to me. I do my best to focus, to pay attention to what Heather is telling me about aligning my upper body and finding my anchor point.

I finally find it: there's a rhythm out here in the archery field.
A kind of gentle staccato that almost helps me forget the tension
between Zach and Winnie, and the gnats, if only for a little while
longer. The sounds of the arrows as they shoot through the air
and make their satisfying *thwacks* as they land.

What's far less satisfying is the way Zach keeps looking at
Winnie.

I can't follow his gaze from behind those douchey shades he
put on again, but there's something in the way he leers and grins
and keeps getting way too close that burrows under my skin. He's
looking at her like he looked at me earlier in the dining hall,
maybe even yesterday when I first arrived. Looking with a kind of
ravenous hunger.

I think of the invitation I accepted. The secret sisterhood I'm
joining. My palms itch and my blood pumps red hot.

I steady my bow, aim, and fire.

Thwack.

"*Yes!*" I scream, pumping my first in the air. A rush of endor-
phins floods me. It's a high like no other, even better than the
giddiness I felt earlier. I jump around and whoop and don't even
care that some of the other kids are looking at me like I'm a total
weirdo. "I did it! I did it!"

I hit the target!

Heather claps for me. "Not bad, Arlee! Not quite a bullseye,
but not bad."

Miss Teresa's bitter voice echoes in the back of my mind: *I'll
never lie to you. The worst thing I could ever do would be to tell you
what your ego wants to hear.* It deflates some of the air out of my
balloon.

"That was amazing, Arles!" Winnie cries, running over to me
and wrapping me in a big hug.

Zach snorts, voice dripping with sarcasm. "Definitely not bad for a total *beginner.*" The last word almost sounds like a swear, the way he says it.

I whirl on him, ripping myself out of Winnie's arms. "I may be a *beginner,* but at least I make an effort. Maybe if you didn't spend so much time bothering girls who clearly aren't interested, you might actually outplay one."

Winnie's mouth falls open. So do the mouths of Zach's groupies.

Zach, however, doesn't even flinch. He only sucks his teeth, gives me a quick once-over, and says, "I could say the same about you, Arlee Gold."

My stomach plummets fifty stories, and for a brief moment, my vision goes white. Zach's friends chortle and go *"ooh!"* and *"oh, shit!"* The groupies giggle and titter. Winnie's eyes grow wide like an owl.

She could say something in retort, but right now, there is nothing to say.

Meanwhile I am glued to the ground, rooted in place, unable to move or breathe. The sun glows so hot and bright that I begin to burn to a crisp. There is static in my ears. Fire in my blood. My fingers twitch, and then I feel it: that familiar twang. That *need.* The thing that called me to the woods years ago, that pulled me closer to the clearing and made me walk past the flies and the horrible sight and the stench . . .

It's not until Winnie pulls me gently by the arm and begins leading me away from the archery field that my ears start to ring and I reawaken, my feet moving once again.

"Don't listen to him, he's a douchebag, like Jane said," she says gently. "He's always trying to get a rise out of—God, I'm so sorry, Arlee."

My throat hurts when I finally speak. "Don't apologize for him."

"I should have said something."

I swallow hard. "It's okay."

Heather calls after us to come back and finish the lesson, but Winnie is practically running now, pulling us farther down the forested dirt path, faster and faster, until we're both sweating and breathless and almost back to the safety of Unit Seven, and the fury that captured me has lifted and drifted off into the air like woodsmoke.

○ ○ ○

Chantal finds me and Winnie on her bed about thirty minutes later, sitting face-to-face with our knees pressed together. She's teaching me the different hands in poker. More specifically, Texas Hold'em.

Chantal clears her throat loud enough to startle me. "Aren't you two supposed to be at archery?"

Winnie stays sweet and smooth as honey. "I cut my finger on a rusty bow. Luckily Arlee had Band-Aids so we didn't need to bother the nurse."

"Mmm," Chantal murmurs, crossing her arms against her chest. She looks even more exhausted than she did at breakfast, as if the dark circles beneath her eyes have somehow grown darker. "I don't see this alleged Band-Aid."

Winnie flips over her hand of cards and points. "See, Arles, that's a straight flush. That's one you want." Winnie sticks her tongue out at Chantal as if she's nothing more than an annoying older sister. "I took it off. The bleeding stopped."

"They were good Band-Aids," I add awkwardly.

"Must've been," Chantal grumps. She opens her footlocker and begins to rummage through it. "Don't be late to your next elective, and if you have another *medical issue*"—she says this in the most mocking tone I've ever heard—"go to the nurse. At least tell a counselor, Winnie. Don't come back here first and let y'alls' parents find out and give them a new excuse to sue the hell out of me and the entire staff. Got it?" She grabs what looks like a change of clothes from the footlocker, and maybe a pair of pj's, then stuffs them in a laundry bag she slings over her shoulder.

The Other Arlee brewing inside me, the girl they don't really know I can be, is tempted to snark, *Another long night away from your job?* but I stop myself and swallow it down. If only for today, I'll be the Arlee they can step on.

Winnie rolls her eyes as Chantal storms out, slamming the screen door. "She's such a square," she scoffs.

"She doesn't scare you at all?" I ask, studying the cards of the straight flush.

Winnie shuffles the rest of the deck and frowns. "Why would she scare me? I've known her for years."

"She's . . . kind of nasty to me, if you haven't noticed. Most of the other counselors are giving me dirty looks and acting like I'm up to something, too."

She shrugs. "She's all bark and no bite. Chantal is Chantal." I can hear the chatty, happy voices of the other girls outside, coming back from their electives.

"She's not like that with anyone else I've seen, Winnie. She . . . glares at me." I think about telling her what really happened in the vacant cabin, but I already lied the other day and told her they were *so* welcoming, so I decide to keep my mouth shut.

Winnie bites at her lower lip. "Sometimes she takes a while to warm up to new people. She doesn't know you yet, is all." I can tell there's maybe something more she wants to say, but she clears her throat and instructs, "Here, choose seven random cards, then see if you can pick the five best ones out of them. The best hand you can."

I do my best to study the seven cards I've selected, but the words and symbols blur together and I can't focus on any of them, can barely even remember the ones Winnie told me made up a straight flush.

After a moment, to my surprise, she adds, "You know who does scare me? Anna."

"Really? Why?" The symbols on the cards stop being so blurry. I see the hand I can make now, clear as day. I lay down five cards in front of Winnie.

"I don't know," she says. "Everyone loves her, thinks she's *so* funny, with that bitchy sense of humor. This may sound sorta *woo-woo*, but I get bad energy from her. Bad vibes. Almost like . . . bad blood. Sorry, that must sound so weird."

She looks relieved when I say, "No, I get what you mean."

Then she finally notices my hand of cards. That crooked grin turns up on her mouth as she reads out loud, "Two pair. Nice, Arlee."

The door bangs open once more, our bunkmates filing in. They say hi and wave, Uma complaining about what a "bozo supreme" her riding instructor is and how she "didn't believe I could make that jump." She tosses her riding helmet against the wall so hard it makes a loud *crack*.

"Uma!" Porter scolds. "Your dads will be mad if they have to send you another one!"

And there stands Olive, leaning back against the cabin doorframe. Our eyes meet, and it's like a lock clicks into place.

"Oh, hey, Arlee. If you still wanted some nail polish, come to my cabin and pick out a color before next elective, okay? I have, like, a billion."

It takes me a second to get she's speaking in code, but by the time I open my mouth to respond, Ginger is raving to Porter about the new song she's writing in her guitar elective, Jane is grumbling about being unable to find her deodorant, and Olive has left and gently shut the screen door behind her.

o o o

Olive's cabin is nearly identical to ours, only much tidier, and with a few rectangular skylights in between the long wooden ceiling beams.

It almost smells like someone's been burning sage in here.

A few of the girls who live in it eye me warily as I walk in, like I've entered a secret club or their personal VIP section.

I have yoga next, so I don't need to change. I can take my time with the fifteen-minute break we have.

Olive is seated on her bottom bunk bed in a corner of the cabin, writing something in her Camp Rockaway notebook. I get a glimpse of her fabulous wardrobe via her open footlocker, which seems larger somehow than mine: shorts made of silk with stripes and elegant baroque patterns. T-shirts and tank tops boasting designer logos and museum-worthy illustrative prints. Pants I could picture someone calling "business casual." Beside the footlocker, she's carefully curated a dizzying collection of shoes: expensive green riding boots. A pair of iridescent flip-flops with little gold charms hanging off them. The kind of rubber rain boots I always drooled over when walking past them with Mom in a downtown department store.

Olive's bed is no less ostentatious, with a patterned comforter that looks plucked straight from some Parisian hotel room, and when she spots me and invites me to sit down, I marvel at how soft her maroon sheets feel against my thighs.

Basic camp-provided sheets aren't enough for Olive Williams, I guess.

All around the railings of her bed, she's taped up photos

of her with family and friends. The kind you might mistake for ad-campaign outtakes. The people in them are just as Polaroid-perfect as she is, with glittering white smiles and glossy hair. Clothes I would kill to own, styled in effortlessly messy-chic ways.

The only thing that ruins the scene is a huge long-legged black spider that crawls across a photo of Olive and another girl at the beach, before disappearing somewhere behind her bed.

I will not think about what I just saw. I cannot throw up. Not now.

Olive closes her notebook and sets it aside. "I'm glad you asked about the nail polish, Arlee, because I really do think some of this is the best of the best, not to brag or anything." She unzips a large cosmetics bag, revealing dozens of colorful little glass bottles. "This brand in particular is so pretty, and it lasts *forever*. Choose one you like." She hands me the bag to inspect.

I feel along the grooves of the polish bottles, realizing we are once again speaking in code.

"This green one looks nice?" I hold up a bottle at random.

Olive frowns at it as if inspecting a diamond. "Hmm. I think you'd like the gold one best, actually. It would really go well with your complexion." She digs around in the bag for a while, then sighs dramatically. "*Damn it.* It's not in here. I must've buried it in some other bag in my footlocker. You know what, I'll get it to you later tonight when I've had more time to search. I should find the fast-drying stuff by then, too, even if it takes me until *exactly midnight*, you know? Who knows, maybe I even left them *in the vacant cabin.*" She says this part slowly and carefully, though her expression never changes. "Anyway, I'm sure I'll find it. . . ."

My heart thumps with glee, but I do my best to keep a neutral expression. This is *it*. This is when I'll get to meet the members of the secret society.

Tonight.

Exactly midnight.

In the vacant cabin.

It's happening.

"Sounds good," I say, doing my best not to beam at her like a pair of headlights. Instead I look at the little silver horse around her neck. *Horse society, maybe? An equestrian sorority?* Maybe, but her fancy green riding boots look more for fashion than sport. "Did you . . . uh, want to tell me anything else?"

It's subtle, but I spot it, a flash of warning in her eyes like a streak of lightning. "I don't know what you mean," she says tightly.

I cringe at myself. I'm being too obvious. Way too obvious. There're other girls in here, girls who obviously don't know about the secret society. "Okay, it's fine, no problem," I mumble. I bump my head hard on my way out of her bunk area, a bright flash of pain making me shut my eyes for second, and I almost bump right into Ruth, apparently this cabin's counselor.

"Oh, and it's Arlee!" she says brightly. She's chewing on a giant protein bar, flecks of granola and chocolate smeared across her mouth. She wipes at it with the sleeve of her T-shirt—definitely not designer, most definitely not in style—and it transfers onto the cheap cotton fabric. Probably staining it forever. "I wanted to let you know I've got extra office hours tomorrow before test prep if you wanted to come meet me a few minutes beforehand. I have some worksheets on concentration I think could be really useful for you, since you brought it up in class and all."

I hear a few of the cabin girls muffle a snicker, maybe some of the same ones who laughed at me during the session this morning. I could die right here, melt into a puddle of shame and stay like a stain on the wooden floors.

Ruth seems oblivious to my embarrassment. She takes another big bite of the protein bar. When she smiles, I see the chocolate on her teeth.

I force a smile. "I'm okay, thanks, though," I say, though my voice comes out wobbly as I head back outside and to my own cabin.

She means well, I know she does, and I feel bad, but if I have any chance of fitting in here beyond the walls of my cabin, if I'm the kind of Arlee Gold who can get tapped to join a secret society . . . I can't let anyone see me struggle.

CHAPTER SEVEN

I t's difficult to wait until midnight.

Right before yoga, I swipe one of Uma's energy drinks from under her bed and keep it stashed for later, gulping it down soon after dinner when I get a moment alone. I need to stay awake. Focused. My whole body is buzzing and humming, alive and burning up with electricity.

There's no campfire tonight. No warmth or light to keep the bugs away and my growing anxiety at bay—though it's mixed with excitement. Glee, even. While my bunkmates wind down for the evening, prattling on about some camp gossip, I slip into bed still fully clothed and pretend to fall asleep early.

"Aww, look at sweet Arles," I hear Winnie say affectionately. "She tired herself out on her first full day." I can't help but smile into my pillow, and for some time, I do doze on and off, keeping my wristwatch close by my ear so I can hear the ticking.

Chantal and Bea sleep in the cabin tonight. They make us turn the lights off by eleven, and then it's only a waiting game.

The crickets. The owls. The sounds of the other girls breathing. My heartbeat. They seem to grow louder.

Finally, midnight arrives. I slip out of bed, slip into flip-flops, and make my way down the slope of the hill, miniflashlight in hand, until I'm at the vacant cabin.

The door creaks as I open it.

I half expect to see Olive inside, standing beside the humming minifridge, smiling at me with a warm welcome.

Instead, it's Anna.

Lit cigarette in one hand, the smoke rising to the rafters, and what looks to be a black cotton blindfold in the other.

Instinctively, I freeze. A deer caught in headlights. A deer standing before a grizzly bear, and the bear is starving.

"You're on time," she says with a grunt. "A surprise, honestly." She puts the cigarette out in a cup resting on the coffee table. "You ready, Arlee Gold?"

My tongue feels stuck to the roof of my mouth. All I can do is swallow and nod.

I think. I didn't factor Anna into any of this. My mind reels.

"Put your glasses up on your forehead," she instructs.

I eye the blindfold in her hand. I feel as though I've just swallowed frigid air. When I exhale, I can almost see the frost in my breath. "They're expensive. If they break, I don't have a backup pair."

"I'll put them in my hoodie pocket, then," she sneers.

"Would they really even be safe there?"

"Ar*lee*." She says my name the same way she said it that first day. "You want to be part of the sisterhood or not? You gotta follow the rules." She reaches for my frames, and reluctantly, I hand them over. The world goes blurry.

Anna makes that worse. She wraps the cotton blindfold tight around my eyes, so tight it pinches and hurts, and my heart is hammering, but I let her do it.

We move outside. The crickets continue to sing so sweetly as she guides me through the now pitch-black night, wet leaves and twigs crunching underfoot. I can't see even a little, the blindfold is so tight and thick. I realize that I'm breathing hard through my mouth in short gasps. I stumble over something on the ground, but Anna pulls me up again and pushes me forward with such force that my chest constricts and my vision goes starry.

This was a mistake. This was a mistake.

The sound of the crickets intensifies as we walk in silence. After what feels like forever, I smell horse manure mingling with the scent of sweaty leather, hay, and fresh pine shavings. Hear the faint whinnies and neighs of the horses. I know where we are. The horse field near the barn.

Luckily, horseflies don't come out at night.

Anna removes my blindfold, but ties my hands behind my back with thick rope that someone hands her.

Shit.

Eight figures stand in a semicircle, their faces obscured by white wooden horse masks. The same masks that I saw before on the path, with the beady black eyes. They wear long gray cloaks. Even without my glasses, I recognize Olive's green riding boots, her curls tucked behind her mask.

My eyes water as I squint, straining to see what's glowing at the center of the semicircle. Dozens of tea candles have been placed over what looks like a large swath of leather fabric, forming the shape of a star—only, the star is slightly crooked.

"Sisters," Anna declares, "I present to you our newest *soror potentiale*: a birth legacy to our esteemed sister of the Order of Equus, Samantha Michèle Gold. May I present for your consideration: Arlee Samantha Gold."

She knows my middle name? I guess it must've been on the intake form Mom filled out, but . . . they also know Mom's name. *Of course* they know mine.

Her name is my middle name, after all.

I hear heavy footsteps behind me, coming closer.

"*Ordo equitum,*" the girls chant. "*Soror potentiale,* be anointed."

Anna spins me around to face another yet figure cloaked in gray, wearing a mask far more terrifying than all the others.

It's also the mask of a horse, only the horse is dead. It's a horse's skull, with wide hollow gaps for eyes. There's a gap, too, where the nose should be, and clumps of thick black hair still stuck to the sides of its temples. Its jaw hangs permanently open in a terrible kind of grin, exposing long slender incisors.

From the stables, a horse that's very much alive gives an ear-splitting screech. It stomps its foot so hard I feel it down to my toes.

The skeletal figure moves closer and closer toward me, taking its time. I can hear the heavy sound of its breath, and it's like those gaps where the eyes should be are looking right into mine, and then I realize that they are. Behind the gaps are human eyes. Eyes that I recognize.

Lisha's eyes.

"All those who see and are seen by the mare of death are bound to her wishes," Lisha says, her voice husky and dark. Hollow like the holes in her skeleton mask. "Arlee Samantha Gold, now you have seen her, and she sees you, but she is granting you a choice. Do you wish to be anointed into our order? To swear by our sacred motto? *Praesidio puellae.*" I can feel her hot breath on my cheek as she speaks. "It means to 'protect the girls.' Watch out for and defend one another at all costs. No matter the price we must pay."

"*Praesidio puellae,*" the others echo. "*Protect the girls.*"

I swallow hard, my throat tightening like a screw. This is all so absurd it should be funny. I should be laughing in their faces, taking them about as seriously as I do the theater students who imitate demons and monsters at the local haunted house.

There's nothing funny about any of this, though.

"Yes or no, Arlee?" Anna snaps beside me. "The Pale Mare has asked you a question. You must answer her."

My brain feels frazzled, like it's buzzing with static. I don't know what I want, not really, except for those blank, blinking human eyes inside the gaps of bone to stop staring me down.

It's okay, Arlee. Mom did this. You can, too.

You wanted this. You wanted to fit in.

But at what cost?

"Yes," I hear myself say, my voice cracking on the word.

Lisha bows her head for a moment. "So it shall be done," she says softly. "*Soror potentiale*, be anointed. *Praesidio puellae.*"

"*Praesidio puellae*," the others echo.

Before I can make a move, Anna shoves me back around so I'm facing the semicircle again, the frenzied blur of white horses, and glimmering tea candles in the shape of a crooked star.

There's a long horrible moment of stillness, of sweetly singing crickets and blurry, beady black eyes, of Anna digging her fingers into both of my arms, even though my hands are tied and I'm frozen to the ground.

I couldn't move if I wanted to. It's like I'm paralyzed.

One masked horse-girl steps forward. She's the closest to me in the semicircle, so at least I can see what she does.

She produces a knife from somewhere inside her cloak. A hunting knife with a thick leather handle. She holds out her bare arm, palm facing up, and presses the knife to her skin. The horse field does a spin. Lisha's warm breath on my neck and the pain in my arms from Anna's grip seems to fade. I taste bile when I see the blood, see the symbol the girl is carving, lightly but enough to make a visible cut. The shape of the crooked star.

Dark blood runs down her pale arm, glowing in the bright moonlight.

The horse-girl holds her arm right in front of me, inching close enough that I smell and almost taste the salt of it in the sweet night air.

I want to run. I want to scream, but I'm still glued to the ground, frozen in fear, every inch of me shaking.

From behind me, Lisha speaks in a terrifying low pitch, like some animal whisper-growl.

"The blood of your sister becomes the blood of your body. Her blood is our blood. Your blood is our blood. Drink deep from the well in her veins, Arlee Samantha Gold, and merge with the Order of Equus. Be anointed."

The horse-girl raises her bleeding arm higher and higher until it's right below my mouth.

"*Lick it*," Anna hisses. She squeezes my neck so tight I can feel bruises blooming.

This can't be happening. This can't be real. It's a nightmare, and when I wake up, everything will be all right.

I stare in horror at the wound in the horse-girl's arm and I just can't, I can't, *no*. It's sick. It's disgusting. It's wrong. I realize that I'm crying, tears pouring down my cheeks, strange whimpering noises coming from my mouth, from some well deep inside me.

"It's okay, Arlee," Lisha soothes from behind me, her voice gentler now, more human. Soft as velvet. "Anna, release her." She does, but I'm still shaking.

The blood is running down the horse-girl's arm in slow, zig-zagging waves. "She doesn't have it in her," she appraises from behind her mask, as if deeply disappointed in me. "We've made a mistake, Pale Mare."

"She's our sister," Lisha insists with patience and calm, as if she's speaking to a child. "Her blood is our blood." She places two gentle palms on my back and begins to rub in slow, soothing circles. "It's okay, Arlee. You are safe. We are your sisters. Taste the blood, just a little. It won't hurt you. It's your blood, too, after all. Taste and merge with us and join the Order of Equus. Be anointed."

"Taste it," the other horse-girls chant. "Taste it. Taste it. Taste it."

Lisha presses against the back of my skull, gently but firmly, leading my head down until my lips graze the warm blood and I jerk my head upward and yank away from her, away from them all, frantically trying to untie the knots that bind my hands.

Anna grabs me again and restrains me. "Stop that!" she growls under her breath, like I'm the one acting fucking batshit, not them. "Chill out. You're fine, Arlee."

"She's your sister," Lisha reminds her. I can hear the smile in her voice. "She's *our* sister now. Welcome, Arlee Samantha Gold!"

"Welcome, Arlee Samantha Gold," the horse-girls repeat. They cross hands, right over left, and begin to sway back and forth. They hum some ancient-sounding melody, as the blood from the girl's wounded arm continues to trickle down and drip into the grass.

A sob spills out of me. I'm so confused. Panicked. Humiliated.

"What the fuck is this?" I cry out. "What's happening?"

Anna steps in front of me. She smiles wolfishly with her mouth but not with her ice-blue eyes. When she answers, her voice is hard, cold, gravely serious.

"Initiation. Welcome, *sister.*"

Then someone finally unties my hands and I can't stop crying and shaking.

There are arms all around me. Strong, loving arms. Holding me. Shushing me. Soothing me. Gently stroking my hair and running their fingers down my back.

The arms of my new sisters.

"It's okay, Arlee," they say. They take off their masks for a moment to reveal their kind faces, though without my glasses and through my tears, it's all a blur. "We're here. We're your sisters. We love you."

"Let it out," one sister whispers in my ear. "Let out the pain."

The shaking ceases as I collapse into their warm bodies. Their love. I let them hug me tight, and cry until there are no tears left in me at all, and then I let out a long, wild animal wail.

They don't laugh. They don't pull away.

They hold me tighter.

"You understand, don't you?" I cry into one girl's arm as they sway and hum and soothe me like an infant. *You know.*

"Yes," the girls say. "We understand you, Arlee Samantha Gold."

It doesn't matter that I don't know them all individually yet. We are a collective. A communal body.

To them, I am not a wild animal. I am a girl who is loved and seen.

My new sisters help me into my new cloak and mask. It's heavy and hot inside the wooden horse face. I can hear every breath I take, but by now it's a comfort to hide my tearstained cheeks, slipping into a kind of solidarity within anonymity. I join hands with them, right over left. Together, we chant, low and then high, up and down a mountain of swelling pitch. In this moment I am no longer Arlee. No longer the shy new girl or the angry ticking time bomb or the daughter of the infamous Sam Gold. I hum and sway until my being fuses to the circle, and a fog inside me lifts, my soul filling with a strange sense of peace.

"I will be watching you, Arlee Samantha," Lisha says. "Very carefully, and I trust you, sister. I trust you will keep us as safe as we keep you."

Safe. They'll be watching, but in a way that keeps me safe.
This is good.
It was so horrifying, but it's okay now.
It's all going to be okay. *I'm home,* I think.
This feels better than good.

o o o

That night, the Order of Equus initiates three more sisters. All of
them younger than me, and all from Unit Five: the rising freshmen of Camp Rockaway. By the time they're brought in one at
a time, the wounded girl's arm has been cleaned and bandaged.
None of the new girls are made to lick her blood.

"New *sorors*," Lisha instructs, "when you see me wearing the
yellow nail polish at mealtime, that means you will come meet us
at midnight in the field for our next ritual."

"Yes, Pale Mare," the other new girls say in unison.

The girls sway and sing some kind of hymn as the candle lights glow and in the near distance, the horses snort and
whinny. Though it's hard to make out without my glasses, I notice
Anna standing beside Lisha on the fringes of the field. Anna's
still in her hoodie, unmasked. I wish I could see the expression of her face and read the look in her eyes. Understand why
she's doing this and what it is she wants from me. Even from a
blurred distance, I can feel something like raw hatred radiating
from her. No, maybe not hatred: *disgust.* Even though she's the
one who held me down and hissed at me to lick another girl's
blood. Even though I'd argue that *she's* the disgusting one.

I'm falling asleep standing up when the ceremony finally
ends. The air is full of excitement. *Euphoria.* The sisters laugh
and hug one another. Some are crying happy tears. I understand
now. I think I'm crying happy tears, too.

We remove our masks and our cloaks. Anna finally returns my glasses to me, though not without murmuring what sounds like "stupid bitch" under her breath, but I'm too mellow now to care, too loved up. It's okay she doesn't see me yet. The rest of them do.

I slide my glasses on and the world sharpens back into focus. Gone is the fuzzy dreaminess of before, the way the darkness somehow looked even darker when it was all obscured. I can see my sisters clearly now, though aside from a girl or two from my yoga class, I recognize none of them except for Lisha, Olive, and Anna.

Then I spot the girl who slashed her arm: tall, rail thin, pale as the moonlight that rains down on us. She's twirling her hair and joking with her sisters like this is a fun, normal camp evening. After all the humming, chanting, and swaying, after the outpouring of love, I admit that I no longer feel as nauseated at the sight of her bandaged wound.

It was only a ritual.

"Thank you for coming, sisters," Lisha says. "Until we meet again beneath the moon."

"Beneath the moon," they repeat.

"And remember, sisters, keep your eyes peeled. Look out for one another. If you see something that goes against our sacred motto, tell one of us. Tell me."

Her head swivels around the crowd, and everyone nods, myself included.

A handful of my new sisters start picking up and blowing out the tea candles that formed the slightly crooked star. They cradle them in their hands like babies as Lisha takes us all back into the barn, where she and Anna place the candles, masks, and cloaks inside a hidden closet that Lisha unlocks. Each girl kisses their mask before putting it inside, so I do the same.

I'm exhausted. A strange, warm drowsiness has taken over me. I only want to sleep. All I can do now is sleep.

"Olive," I say, approaching her. She's in the middle of a conversation with another sister, both of them laughing, animated, like none of this was the least bit strange or scary. "Can you please walk me back?"

Olive's face softens at the sight of me. She reaches out her hand and I take it. "Of course, *soror* Arlee. Sisters, until the new moon!" She waves to them, and they wave back.

"We love you, Arlee!" they say.

"We can't wait to see you again!"

I feel myself smile, though as I click on my miniflashlight and Olive does the same with hers, and we make our way back down the forested path, into the cool darkness, an odd feeling blooms in my belly. A reminder.

"Why did they make me do that?" I ask. "Lick the . . . blood? Why me and not the younger ones?"

Olive gives a sad smile. "I think it's because you're older. You joined late, so you needed to be anointed. You're a *legacy*. Listen, I know it's super weird, but it's just a ritual. A silly old blood ritual." She laughs a little, shaking her head. "Danielle is fine. She's done this so many times before. It's all consensual. I'm so sorry it scared you so much. You're okay, Arlee." Her voice is like a soothing balm. "It's just a ritual. I know, it creeped me out, too, when I went through it."

"Did they make you lick blood?"

Olive laughs a little. "No, but I saw them do it to one older *soror*. It's natural to feel grossed out. Blood rituals are taboo in our modern society, you know? But this ritual goes back centuries, to before the camp was even here. The Order of Equus has a long and beautiful history. You're going to see. You'll understand. The connection runs so deep."

I feel a sudden hot wave of shame. I was being a child. A petulant child who cried and carried on over a little blood and some creepy Halloween masks. At the fact I was treated a little rougher than the younger girls. I realize now the costumes did look pretty ridiculous. Maybe even a little cheap, too. How did I ever find them so scary?

Those same younger girls played along, chanting with the others. They joined the Order without terror. Without incident.

"I'm sorry," I say quietly. I'm not sure why, but I mean it.

"Hey, it's okay. We're your sisters now, Arlee. We won't hold it against you. The Order of Equus is special. It goes past summers. It's for life."

She's so earnest and sincere, but something in the back of my mind pokes at me over and over as we pass an owl hooting in the trees.

"Was Vidhya in the order?"

She chews her bottom lip. "She was. She loved it, though. Like you, she was a legacy." She frowns, lost in thought. "Her mother was a *soror*, as was her grandmother, but no one in her family was as legendary as . . ." Olive trails off, leaving her thoughts unfinished.

Fatigue prickles behind my eyes.

"As legendary as my mother?" I ask.

Olive bites at her lip even harder. "I don't want to speak badly about your family. . . ."

"Just tell me. What did she do? Why does almost everyone else act like I'm some pariah because of her?"

"I—I don't know," Olive says quickly. "I'm sorry, Arlee. I don't really know the details." She's lying, and it's obvious, but my eyes keep slipping shut and I'm so exhausted that I don't have the will to keep pressing.

I'll find out one way or another. Eventually, one of them will have to tell me the truth.

"I can't wait to go home," I murmur sleepily.

"We're almost back to Unit Seven."

I didn't mean my cabin or Unit Seven. I meant home in Raleigh, in my own bed, downtown, surrounded by neighbors I know and artificial lights and the gentle hum of the city—*No*, I tell myself, forcing the thought out of my mind. You don't want to go home. *For the summer, this is your home. And you've finally found your family.*

When I return to my cabin, I strip down to my underwear and collapse under my sheets, buzzing with adrenaline. Now, I can finally be part of something special and true.

Mom was right.

There's nothing here to fear. It was all in my head.

I'm finally home.

o o o

I wake up the next morning hungover on happiness.

It's a beautiful feeling. A pulsing, shimmering rush to carry me through the rest of the whirlwind of Camp Rockaway.

I think I'm different now. A different person. A different Arlee. The Arlee before initiation is not the same girl whose skin I inhabit now, and I like it that way.

The first day after initiation begins with the same 8 A.M. bugle call. The same clanging of the haunting, hollow bells and the count-off at the campfire circle in the chill of the morning air. They no longer sound so menacing.

My skin glows. My smile is bright.

All this time spent in the sun is starting to do me good, I

think. It's only been a few days, but the hills we walk up and down all day are now a little easier.

After breakfast, Winnie and I walk together to test prep, trailing behind the rest of the group. I savor each moment like this we get to be alone together. I wish I could share what happened last night with Winnie. The beauty and the horror. I hate that I have to keep secrets from her.

"I'll never get over it," I hear myself say, inhaling deeply. The air is so rich with sweetness.

"What?" She grins at me, like she's already going to be endeared by my answer.

"The scent of *fresh-cut grass*. Blossoms. Flowers. We have it in Raleigh, obviously, but it's so much stronger down here."

"Yes, it is quite aromatic," Winnie says, and for a moment my brain registers the word as "romantic" and I nearly trip over a pinecone. Or maybe . . . that's just the way she says it.

"Nice SAT word," I tease.

She bumps her hip against mine, very much on purpose. "I should hope so. I study flash cards every night before bed."

"No way? Even when you're drunk?"

She snickers and winks at me. "*Especially* then. Hoping I can crystallize memories even while intoxicated. But yeah, I . . . sort of have to. I'm one of the few campers here on scholarship."

Her eyes fall to the path.

"Oh" is all I can say.

"Yeah," she says. "I have to maintain a certain GPA every school year so they keep giving me the money."

No wonder she hunched over her notebook during test prep, taking such furious notes, her eyes fixed on Ruth. I told myself that I would study, too, use this opportunity like I promised Mom I would . . . because, like Winnie, I do need to keep my grades up, get my scores high. . . . But Ruth's voice still sounds like a lullaby, especially this morning. I find my-self drifting from thoughts of algebra and data analysis*to fields full of horses.

I discover by the time I arrive to aquatics that Melody switched out, obviously due to me, but who cares?

I'm a *soror* now. I have a whole sisterhood behind me, watch-ing me, protecting me.

I push myself hard in the pool, doing laps as Eric cheers me on, not giving a shit about the boys who try to get in my way and fuck up my rhythm or splash me whenever they feel the impulse. Fuck 'em. They can keep going at me, but I'll just keep growing stronger. Tougher.

I've survived initiation. I can survive anything.

I'm steadier on my horse, Velvet, in the ring, and my thighs aren't nearly as sore after riding. Olive and I pass each other secret smiles in the tack room, horseflies buzzing in the hot summer air, unable to touch either of us.

I see my fellow campers now as though I've fully zoomed out on the screen of our lives. As if a light switch has been flipped on, only that light is not a soft bulb but burning neon. We are the children of Wall Street stockbrokers. Lawyers. Politicians. Ambas-sadors and senators, like Jane's mother. She casually slips it into conversation during a card game after lunch. Ginger comes from a famous musical family and is all but guaranteed a record deal with a major label. Scouts are already calling her the next Fiona Apple. For a moment, I feel unworthy of sitting on the floor next to them in my messy hair and off-brand clothing, until I remind myself of the Order of Equus and the way my sisters held me in the horse field.

The way they *saw* me. I've never been seen like that before.

I realize that I want to burn brightly, too, if only for the summer.

Zach is once again a creep during archery. He makes slick

comments with Michael and his obnoxious bros about Winnie's legs. They yell like wild animals to try to distract her whenever she takes a shot, hoping she'll miss her target.

She never does.

Then Winnie lands a bullseye so swift and true it even makes Heather squeal with pride. And then I catch it, amid the applause and cheers of the other campers: Zach reaches out, discreetly, and pats Winnie's ass.

Winnie steps away from him, closer to me and the other girls here who aren't his groupies. She's smiling and acting like she didn't even notice, but by now I know her well enough to see the hurt beneath the sweet façade.

The hurt that's slow boiling to rage.

I know it all too well. It reminds me of myself.

I want to take my bow and shoot him in the eye. Whack him over the head with it and kick at his disgusting excuse for a self. I want to mention it to Heather, what I saw, but I don't want to embarrass Winnie. Especially now that it seems to have been forgotten, and Winnie seems happy again.

I don't want to take away a single moment of her happiness. If she's going to let it go, I guess I will, too.

For now.

Keep your eyes peeled, Lisha told us. *If you see something that goes against our sacred motto, tell one of us. Tell me.*

I stare Zach down, the thunderstorm of fury in my belly calming slightly as I think, *Oh, I will.*

I smile to myself. I can't wait until we meet again, me and my sisters. Until I find out more about what this all means, and what it means for me.

I'm on the brink of really being part of all this. Part of Camp Rockaway. I feel a warm glow of pride, thinking of Mom. She was right to push me to come here. She *knew.* I write her a letter with my fancy Camp Rockaway pen, humming Ginger's song to myself as I go:

Summer sunshine in my eyes
Bright as hell, those blinding skies
They say this is where good girls go to die
Too bad I've never been a good girl

The song is stuck in my head during the rest of that whole surreal week after my initiation. Chantal surprises us on Friday night with another Unit Seven campfire feast. I feel confident enough to ask, and Ginger lets me hold her beautiful guitar. I almost start bawling like a baby then and there, sitting among all these girls. I strum a few chords, doing my best to remember what I learned in all those haunted years I played piano.

"Can you teach me?" I ask Ginger. Once again, she's braiding Porter's hair. Uma's making friendship bracelets with Jane, Olive, and a few other girls in our unit I don't really know. The fire crackles warm and bright on my face, keeping the bugs away, keeping my body feeling safe and protected. The air smells like woodsmoke. It's the most beautiful thing I think I've ever smelled.

"Of course, Arles!" Ginger says, bouncing up and down on her seat on the campfire bench. "I can teach you basic chords tonight, if you like. You played piano, right? It's different, but if you can play piano, you can learn guitar."

She spends the next few minutes refreshing my limited memory of guitar chords, showing me a few I remember and teaching me some I'd forgotten.

When I feel confident enough to, I strum a chord, the music flowing through me, stirring my musical imagination.

Then I hear the sharp whisper: *Put it down, Arlee. You will always be mediocre at best.*

I whip my head around, a bright flash of heat in my belly, searching for the source of the voice. But there is no one around here, no one but me and the other girls and counselors of Unit Seven. The voice, though. I swear, it sounded as if someone were right behind me.

Shivering, I swallow and strum a few strings in defiance. I know that voice. It belongs to Miss Teresa.

"*Fuck you*," I whisper back to her as I strum again, rapturously, until I'm playing something by ear, even though I don't really know the chords or the strings that well. Some intrinsic part of me kicks in and I'm playing and playing and my heart bursts with love because this is it, *this* is the music I've always wanted to cut open my veins and bleed for. Music I feel in my soul. I play a wordless song I write as I go, about fathers who leave and flies that hover. About madwomen and the dark, deep secrets burning within them.

I stop and realize everyone else is silent. Watching me, though this time not with suspicion.

"Wow," Ginger whispers, tears in her eyes. "Arlee. You have a gift."

Winnie walks over to me, warmth blooming in the spot where she touches my shoulder. "You're amazing, Arles. Are you really not fluent in guitar?"

"Seriously, you should consider playing with my band in the Midsummer Concert," Ginger says.

"I . . . uh, yeah, maybe." I blush and pluck at one of the strings. I never did well with compliments.

Chantal's eyes are on me, too. Only she isn't looking at me in awe, or even disgust. She's looking at me as a deer might when it spots you across a forest trail, eyes wide, head up, tail swishing with . . . alertness?

Apprehension.

I stare back at her. In this tiny moment, I love that I have the power to make her uncomfortable, that all her snark and bravado has been reduced to something raw and animal.

She's only seen the half of what I can be.

I show my fangs when I open my mouth to flash her a smile.

CHAPTER EIGHT

That night, after the campfire, my bunkmates and I throw our own little house party.

We're not the only cabin doing it. Bea and Chantal are in the vacant cabin getting drunk and high with some of the other counselors. We're supposed to be in bed by eleven at the latest, but now it's quarter to one, and I'm drinking from a flask while the other girls whoop and cheer me on.

I feel so free now, all warm and fuzzy and floaty. All the anxiety and fear I felt has evaporated from my pores, and now I'm just filled to the brim with liquor and laughter. Ginger gets out her deck of cards and we play round after round of blackjack, placing bets over giant bags of candy and, of course, more shots of booze.

Everything feels lucid and strange, like I'm ensconced in a delightful dream. When I stand, I find I'm wobbly, and I can't stop laughing.

"I need to go the bathroom," I slur, giggling as I try to stand and trip. Why is everything starting to spin?

"Careful, careful," Uma warns.

"I got her." Winnie laughs. She stands and I extend my arms toward her, falling into her embrace. I can't stop giggling. "Winnie! Winona! Come be my caretaker!"

"The trusty bellhop is at your service, *m'lady*," she says with a curtsy, wrapping one arm around me.

Jane throws a gummy bear at her. "You're a fucking dork supreme!" Winnie flips her off and I lean deeper against her warm body, loving the feeling of her hip pressed against mine.

"Careful," Winnie tells Jane. "I'll kick your ass next round and you'll be begging for me to return those gummies after I win them all."

We step out into the warmth of the night, the screen door creaking and slamming behind us. Winnie clicks on her flashlight and tries to guide us down the hill one step at a time, but I realize how much fun it would be if I ran, so I practically bolt to the bottom, stumbling on the way down and skinning my knee on a sharp rock. I barely feel a thing. Another drunken laugh spills out of me.

"Jesus, Arlee!" Winnie sprints after me, but now she's laughing, too.

"Race you to the bathroom!" I cry, and I'm up again and flying through the darkness like a bat, fearless, not caring what I run into or stumble on. I've never felt more alive. More awake.

Winnie waits for me while I pee, leaning against a sink and watching as I wash my hands. When I see myself in the mirror, I take in how drunk I really am, how wobbly I feel. My face almost looks surreal, distorted. I reach out and tap the glass.

"I'm cute," I say to my reflection, then hiccup.

Winnie grins. "Yes, you are cute."

"And you're cute, too, Winnie." I dry my hands on a paper towel and sidle up to her, craving the way it feels whenever our bodies are pressed together. This indescribable love is bubbling inside me, threatening to burst and spill all over her like hot lava. Tears fill my eyes, blurring my already foggy vision. She's still grinning, but there's a softening in her gaze. Maybe even a small look of surprise.

I lean my head against her shoulder and sigh deeply into her warm skin. "I'm so, so glad you're here this summer. I don't know what I'd do without you." Her T-shirt smells so good, like candy and bug spray and sunshine.

I close my eyes, feeling Winnie's fingers gently stroke my hair. "I'm so, so glad you're here, too, Arlee," she says softly. "You know, it's funny, when I first saw you, I thought you looked so terrified. Like a kid on their first day of school."

"That's exactly how I felt! Are you a mind reader? Because it's like you read my mind!" I giggle and slide down to the floor. Winnie slides down with me, her fingers still in my hair, my head still resting against her arm. I can hear her heartbeat, feel it pulsing against my skin.

"You looked terrified," she continues. "But you also looked hopeful, like you wanted us to like you and accept you. I could tell right away that you were a nice person. A genuinely nice person. I knew right away I wanted to be your friend."

"You're my best friend here," I slur. Even with my eyes shut tight, I can feel the room tilt beneath me.

Her nails are on my scalp, scratching lightly, leaving traces of love on my skin. Then I feel her lips brush my cheek.

I open my eyes and tilt my head toward hers. My heartbeat pumps louder. The warm bathroom lights flicker once, twice. Four times. Something tickles my hand, which is resting on her thigh.

A moth.

A massive, gigantic, horrifying moth. Patterns like gaping owl eyes on its wings, and the wings are so large and grotesque and they're much too big. No, no, *no*, they're so massive and curved at the ends and something snaps inside me and I finally release a bloodcurdling scream.

Winnie recoils from me. The moth flaps its dusty wings and

flutters to the ceiling of the bathroom, cocooning its body over the yellow light fixture, which flickers again.

I don't think. I just react. I leap to my feet and sprint out of the bathroom and back into the night and as far away as I can get from the horrible, horrible moth. It's so crushingly dark out here and the crickets are so loud and I can feel it on me. *Oh my God, it's on me! Is it on me?* Every muscle in my body shudders and spasms as I whimper and choke back a sob, the sharp afterimage of the moth superimposed on every patch of darkness until it's all I can see. Over and over, like a fevered hallucination, the giant moth. Its massive dusty wings covered in owl eyes.

I slam into a tree and clutch at it, the bark scraping my skin. I retch and vomit all the liquor and candy into the grass and dirt, my stomach squeezing and searing with pain and my eyes full of tears and all I know is I have to get it all *out, out, out* of me.

"Arlee!" Winnie calls. I hear her panting and running up behind me, one hand on the small of my back, the other gently holding back my hair as I puke. "Oh, Arles, it's okay, that's it. Just let it out. Oh, gosh, we gave you way too much. I'm so sorry, Arlee."

The forest is still spinning but at least the afterimages are gone, my eyes more adjusted to the darkness.

"How did you find me?" I croak. I can't believe she's seeing me like this: puking, crying, pitiful. I should be ashamed, embarrassed, but instead I feel safe. Loved. Like as long as Winnie is here, I'm okay. She'll take care of me.

Winnie clicks on her flashlight. I can hear the smile in her voice when she says, "I brought *this* with me, silly, and I could hear you. You got pretty far from the unit, but not so far I couldn't spot you."

"I think I'm done puking," I moan. "Wait . . . no. I'm not." I retch and vomit bile, because there's nothing left, no more candy or liquor. Nothing inside me but the juices in my stomach.

"My head hurts."

Winnie links her arm through mine and leads me through the makeshift trail in the woods I made and onto a dirt path. "Let's get you back to the cabin. Get you some water. Uma has a secret stash of Tylenol *and* Excedrin if you want any. Though I'd recommend the Tylenol since the Excedrin will keep you up all night."

"Thank you for taking caring of me," I murmur. It's like there's an ice pick in my brain, stabbing at my forehead over and over. I want to lie down and never get up.

"Of course, Arles," she says. "Always."

"And thank you for not judging me. About the moth." I shiver.

We've made it to the sloping hill, our cabin at the top of it. Before we reach the small flight of stairs, she grabs my hand and squeezes. "We all have our fears."

Like this, I think. *I'm scared of how I feel about you.*

The lights are still on in our cabin, but Porter and Jane have migrated to their beds and fallen asleep. Ginger strums at her guitar. She and Uma are on the floor when we walk in, sitting in the aftermath of our cabin party: candy wrappers, bags of chips and cookies. Crumbs cover the blankets, and will no doubt bring more bugs, but right now I'm too dizzy and faded to care.

"You okay? You guys were gone a while," Uma half whispers.

"Just a little too much alcohol," I hear Winnie say, leading me back to my bed. Things are so fuzzy, time slipping in and out. Luckily, I'm already in my sleeping shorts and tank top, so I slide in between the sheets and rest my spinning head on my pillow. Winnie refills my water bottle in the fountain spigot outside and brings it to me, helping me press it to my lips.

I chug down the water. She tucks me in, and I doze off to the sounds of gentle conversation and Ginger strumming some sad, faraway lullaby.

That night I dream of a field. A field full of dozens of wild white horses with massive brown moth wings.

Their eyes are beady, black, and unseeing.

o o o

I'm the last of my bunkmates to wake up the next morning.

For a moment, I'm disoriented, as if I half expect to see the pink seashell lamp and San Francisco poster in my bedroom instead of the inside of this cabin.

I'm drenched in sweat. My sheets and pillow are damp. My head feels fuzzy and stuffed with cotton.

Those dreams I had . . . they did a number on me. I sit up slowly in bed and stretch, stars dancing in front of my eyes.

All I want to do now is shower in freezing cold water.

There was no 8 A.M. bugle call. No rushing to the bathroom to brush our teeth and wash our faces in preparation for a big day at camp.

It's finally Saturday, and that means no electives today, no test-prep session. Brunch will be served at eleven, and it's only quarter to ten. After brunch we can take part in any makeshift activity that might be going on around the campgrounds, be it sports or crafts or music practice, but otherwise we're free to wander so long as we tell a counselor where we'll be and we go everywhere with a buddy.

Jane is bouncing around, already high on sugar. Ginger is writing a new song, mumbling lyrics to herself from her top bunk as she strums her guitar. Uma and Porter are sitting on the floor, leafing through some trashy celebrity magazine and whisper-giggling over every page.

Winnie is, oddly, nowhere to be found. She's usually the last person to wake up, not me.

I swallow down a lump in my throat. Last night was almost perfect. We finally got alone together and we almost . . . kissed.

Did I drunkenly imagine that?

All I want to do is feel that wonderful rush of love I felt the other night. I wish she was here with us now. With me. I have to find a way to get her alone again, if only to restore that shattered moment. . . .

Fucking moth.

"Should I wear this for Sundown?" Porter asks as she twirls around the cabin, holding up a yellow sundress for us all to see.

Sundown Ceremony. It's the only firm thing we have scheduled this weekend. This mysterious, required ceremony held tomorrow night in the Grand Amphitheater.

"*Love* that!" Jane says. She's sitting on her bed, flipping through a Wonder Woman comic book while digging through a bag of gummy worms. "You can borrow my braided sandals if you want, Port. They'd go so well."

"You're truly a genius, Jane," says Ginger. "A style genius. Forever Freya is shaking."

Jane flips her hair and scoffs dramatically. "It's the wisdom of all those middle-school modeling camps!"

I've heard a few whispers about it throughout the week, but no exact explanation of what Sundown Ceremony is. As I pull my fuzzy robe around my sleep clothes, I ask, "What is it, exactly?"

Uma shrugs. "It's this weird thing they do every summer," she says. "Another meaningless Camp Rockaway ritual."

Porter shakes her head and insists, "It always means *something*. We don't know exactly what, but it does. It changes a bit every summer."

"It's, uh . . . you ever seen a really weird, artsy play, Arlee? The kind that feels oddly menacing even though you know it's not meant to be?" Ginger asks. I shrug, nod, and fish around in my footlocker for my bug spray. "It's kind of like that. Only . . ."

"Creepier," Uma finishes.

"It's, yeah, it's not my favorite activity," Ginger admits, plucking a string that sounds vaguely out of tune.

The door bangs open and in walks Bea in athletic leggings and a fitted sports tank, her skin glistening with sweat. "Oh, good, you girls aren't still drooling in your beds," she says.

"Where were *you*?" Uma asks.

"Morning yoga by the campfire. I told you girls about it last night before you had your little party, but as always, none of you listen."

"We listen, we just prefer drooling in our beds, especially after we *party*," says Ginger. "Hey, Bea, do you like this verse I came up with?" Ginger begins to play something for Bea as I gather my towel and shower caddy, then head to the bathrooms down the hill, eager to wash off the sticky-hot sweat and get some of the fuzziness out of my brain.

A few other girls and counselors are gathered near the campfire circle, rolling up yoga mats, Chantal included. Winnie is not among them. Maybe she's in the bathroom.

I call her name once I get inside, water hissing and steam rising from a few of the stalls, but no one answers me.

For some reason, it gives me this brief feeling of . . . panic.

I remember the black, beady, unseeing horse eyes in my dreams and shudder.

God, I hope she's okay, I think—even though I *know* I have no reason to believe otherwise—as I lather shampoo through my hair again and again and again, my eyes scanning the walls nervously for insects.

I can't help but remember the moth.

I blast the cold water and gasp when it slaps against my skin. *Keep your eyes peeled*, Lisha told us. *Look out for one another.* Am I not meant to be looking out for Winnie?

No, Arlee, she's fine, I berate myself. *You're imagining things. Everything is fine. You got too drunk and you freaked out and Winnie helped you back into bed. Stop spiraling.*

It was only a damn moth.

I gently shift the water to warm and breathe deeply for a few minutes. Eventually, the fuzziness in my head begins to fade, and my heart rate starts to drop. I envision myself and my sisters in the field, imagine that the warmth of the water is the warmth from their loving embraces. My wet hair up in a towel, I step to the sinks to brush my teeth.

I freeze. My shower caddy clatters to the floor.

There's a huge, massive, horrifying long-legged spider nestled inside the basin of the sink. Like the one I saw crawling across Olive's bed, only, somehow, ten times worse. Even worse than the moth from last night. . . .

Its legs are twitching—oh God, *oh God*—stretching across every inch of the sink bowl. No no no *no. Fuck that.* I retch and swallow back the impending vomit, my heart thumping against my rib cage like a sledgehammer. I want to race out of the bathroom as fast as my flip-flops will take me. I'll brush my teeth outside with fountain spigot water, or I won't brush them at all today because good God.

Then I feel it: a sudden wave of rage mixed with the repulsion.

I want to kill it, I think.

I want to *smash* the spider with my bare hands.

I lift a shaking palm in the air, trying to steady myself. I can do it. I can kill it. End its sick, sad little life. It's only a spider and it can't hurt me and—

No. I can't. I can't. I'm a coward. A failure. I run out of the bathroom, visions of the smashed spider dancing behind my eyes.

I can still feel it as if it were on me. I can't do it. I can't bring myself to. A wave of shame follows the rage and repulsion. They'll always own me. Control me. Why did I ever think that I could make it here, with all the fucking bugs? Now there's more humming in the air, gnats and flies circling the trash bins near the front of the unit. They fill my head with their buzzing until my ears ring.

It takes me a few moments to realize that I've dropped my towel somewhere in the grass, and remember that I left my shower caddy behind. That I'm panting in my bathrobe and flip-flops, looking absolutely ridiculous. My hands and feet can't stop tingling, my toes recoiling even though I'm so far from the sink spider.

I can't believe I came so close to killing it.

Christ. Here I am, losing my shit in a bathrobe with soaking wet hair. No wonder people think I'm bananas. No wonder they whisper.

A few girls still clustered around the campfire are staring at me. Including Olive. She holds her hand up and lets it linger there. It's not quite a wave, but an acknowledgment, nonetheless. She smiles a little.

She sees me. I should relax. With her, I'm safe. With my sisters nearby, I'm always safe.

But why can't I stop shivering?

My teeth clattering, I force myself to walk back to the bathroom and collect my things, but no. I can't face the spider again. I can't. The too-many legs, the massive, ungodly body I was too pathetic and terrified to smash—

"Arles?"

Winnie stands in front of me. *Winnie.* Relief washes over me for a moment, but only barely dampens my anxiety attack. Like me, she's wearing a bathrobe, only hers is personalized with WINONA DE LEÓN embroidered across the front in gold letters. She's holding my shower caddy, everything neatly tucked inside, which I stare at gratefully.

"I heard the commotion and saw all your stuff on the floor," she says. "I figured . . . was it the spider? Oh, Arles, I'm so sorry. Some of the ones in these particular woods are really terrifying, I know that."

I swallow hard and nod, my cheeks flushed. I'm unable to speak. *Act normal*, I tell myself. *Be cool.* That gets slightly harder when she smiles and steps closer to me, touching the part of my arm where the sleeve of my robe has slid down.

"Listen, after brunch I'm thinking of going for a swim in the river. If you're not doing anything else, you should come with me."

The warmth from her hand travels to my heart, cracking open there like some strange heated blossom.

I clear my throat. "I'd love to," I finally manage to say. I reach out for her, and she folds her fingers around mine. "Thanks for grabbing my caddy, by the way. I'm . . ."

"Afraid of bugs." She makes it sound so simple. No judgment. No strange looks, no scoffs or a roll of her eyes. No words like "weirdo." Just a fear. A simple fear that a lot of people surely have, too. "Let's go get dressed and ready for brunch, okay? I find I'm a bit jumpier when I'm hungry."

I almost leave the pink towel in the grass, forgotten, but Winnie grabs it just in time. She's always here. Always taking care of me. I should take better care of her. My sisters should know about Zach. . . .

She slips her arm around my waist and together we walk up the hill, butterflies flapping wings made of sparklers inside my stomach. I could walk like this with her forever.

When we pass Olive, she and I nod at one another, as if to say, *I'm here. I see you.*

I see you too, I think.

o o o

That afternoon, just as she suggested, we wander down to the river for a swim, just the two of us.

Jane wanted to join some of the other campers and counselors for an impromptu soccer game. Porter went off with Uma as her reluctant third wheel to visit the boy in Unit Three she's been making eyes at across the dining hall. Ginger is with her makeshift rock band, practicing in preparation for the Midsummer Concert.

And I have Winnie all to myself, the skies cloudy with warm streaks of sunlight peeking through as if the world is saying, *It's all gonna be okay.*

I am in awe of the way Winnie exists so effortlessly in the world. She walks with confidence, back straight, head high—and it's not like Olive's regal confidence; there's an easiness to it—even though she's only wearing a nautical navy-and-white one-piece swimsuit and nothing else. As we pass by other units and impromptu sports games and pairs and groups, boys and girls alike stare. I know they aren't staring at me, in my baggy Camp Rockaway T-shirt and cotton shorts, my head down, eyes mostly kept to the dirt. They stared at me when I first came here, but that was only out of curiosity. They stare now because they've figured out who I am, but they don't stare at me like they do at Winnie. I am the strange girl. The source of their suspicion. The one with the nightmare mom. Winnie is the beautiful one. The elegant one. The girl who laughs openly before shouting snappy comebacks to any boy who dares to whistle or catcall her.

"Your body would look good next to mine!" one hollers at her.

"But your tiny dick sure wouldn't!" she shoots back.

This always causes the boys to go "*oooh!!*" and "*oh, shit, bro!*" and rib their friend who was bold enough to harass someone as powerful as Winona de León.

The brackish smell of the Echo River hits my nose before the wide expanse of water comes into view. I love the sand on the river's beach, gritty but soft enough between my toes. The trees and patches of grass that surround it like a sacred grove.

And oddly, there's an old piano.

It sits alone beneath the protective branches of a massive willow tree. Light yellowing wood, recalling an old parlor style. Or maybe some kind of saloon. I can practically hear the ragtime music that might've been played on its keys. The piano is pushed back enough far from the beach that you don't notice it right away, but once you see it, you can't *unsee* it.

I ask her about it, but Winnie only says, "It's been here a very, very long time. Possibly before the camp existed. No one really knows why the owners keep it on the grounds. No one plays it, to my knowledge. It's sort of a Rockaway mystery."

The piano calls to me, softly at first, and then with an urgency I can't dismiss. Soon it's practically shouting my name. It calls to me to lift the lid and run my hands across the keys.

I shudder and spread my towel and lie out on the sand, spraying myself with extra sunscreen and bug spray. Winnie slips out of her flip-flops and puts her feet in the river. She raises her arms to the sky and exhales deeply with a satisfied "*Ahhh!*"

A dragonfly skims across the water's surface and flies right past her. In that moment, it doesn't frighten me. Not one bit.

The sun hits Winnie's skin as if she's made of stained glass, and I see fractured rainbows dancing across her skin. She shouts out with glee. Elation. She is pure joy. She is something that lies beyond what beautiful ever could be.

Something I could never ever dream to be.

She is . . . perfect.

My chest constricts, moths flapping their ghoulish wings inside my belly. I stand, strip out of my clothes until I'm in my bikini, in a body I don't feel proud of or even like much, even though I feel like I should. Even though every Instagram infographic decorated in soft pastels practically begs me to. That proverbial self-love, and the calm, assured self-acceptance it brings. It sounds to me like some old folk tale. Enchanting to think about, but not something I can ever quite grasp for myself.

I leave my glasses on my towel and wade into the shallow water. I stand beside Winnie, the warm rocks massaging my feet.

"It's perfect here," I say, even though things are out of focus now, but I kind of like it that way.

She shuts her eyes. "It's my favorite place in the whole world."

As soon as she catches me staring, I quickly look away and blush, staring down at my own stomach. How it sticks out and grows puffy after I've eaten. How it'll never be flat. How I know deep down there's nothing bad or wrong about this, but I can't help but feel defective all the same. And then feel defective about feeling defective.

"I'll never have a body like yours," I hear myself say. I don't know what it is about this place, because I would normally never be so bold as to say such a thing, let alone admit it to someone I've only recently met.

Winnie's face falls. "Arles . . . what do you mean? Your body is your body. Mine is mine. I mean, *duh*, but you know what I'm saying, right?" She moves a little closer to me. She smells like sunscreen and river air. "Your body is beautiful, Arlee. Everything about it is. It's okay if you don't love it now, or accept it as it is, but why don't you put aside for a moment what you think you *look* like—which, by the way, is stunning—and focus on how you feel?" She lifts her arms once more and closes her eyes. "How does it feel to have the warmth of the sun on your body? How do your feet feel against the rocks? Doesn't it feel so amazing? You know what feels even better?" She turns and grins at me before wading further in.

Comments like these might feel patronizing from someone else, or even a tad cliché. From Winnie, though, they somehow sound profound.

I follow her as she goes deeper and deeper, then dives beneath the surface of a wave. When she breaks for air, droplets spill from her hair like summer rain.

"My God, I feel alive again!" She laughs. "Come on, Arles, you'll see what I mean! It's amazing!"

I grin and dive in after her, enjoying the way the river sucks me in and sends shock waves through me from the cold. I sink to the bottom. When I surface, she's right there, swimming toward me. She splashes me, and I splash her right back.

"You look like a mermaid," I blurt out, then feel my face flush when she parts her lips in surprise.

"So do you," she says with a smile.

The moths in my belly flap their wings even harder.

Winnie floats on her back, so I do the same. With my ears underwater, everything becomes achingly quiet and still. I relax into it, that peaceful feeling. I think of last night, of our interrupted moment of bliss. Of racking up the courage to try kissing her again . . .

"Chantal's here!" Winnie yells, waving at the beach. "Hey, Chantal!" She smirks at me as I pop up out of that blissful quiet. "And she's got her man with her."

Chantal is, indeed, with a guy.

I squint and make out the shape of Eric, my handsome aquatics instructor.

They're blurry, but I can sort of make them out. Sitting together beneath the willow tree, half-obscured by its long low-hanging branches laden with green leaves.

"Ugh, she can't hear me," Winnie grumbles. "Let's go say hi."

"I didn't know she had a boyfriend."

"Oh, yeah, Chantal is a lady of many mysteries."

To my dismay, Winnie swims to the riverbank. I follow, though I wanted to stay out there longer. Let her tell me all the good things I should think and feel about myself.

While Winnie approaches the couple, I stall and wipe myself down with my towel and put my glasses back on. My vision sharp once more, I focus in on the couple under the tree: Eric's fingers intertwined in Chantal's, one of his hands crawling up her thigh.

I watch as she and Winnie chat happily. Winnie beckons me over. I have a sudden violent urge to run back to Unit Seven and hide under my bed. I've done a great job of mostly avoiding Chantal all week, ever since my outburst. Still, she makes me nervous.

But I can't keep hiding from everything that scares me. I'm a sister now of the Order of Equus. I have a whole group of girls behind me, protecting me, I remind myself. I can handle anything.

Protect the girls.

I take a deep breath and approach, the yellow-and-blue seahorse beach towel Mom gave to me wrapped protectively around my body.

Chantal and Eric are in love. I somehow know this right away from up close. She's glowing, he's glowing, her whole body and face so relaxed. She nuzzles her head into the crook of his neck, the smallest of smiles on her usually pursed lips.

I don't know if I've ever been in love, but I can feel it from them. It feels good and pure and true.

"Arles!" Winnie chirps. "We were just discussing what weird shit Caroline might have up her sleeve tomorrow night."

"Mmm, she better not recite spoken-word poetry for ten minutes and then randomly burst into song," Chantal scoffs. "Remember that one?" She and Eric laugh over the memory.

"Is that what she usually does?" I ask, feeling awkward and a little chilly in the shade of the willow tree. I want so badly to be back out in the water with Winnie.

Chantal cocks her head at me. "Oh, right. You've never been to Sundown Ceremony." The way she says it, I can't quite tell if she's mocking me or being serious.

"So, it's as weird as it sounds?"

She grimaces. "It's weirder, if you can believe it. Though it . . . changes."

"Changes?"

"It's a little different every summer," Winnie says. "Though Chantal has seen more of them than I have."

"Should I be scared?" I half joke.

Chantal scoffs and laughs. "Girlie, you have no more reason to fear Caroline Rhinelander than you do that piano," she says, nodding to the yellowed instrument. "She's kind of kooky but totally harmless. She's a great leader around here."

"Yeah," Eric adds. "We love Caroline."

Even though it's fairly far away from us, the piano seems to be inching closer and closer across the beach . . . and I can almost hear the sound of its mellow keys.

"You two should head back soonish," Chantal says, melting her back into Eric's shoulder. "Change and get ready for dinner. We're eating early tonight, and I doubt you'll want to go smelling like river water."

I check my watch. We should have plenty of time to stay at the river, and I start to say so, but Winnie yanks me away as she says goodbye for both of us, then whispers in my ear, "That's her code for 'I want some alone time with my man.' Let's take a little walk farther down the beach before we head back. Chantal's right. We should shower before we eat."

My heart sinks at the thought of going back so soon, but I don't want to sound clingy or needy. Annoying. Instead, I ask, "Don't they spend tons of *alone time* together?"

Winnie giggles and bumps her bare shoulder against mine. "It's never enough for those two."

I shiver again, a full-body shiver that hits me like an electric shock, but this time it's not from the coolness of the shade.

○ ○ ○

The path to and from the river is flanked by black wrought-iron lampposts.

Elegant and tall, they look as though as they belong to a bygone era, not on the grounds of a teen summer camp. They flank the path to and from the dining hall, too, and as we walk back from dinner, I step closer to get a better look. Each lantern emits a soft glow, and each attracts a wealth of creepy-crawlies drawn to the light as though it were the sun itself.

Wrapped and twisted around one is a massive spiderweb.

Corpses of brown moths hang by their feet from the silk, lit by the orange shine of the lantern. I lean closer, vomit in my throat, television static roaring in my ears. Though my brain is screaming at me not to, I reach out and gently tap one, startling when it wiggles, its antennae flickering back and forth. It's not a corpse, after all.

It's still alive.

Above it in the center of the web is a truly dead moth, its

body divided by the spider clean in two. It floats between the silk strands like corn husks in a southern wind.

Do the moths that remain alive after they are captured accept their fate? Do they know they're done for? Have they lost the will to stop pumping their fragile wings, beating their little legs, struggling to fly free?

Are they as scared as I feel right now?

The moths horrify me, dead or alive, whether hanging as husks or soon-to-be corpses.

But they feel familiar.

As familiar as . . .

I stare at the still-alive moth that disgusts me in every way possible and wonder, even though I can't seem to bring myself to:

Should I try to free it?

As dusk inches closer, I start to notice them cropping up despite the layers of bug spray I've slathered on: little white bumps all over my arms and legs. They itch so bad, these mosquito bites, and I do my best to block out the thought of the sharp tips of their straw-like mouths, sucking in my blood and injecting their saliva in its place. . . .

Goose bumps appear beside my bites by the time Winnie and I reach the cabin, me lost in the static, nodding and pretending to listen to her long-winded story about some friends of hers from back home.

I know from my research rabbit holes late into the night that the only mosquitoes who bite are the females. They need our blood so they can make their eggs and spawn a billion more with slender legs and long, translucent wings. I know from my research, too, that they are, in fact, flies. They live on liquid diets, they can walk upside down, and they're able to see behind them.

I want them dead. I want them all dead. One is one too many. One means dozens more.

CHAPTER NINE

That night, once again, I'm having the strangest dream. I'm immersed in total blackness, something sticky, warm, and wet in my hands. I dig in with my hands, deeper and deeper, and I'm almost to the truth when a burst of light startles me awake.

I squint into the flashlight shining into my eyes.

"Sorry," Winnie whisper-giggles. "Secret mission tonight. Want to be my buddy?"

I groan. "Where?"

"The barn," she whispers, smile as bright as her flashlight. Tiny insects swarm in the light's gleam, but I do my best to pretend they aren't there, even though I can almost feel them burrowing beneath my skin—

Wait, could it be? Is Winnie part of the society, too?

No. My heart sinks when I remember that's impossible. She wasn't there, at the initiation.

"You mean the barn party?" I whisper. "Won't Zach be there?"

She pouts at me. "*Please.* Don't let his disgusting presence dissuade you, Arles."

"Stop shining that in my eyes and maybe I will," I say, kicking at her under the covers. She giggles and snorts and soon we're both laughing.

"*Shut up!*" Uma snaps from her bed.

"Keep your pj's on, lady!" Winnie hisses. In the glow of her flashlight, I put on my glasses, pull on a hoodie, and slip into flip-flops. On the way out, as we're careful to tiptoe over the squeakiest floorboards, I notice Chantal's bed is once again empty, though Bea is sound asleep in hers.

"Cooler tonight," I note, zipping my hoodie up all the way. The stars shimmer, and I'll never get over how bright and clear they are down here. How fresh and sweet the air smells. I catch a whiff of pine, and then, as Winnie turns her head, her tea tree shampoo.

"It's so nice out, isn't it?" she asks, inhaling deeply. "Atlanta is so congested, especially where I live. So many lights. So much pollution. Here you can really *feel* the air, you know what I mean?"

I nod. She is so beautiful, standing there with her flashlight in her cotton shorts and pink flip-flops. Everything about her is so beautiful. "I can see more stars here than I've ever seen in my life."

I follow her down the slope of the hill and through the darkened path, our footfalls soft on the dirt. The whole way, we don't speak, just enjoy the sounds of the forest at night. The frogs that croak in the small pond we pass. The hoots of the owls in the trees.

The familiar whinny of the horses.

Even from a distance, I can hear the pounding bass and see the flashing colored lights coming from the barn and spilling out into the night. Yellow, red, blue, green; they alternate like the ones inside a nightclub, or at least the nightclubs I've seen in movies and on TV. Just beyond, the horses agitated and anxious in their stables. Kept awake by the music and shrieking loud voices from the party, even though they're plenty far away from the barn.

The barn doors are ajar, a few people clustered around the sides of it. I spot a familiar-looking girl, red Solo cup in hand, leaning against the wooden slats and chatting it up with an older guy counselor I've seen a few times. Then I realize why she looks so familiar.

I saw her the night of my initiation. Bright red hair. Baby-blue eyes. Winnie notices me staring and lightly jabs at my side. "Forever Freya finally catch your eye?"

"Huh?" I blush, glad she can't see my face begin to go red in the darkness.

She laughs. "She's a famous beauty influencer. I think she's got, like, a hundred thousand followers on Instagram alone."

"Huh." I shift my eyes away from Freya and onto a group of guys having an intense debate about something that definitely isn't school-related. They, too, hold red Solo cups, taking swigs.

So one of my sisters is famous. An *influencer.*

"My sister," I accidentally murmur, and when Winnie bunches her nose at me in confusion, I cough and clear my throat. "Never mind. Sorry. Sometimes I talk to myself."

My blush is even worse now.

"It's okay," Winnie says, weaving her fingers through mine, and my heart does a backflip. "Let's go check it out."

As we step closer to the barn, I notice a curl of thick smoke coming from one of the debating boys' hands and the glow of an ember. I catch the skunky smell. Marijuana.

I shouldn't be surprised. It would be fairly easy to sneak drugs into camp, now that I think about it, and weed is simple enough to get. Still, there's something about the way those boys keep glancing over at us in between hits of the joint they pass around. Massive laughs and loud, aggressive-sounding voices. Wide, powerful stances. Like they own the camp. Like they own the whole world.

The closer we get to the barn, the louder the bass and pounding music grows, until I can barely hear Winnie at all when she asks, "What do you want to drink?"

I was hoping by now she would explain to me what we're doing here, or who we're here to see, but instead she raises her eyebrows at me in question, as if I was the one who dragged her here to this forbidden midnight party. As if I'm the one who's desperate for alcohol.

"Uh . . . what do they have?"

She smirks at me, her eyes twinkling with amusement. "Jungle juice, most likely."

"What's that?"

She laughs. "Come on, I'll show you. It's amazing but *horrible*."

Then the barn doors swing fully open, campers spilling out. Loud, animated, booze slipping from their red Solo cups.

We step inside, where it smells of sweat and liquor and bodies.

Chaos.

A disco ball spins from a hook dangling from the rafters. Fractured lights sparkle and spin against the walls and the floor as the room alternates between neon candy colors. The music is pulsating. Joyful. A girl in 3D glasses deejays from a far corner of the room on a shiny laptop resting atop a hay barrel. Portable speakers pound with a bass that rattles the ground.

Older campers and counselors alike are jumping, dancing, pumping their fists to the beat. Grinding against each other. Pouring alcohol from a giant keg and taking shots. Sloshing drinks everywhere. Smoking from pipes and joints and bowls. Making out against the walls. On the barrels of hay. In one section, a game of dice is being played with real money piled on the floor. A lot of money. Hundred-dollar bills. In another, a game of poker with equally high monetary stakes.

Holy shit.

Winnie grabs my hand and pulls me through a throng of

people until we're at the keg. She grabs us some cups from a tall stack and begins to pour me a drink.

When she hands it to me, her smile is so dazzling and wide as she taps hers against mine in a toast that I don't think, I just take a sip.

It's bright and fruity, and I can't taste the alcohol. It doesn't burn going down.

"Welcome to Rockaway!" she screams, grabbing me, hugging me tight, jumping us up and down in time to the music. I scream, too. I feel free. Alive. The lights cast mirrored rainbows across her face and I could kiss her right now, I think. Pull her in close to me and touch her lips to mine.

I take another long drink from my cup. I feel fizzy. Elated. Bold. Our noses touch when I turn my head toward her, and then our lips brush and part.

I go for it. I kiss her.

She kisses me back.

It's my very first kiss, with the music and the scents of smoke and booze and the neon-colored Americana dreamland of Camp Rockaway all around me. Around us.

Then she pulls away.

"B-r-b," she whispers in my ear, and I startle, surprised. I smell the fruity sweetness on her breath. Before I can ask where the hell she's going, she's off into the crowd, and I'm standing alone, the music thumping, people bumping into me.

My mouth goes dry and my heart drops. Did she not like it? Did I scare her?

Did she think we were only playing around? Kissing like girls who are friends sometimes do?

Did she think it was all for attention, that I was using her to try to get attention from boys? I've seen other girls do that.

A few are staring, shooting me long, curious looks from across the makeshift dance floor.

Including a boy, part of the poker game, who's sneering at me from across the room, like he saw us kissing and was getting off on it.

I take an angry chug of my drink and turn away from him. I won't let him—*any* of them—get to me. I sway to the beat as song after song goes by, but the more time passes, the more I feel awkward and uneven. It's not the same without Winnie. No one around me is letting me into their circle. No one seems to want to talk to me or even be near me.

Tears well up in my eyes.

Maybe Winnie doesn't really want me either.

The smell of weed and cheap beer is overpowering. Nauseating, even, and whatever's in my cup isn't making it better. That sickening sweetness threatens to climb up my throat, and I refuse to drunkenly puke two nights in a row. There's a girl on Rollerblades swerving through the gaps in the crowd, making me dizzy. I keep thinking I can hear people saying things like *"There's that weirdo girl"* and *"God, she gives me the creeps,"* but it's so loud and chaotic, it's hard to tell what's real. My heart speeds up and I feel my fists clench at my sides, my Solo cup crunching in my hand.

I need to get out of here. There's no trash can that I can see, so I just drop my cup on the floor and push past all the people, past the rowdy game of king's cup that's triggering cheers and shouting arguments, and back out into the fresh air of the night.

Small packs of boys and girls are huddled about, sharing joints and cigarettes. One is even wearing a massive pair of deer antlers, like some kind of bizarre headband. I recognize a few people from my electives, but everyone at this party seems to be on the older side. Counselors and the girls from Unit Eight and the boys from Unit One. Forever Freya, of course. My famous sister, though I'm too intimidated to go up to her outside of our society meetings. I scan the small crowd, but there's no Winnie in sight.

Jesus, I hope she's okay. I hope she's not mad at me, or disgusted. I'm so ready to go back to the cabin and go to sleep, and—

"*Arlee?!*"

Lisha is huddled in one of the small groups of people, along with Michael and a gaggle of girls who are probably from her unit. They don't smile at me like she does, just sort of stiffen and stare, and I feel my jaw clench tight. They're all dressed as impeccably as one can be at a sleepaway camp: high-waisted shorts, crop tops, and cutout tanks that cinch their waists. Rompers with frills that were definitely not from some local mall. Lisha is the only one dressed in all black.

I take a cautious step forward. I'm happy to see Lisha, but the others . . . they definitely don't seem happy to see me. The muffled bass thumps from inside the barn. Lisha beams and beckons me into their group, and the five or so other girls only move an inch or two to let me into the circle. Michael, though, leans a little too close into me for comfort.

"I'm so glad you came! Where's your drink?" Lisha asks, taking a sip of hers.

I shrug, the harsh looks of the others girls only making me feel more on edge, even though my sister is here with me. There's a gnawing in my gut, something familiar clawing to the surface slowly but surely. "Must've misplaced it."

"Aren't you Arlee Gold?" one of the girls asks, a curly-haired brunette with cold blue eyes. She wrinkles her button nose at me. For a blip in time, I imagine what it would feel like to punch it so hard it breaks.

Then I blink and the ultraviolent thought is gone. I shiver, repulsed with myself.

Get it together, Arlee.

"I am," I say, straightening a little and sizing her up. "Can I help you? Is there a problem?"

Lisha looks impressed. A few of the girls laugh, acting surprised. They didn't expect a mouth on me, I guess.

"Maybe there is," says the brunette. She takes a step toward me and I can smell the liquor on her breath.

"Woah, woah, chill, Paula," Michael says, holding her back. "Arlee's cool. She's not like that."

Like what? I think.

Obviously, this once again has something to do with my mom. Sam Gold. The resident camp pariah, even though she hasn't been a camper in well over two decades. Even though no one will tell me what the fuck she's done that's made her—and me—so repulsive to them.

The look in Paula's eyes is starting to become all too familiar. Fear masked as rage.

Fear. I try on that idea, that I can inspire fear. It makes me stand a little taller, hold my head a little higher, and maybe I imagine it, but Paula shrinks away from me.

"Arlee's awesome," Lisha agrees, and this seems to relax a few of the other girls. "Frankly, I'm glad you came to liven this party up a little bit. I haven't seen Paula so pissed since Iris stole her last-summer boyfriend."

"*Fuck you,* Lisha!" Paula throws her drink right in Lisha's face. A few girls gasp, me included. Lisha takes it like a champ, not even flinching as the alcohol drips into her eyes. She runs her finger across her cheek and licks it.

"*Mmm,* my favorite vodka flavor," she says with a chuckle as Paula storms off and the other girls disperse, some to follow and comfort her, and some who've clearly had enough of this drama.

Lisha looks right at me and grins like we're best friends. "I told you, people don't like me, Arlee."

"I guess that makes two of us," I say. "Thanks for backing me up and all."

"You're just blunt, Leesh," Michael says. He's lingering still, his eyes bright, a grin on his lips. Like he finds all this so funny. "And she's just wasted and kind of a bitch. Ignore her."

"Things I'm already well aware of," Lisha says dryly, taking another drink from her cup. "Paula's not a bitch, though. I probably deserved that splash of Stoli. Sore spot for her. Here, Michael, get me a refill?"

He rolls his eyes and scoffs but takes the cup from her. "You owe me a Xanny for this," he grumbles before stalking off into the crowd.

Lisha wipes the rest of her face and hair with the fabric of her T-shirt. It's incredible: she isn't bothered by any of this. I inch closer toward her, craving her cool calm. Her confidence and ease. The way she acts as though drinks are flung in her face every single day.

I can definitely learn from her.

I briefly wonder if she, too, inspires fear. She must, I think. She's a great leader. She wears the skull of the Pale Mare all too convincingly.

"Have you seen Winnie?" I ask.

"Mm, yeah, earlier," Lisha says. "Want me to help you find her?"

I could melt with gratitude. "Yes, please, and thank you, Lisha. It's nice to have someone talk to me like a normal person."

Lisha links her arm through mine and smiles. "You *are* normal, Arlee. Maybe everyone *else* here is bonkers." I smile back and off we go, scanning the party together, indoors and outdoors.

The drunken, rowdy, stoned assortment of older kids and coun-selors. It feels so nice to have Lisha by my side, guiding me through the madness.

"So did my mom, like, spit in too many people's spiked lem-onades or something?" I ask her as we leave the Winnie-less barn.

Lisha throws her head back and laughs. "Oh my God, Arlee! Don't pay attention to these losers. Your mom is a legend. Anyone who says otherwise is riddled with nothing but envy."

Envy. That's certainly not what this feels like, but Lisha seems to know what's up, so I nod and follow her around the perimeter of the barn.

I think again of the sacred motto I agreed to uphold: *Protect the girls.* Of how I promised myself I'd care for Winnie. Tell my sisters about the asshole who keeps harassing her.

"You should know, by the way, Zach's being . . . a complete douche to Winnie lately. A creep, really. I know you sit with him and are friends with him but honestly, I can't stand that asshole." I think I hear his smarmy laugh right then and there from inside the barn party, but I know I'm imagining it.

"We're not friends," Lisha says stiffly. "And we've got that all covered." Right as I'm about to ask what she means, she points and adds, "There's our girl."

I squint and spot Winnie over by the stables, bathed in the yel-low glow of the outdoor lights. There's a dreamy look on her face as she strokes the Appaloosa she's been raving about all week. Her horse for the summer. We hurry over.

"Oh my God, Arlee, you found me!" She giggles and stum-bles backward, landing hard on her butt. Her horse whinnies and nearly kicks her right in the head. Lisha and I help her up and get her away from the frightened animal, but all the while she's still giggling.

"Ugh, Winnie, you know better than to stand directly behind a horse," Lisha scolds.

Winnie throws her hands in the air and shrieks, *"C'est la vie!"* Then she bursts into another fit of giggles.

"Jesus, Win, how much did you drink?" I ask, kneeling down to her level to help her to her feet.

"Not *nearly* enough, Arles." Her eyes are going in two different directions, even when they attempt to focus on me. Her breath smells like sour booze, and she keeps stumbling while Lisha and I do our best to guide her away from the stables.

I guess tonight is her turn to get wasted and for me to help her. Was I this bad the other night? Somehow, I doubt it.

"See, what neither of you understand and what no one in the whole world understands," she slurs, "is that this is probably the very best I've ever felt in my entire life." She tugs on my arm so hard I feel my shoulder muscle give a painful pull. I wince, tears stinging my eyes and blurring my vision, as Lisha and I take her past the barn with the party still raging on.

"I'm so very glad for you," I say. "But I think it's better to call it a night."

"No!" Winnie cries. She stomps her foot like a toddler. "You don't get it, Arles! The *better* has just begun!" She grabs me in her arms and pulls me up against her. My heart reaches my throat as her lips go right to my ear, reminding me of our kiss. "Don't you want to party, Arles? Don't you want to experience a *real* Camp Rockaway night?"

"Sure, um, but let's do it another night, okay? You're smashed, Winnie. Shit . . . where's Lisha?"

She's gone. Vanished back into the crowd without saying goodbye, leaving me alone to deal with this.

Weird.

And what was that about "we've got that all covered"?

I admit, the way she said it . . . it scares me.

I'm sweating profusely now, doing my best to wrangle Winnie and guide her past the small groups still mingling outside, smoking and drinking and laughing. A few boys whistle and catcall as we pass them.

I hear Zach's voice, rising above the drunken laughter. "Winnie, you look *hot* wasted! I hate to see you leave, but I love to watch you barely walk a straight line while you go!"

"Fucking asshole, hope he chokes on his own saliva," Winnie mumbles, then giggles as she trips and nearly takes us both down with her. I pull my miniflashlight out of my pocket and snap it on, tugging at her arm.

"Come *on*, Winnie! One foot in front of the other." But she's too heavy and uncoordinated for me to tame, especially with my flashlight in one hand. She pulls us both to the ground and wraps her arms and legs around me, cackling with laughter. The boys hoot and holler some more, and then the rush of fatigue hits me all at once. I don't want to be here right now, on the ground with Winnie like a circus sideshow. A spectacle. I hate the way people are laughing at us, and the way she seems oblivious to it. She rolls off me, accidentally exposing her bra.

"Yes, baby girl, give us a show!" a boy cheers. I scramble to my feet as Winnie lies on her back, eyes slipping closed. I pull down her shirt and cover her chest. She's beyond gone, and a couple of boys are advancing, like sharks that smell blood in the water. I try to lift her but she's too heavy. I'm breathing hard. I can't do this. Not alone. I can't—

"Well, well, well, look what the cat dragged in." I swivel around, my flashlight shining right into the face of Chantal. Shit. She lifts her hand to shield her eyes. "Um, you mind, Arlee? I'd like to keep my vision intact if it's all the same to you."

"Sorry," I murmur, lowering the flashlight. She stands there with her arms crossed, not holding a drink or cigarette. She stands solid, and by the looks of it, stone-cold sober, though she's dressed differently than I've seen her so far.

Tight black leather skirt. Maroon-colored camisole that reveals a hint of stomach and more than a hint of cleavage. Hair tied back into a bun that makes her cheekbones look even sharper.

Beside me, Winnie moans and struggles to get to her feet.

"Here, baby, let me help you up," Michael says, his voice all honey, reaching down for her hand. Chantal steps over and smacks his arm so hard he yelps.

"Ow, what the *fuck*, Chantal?"

"Perv elsewhere, *por favor*. This is my girl. You touch her again, I'm telling your unit head about the secret iPhone I know you've got stashed inside a pair of those Calvin Klein boxers your mom still buys for you."

Michael snorts and mumbles something like *"Eric's fucking you, so of course he'd take your side. . . ."*

"What was that, little boy?" Chantal snaps.

Michael mutters something else that contains a word far worse than "bitch," then stalks off back to where the party is still raging.

Winnie moans from her spot on the ground. "I wanna go to sleep. . . ."

I expected Chantal to lecture us, get angry. Launch into a thousand pointed questions like she did with me in the vacant cabin. But instead she sighs and pulls Winnie to her feet, says, "Come on, girlie," and together the three of us find our way back to the forested path.

Chantal is surprisingly strong, and I let myself relax a little as she takes the brunt of wrangling a drunken Winnie.

"You didn't lie about liking to party, Arlee," Chantal says with a snort.

"I . . . I only came here for her," I say, then bite my tongue, realizing I'm shifting all the blame on Winnie for us being out so late. Yeah, it *is* her fault, and she *is* the one wasted, but I agreed to come with her. "I mean, it was both of our ideas, but I didn't really want to drink or—"

Chantal sighs like I'm exhausting her. "You think you're the first newbie I've railed on that's snuck out to one of these things? Almost everyone here has been at least once. It's not exactly hard to find." She pulls Winnie up straighter. "Come on, girlie," she says gently. "I've got lots of water for you back at the cabin, and a really nice place to lie down."

"Lie down sounds . . . very good . . . ," Winnie slurs. She slumps forward, still wobbly, but nods and leans her weight against Chantal for support. Winnie is so easy with her, so relaxed. Winnie trusts her.

"So, you rail on everyone new, not just me?" I ask.

Chantal ignores my question. "Please point that tiny flashlight straighter so I can see."

We're getting closer to our unit. I'm so tired I could sleep for a thousand years, but I'm also insatiably curious. What does Chantal have against me, if anything? Is she only prickly with me because I'm new, or because of the mysterious legacy my mom left behind? I try another angle.

"Did they have these barn parties back when my mom was a camper?"

Chantal frowns in confusion. "How should I know?"

"You seem to know enough about my mom to prejudge me. You and everyone else here."

Chantal stops walking, and Winnie nearly falls flat on her face before she stops her.

"Why did we stop?" Winnie moans. "I want to go to sleep. I want to sleep forever."

"We will soon, girlie," Chantal hushes her. "What I need you to do for me now is walk, okay? You can go slow, but please try."

"Why won't you answer any of my questions?" I ask, this time more sharply. I can feel it again, that rage that lives inside me taking over, slowly but surely. The taste of metal in the back of my mouth.

Like blood.

When she turns to face me, my flashlight is bright in her wide eyes. Once more she looks like a deer caught in headlights, and I see it now so clearly like I saw it on Paula's face: fear. She's *scared* of me. Confident, in-charge Chantal, who does and says what she pleases. Who happily bosses us around every day but sneaks off by night to do God knows what, shirking her duties on a whim. Who drilled me like a sergeant my very first day here, and wears leather skirts out at forbidden parties she herself forbade. She's scared of *me.*

Once more, it ignites something deep within me. A curious, inviting feeling, like the lure of a burning stove top, or the impossibly long way down from the roof of my apartment building to the concrete below. . . .

"Please, Arlee," she says quietly, as if begging, "can we just focus on getting Winnie back to bed right now?"

I should take a deep breath and calm down, help her with Winnie, get us all back to our cabin as quickly and safely as possible. Apologize for my tone, for sneaking off, for disobeying her rules, no matter how hypocritical she is about them.

Instead, I take one step closer to her, and relish the way she backs up a little, much like Winnie's nervous horse.

"We can once you tell me why everyone hates my mom and looks at me like they hate me, too."

Chantal swallows, eyes darting around, as if checking the forest for watching eyes or listening ears. As if it's bugged.

"Your mom was part of something," she says slowly. "Something that . . . something very bad happened. Very bad things."

My pulse quickens. I feel a strange flutter of pride. *The society.* Was it something she did with the Order? My curiosity only deepens.

"Arlee, please back up," Chantal says carefully. "And get that out of my eyes." She holds up her hand to shield her vision.

I want more. Answers. *Bad things.*

"What kind of bad things?" I press. I don't back up, and I don't drop my flashlight. Chantal winces and tries to move away from me. "Tell me!"

Chantal swallows hard. "Look, I wasn't there, okay? But . . . they say a boy's arm was broken, after he broke her best friend's heart."

That's when Winnie bends over and pukes everywhere.

It splashes onto Chantal's shoes. "Well, fuck," she says. She glares at me, the fear gone now. "Help me or don't help me, Arlee. She's your bunkmate. *Our* bunkmate, and presumably your friend, but you aren't acting like a very good one right now."

She's right. I'm still pulsing with this feeling, this thirst, but Winnie needs me. I can get answers out of Chantal later. I swallow back my rage and stay quiet as we nearly carry her up the hill, into the cabin, letting the screen door close as quietly as we can behind us.

Winnie stumbles over to my bed and collapses facedown.

"Is she okay?" Porter whispers in the dark.

"She's fine, go back to sleep," Chantal reassures her, then brings Winnie a bottle of water and places an empty trash can beside her head in case she pukes again, then opens her own footlocker and pulls out her nightclothes.

"You're not going back to the party?" I whisper.

Even in the darkness, I can catch her look of annoyance. "No, Arlee. I'm not going back to the party. Like I said, she's my girl, and so are you. Go to bed."

While Chantal slips out of her sexy clothes and into her sleepwear, I climb to the top of Winnie's bunk and curl up inside her comforter, inhaling the sweet scent of her as I finally begin to drift off.

Warm, acid-laced honey. That's what this feels like, coursing through my arms and legs, filling me up with its strange, delicious, terrifying feeling.

Could Mom really have broken a boy's arm? Is it a rumor or is it true? Or worse? I picture her as I slip into a half dream: Mom the successful lawyer in a power blazer with perfect eyeliner and scarlet lips. Mom who fights each day for the rights of her clients. Who stays up late slugging espresso and doing research for her clients, mostly women, mostly in dire situations. Who often works pro bono. Who's the most ethical person I know.

Well.

I remember the piano. The way she grabbed my arm that day with the squirrel.

I briefly remember the things she did, the things that for so long I kept buried. . . .

No. I won't go there. Can't go there.

Once upon a time, Mom maybe did some very bad things.

So what?

So have I.

CHAPTER TEN

When I wake the next morning, I'm on the top bunk, in Winnie's bed. The sheets and pillow smell like her.

I think of the kiss we shared last night and feel hot and flushed all over.

The day is slow and lazy once more. Winnie is a little hungover, so I don't speak of the kiss, even when we join Ginger and Jane for a walk down to the river.

Maybe she doesn't even remember it.

"The Echo River can cure any headache," Jane assures us. "It's magic."

"It's *cold*, is what it is," Ginger complains. "Y'all swim, I'll watch. Also . . . there's someone I've been meaning to talk to." She nods in the direction of a tall, gangly boy sitting with a small group of friends by the willow tree, and Jane laughs.

"Go get him."

With Jane and Ginger with us, and so many other campers and counselors at the river this time, there's no way I can talk to Winnie now. I swallow down my feelings as hard as I can.

Still, she touches me a lot that day. Holds my hand in the water. Pushes me playfully into an incoming wave and shrieks with laughter when I splash her and then chase her to the bank. It's a sweet, beautiful, lazy Sunday, and tonight we have Sundown Ceremony.

The yellowed piano watches us from the beach. It seems to be waiting for me.

I know the dead moths hanging from the lamppost lanterns on the path back are waiting for me, too. After we towel off and head back, I try my best not to look at them, though I sneak a glance and see: there's dozens of corpses now where there only used to be a few.

I gag and retch.

"Are you okay?" Winnie asks. She touches my wrist.

"Fine," I lie. "I'm fine."

After an afternoon of lounging around in the cabin, playing cards, eating tons of Jane's candy, and then a late dinner, Sundown Ceremony is held in the Grand Amphitheater, at the very center of the camp. The same place, I've been told, that the Midsummer Concert will take place on the fourth of July.

The long benches that lead down the hillside are made of dark wood, as is the openmouthed pavilion at the bottom of the slope. Much like the Little Amphitheater, the seats are carved with depictions of owls and deer and horses, but there is no large canopy to shield us from rain or sun. We are exposed to the open expanse of the sky.

A red curtain hangs from the pavilion's rafters, as if we're all about to watch some kind of live theater. Or maybe something like an experimental play, like Ginger suggested.

In the center of the stage is a classic vintage microphone, similar to the kind you might see in old movies or at a jazz club.

Will Caroline emerge from behind the curtain in historical garb and start reciting self-written poetry? The thought is both eerie and hilarious.

From where Unit Seven is sitting toward the rear, we have a

perfect view of the sun turning the clouds to blushing pinks and purples.

I'm sandwiched between Winnie and Jane, who are taking occasional sips from a flask that they keep passing between them.

"Really? Wasn't last night enough for you?" I murmur.

"Never enough," Winnie mutters back, though the smile she shoots me is dampened, a strange sadness in her eyes.

I feel the cool metal pressed against my thigh and see the flask in my lap. Winnie whispers in my ear, "It's whiskey and Coke we stole from the vacant cabin," and I smile in spite of myself, unscrew the cap, and chug, hoping to quiet the racing thoughts that keep buzzing and bumping around in my brain like horseflies. The liquor burns on the way down, but I relish the sweetness of the soda. The way Winnie's hair keeps brushing against my shoulder isn't half bad, either.

"Attagirl," she says. She pats my shoulder and a warm glow runs through me. Even though deep down I know we probably shouldn't be drinking like this. Night after night. Expecting a different result.

Secretly, I hope it leads to another kiss between us.

"We're so glad you can hang," Jane says, flashing me a smile of approval. "Seriously, Arles, you're always so much fun."

"Honestly, way more fun than Vid—" Winnie starts, but then quickly stops herself. Olive, who is sitting in the row in front of us, doesn't seem to have heard Winnie's slipup. Or, if she has, Olive gives no indication. Winnie clears her throat and takes another swig from the flask.

Would Olive be angry if she overheard? Sad?

Would she ask the Order to retaliate against Winnie for her comment? Is that how it works?

The thought alone gives me goose bumps. There are too many secrets here at Camp Rockaway. Secrets laced with poison.

The stage lights snap on.

Two counselors, Forever Freya and a boy—both wearing bright red Camp Rockaway T-shirts—walk onstage and lift a hand to quiet the chatter.

"Welcome to the Sundown Ceremony," Freya says into the microphone, and a cheer ripples through the crowd. "I'm Freya, head counselor of Unit Eight"—a cluster of girls hoot and holler, including Lisha—"and this is Caleb, head counselor of Unit One." Boys near the middle pump their fists in the air and whoop with pride. I spot Michael's snapback where he sits with the rest of Unit Two, but I don't see Zach with his unit. Which is strange, because he was at the barn party last night. Maybe he claimed a headache to hide his hangover and get out of it? I wouldn't be surprised. "For those of you who are returning this summer—and I see a lot of familiar faces—welcome back. If this is y'all's first year with us, please raise your hand."

A group of what appears to be the youngest-looking girls all raise their hand, as do the boys in the front row. The rising freshmen. Aside from them, I'm the only one to slowly raise mine.

I can feel the eyes of the other campers on me, and hear their murmurs, but I keep my eyes ahead, focused on the counselors. Let them gawk like I'm a circus sideshow. Let the rumors continue to fly. Fuck them. I'm starting to feel a little fuzzy around the edges, warm and weightless inside my body. I take another pull from the flask. This time, it doesn't burn going down.

"Welcome to all of you," Caleb says into the mic. "New friends and old. This is a very special place, and Sundown Ceremony a very special night. I'm so glad you're all here. Rockaway forever."

"Rockaway forever," everyone chants, as if on cue. "Rockaway forever and always."

"You're here to learn, of course," Freya says. "But you're also here to challenge yourselves. To grow, and make lifetime friends and memories."

"And this is year eighty," Caleb adds. "Eighty years of excellence. Rockaway forever."

"Year eighty," chants the crowd, and this time I feel my lips moving as I join in. "Rockaway forever and always." I start to sway in my seat, the liquor loosening my nerves.

"As such," Freya says, "I'm told that tonight, we have a very special presentation for you all, courtesy of our wonderful camp director, Caroline Rhinelander." On her last few words, the mic rings out with shrill feedback. Some people cover their ears. "I'm so excited to see what she has in store for us! Some years, she's certainly been . . . well, creative."

Laughter ripples through the crowd.

"Hopefully this year is just as . . . er, exciting," says Caleb.

They both step off the stage.

There's a long, strange pause in which nothing happens. Absolutely nothing. The sounds of the crickets in the trees seem to grow louder. Then there's a faint rumble of thunder on the horizon among some darkening sunset clouds, but no one seems to pay any mind. All eyes are glued to the stage.

I don't know why, but suddenly this is all so *funny*. Hilarious, even. Everyone waiting and waiting, all this buildup and nervous tension and . . . nothing. A laugh climbs up my throat and comes out of me before I can stop it, loud, harsh, definitely attention-drawing, just as the red curtains begin to part. I pretend to muffle it with a cough, but still draw a few stares, including one from Melody a few rows down, who scowls when she sees that it's me.

I'm tempted to flip her off. Tempted to flip off everyone at this fucking camp, save my sisters and bunkmates. So judgmental.

They all think they know who Arlee Gold is, but they have *no idea*.

"You okay?" Winnie whispers, gently shaking me by the shoulder. "Arlee, seriously, *chill.*"

"Someone's not driving home tonight," Jane mumbles.

"*Shh!*" Chantal shushes. She turns around and shoots death glares at the three of us. Winnie tucks the flask behind her legs and sits up straighter. She gently swats at my arm and I swat her back, though it's difficult, to say the least.

Goddamn, I'm *tipsy.*

I need to control myself, the jumpy feeling inside my skin that's growing stronger and stranger by the moment. I need to be serious. Still. Focus on the three people who've just stepped onto the center of the stage.

They are wearing long gray cloaks, black riding boots, and bone-white masks carved from wood, with long faces and unseeing black eyes. One owl, one deer, and one horse.

Horse. The Order of Equus. Are they also my sisters?

The horse-masked figure removes theirs, revealing the face of Caroline Rhinelander. She has a massive burlap sack slung from one shoulder.

Oh my God. Is Caroline in the Order, too?!

It would make sense. The way she was with Mom . . .

She blinks a few times, her eyes adjusting to the harsh brightness of the stage, and then beams at all of us with her snow-white teeth. The owl and the deer stand behind her, their human hands folded in front of them, heads slightly bowed.

Caroline places her mask in her sack, but there's something else in there, bulging. Heavy.

"Welcome to another glorious summer at Camp Rockaway," Caroline says brightly into the microphone. Another burst of feedback screeches through the evening air. "Year eighty. A beautiful number. One that is even and whole. An age we all should wish to see. Life is full of different stages. We have our youth and all its boundless energy." The deer steps forward. "The wisdom that comes with age and time." Then the owl. "But who is it that gives us life? Who is it that is meant to protect us, to keep us living long and healthy?"

Her beam fades to a frown, like mud flowing into a riverbank. Her eyes are haunted, her expression dour. Sad. Even from here, I can see that.

She and the figures raise their arms to the sky. The three begin humming in a low, buzzing monotone that makes me think of flies. Of initiation.

For a few seconds I feel as though I'm filling with helium, floating up above the bench, above the amphitheater and all the other faces and bodies below. I'm hovering in the sky, suspended midair.

It's nothing like I've ever heard or felt.

Then the humming stops and I'm back on the ground. My head rushes with horrible dizziness.

Caroline reaches deep into the sack and slowly removes something large and pinkish, blue and white with both hands. A few campers gasp—likely new ones like me, who've never seen this before—but otherwise they remain quiet, attentive. Beside me, I think I feel Winnie shudder ever so slightly.

My eyes focus on the thing in her hands and, oh God, it's . . . a little . . . *too little* . . . baby . . . God.

No.

Caroline dangles it before us by its neck. It flops down, long and flaccid, limbs dangling like broken puppet strings. Its eyes forever sealed shut, with a mouth that cannot make noise hanging slightly ajar. I can't see every detail from this far back, of its furless pink-and-blue-speckled flesh, but . . .

A horse.

A fetus.

"What the fuck . . . ," I whisper, because right now I can barely control my mouth.

A group of boys a few rows down spew profanities. Their counselors shush them, but I catch a glimpse of their expressions. Shocked. Bewildered. This is not what they were expecting. Even Chantal swivels around in her seat, mumbling to herself as she counts each of us in her head. That's what it looks like she's doing. Making sure we're all here.

She looks as dumbfounded as I feel.

There are murmurs from all around, a swell of rising voices.

"What the fuck, *what the fuck*?" someone screams.

"Is it dead? *Is that a baby horse?!*"

I taste metal on my tongue and reach my hand out behind Winnie's legs, grasping frantically for the flask, but Winnie stops me. Holds my wrist firmly in place.

"It's gonna be okay, Arles," she says in my ear. Calmly. Too calmly. There's something else beneath the placid surface of her voice, a trembling unease to match my own.

"Jesus Christ," Jane hisses beside me. "This is gnarly, especially for her. What the hell, Caroline?"

Porter starts to cry, tears dripping down her cheeks. Uma has an arm around her.

"Yo, that's fucked up!" one of the Unit One boys cries from the front. "Put that shit away!"

Caroline doesn't flinch. Doesn't react one bit to the uproar. Neither do the masked figures onstage beside her. If anything, her smile seems to grow wider, her gray eyes brighter. It's like she's oblivious to the shift in mood. Oblivious or . . . maybe she doesn't care at all.

"This little girl was born prematurely, the umbilical cord wrapped around her neck like a noose," Caroline says. The limp foal's body droops down toward the amphitheater floor. "She never got to breathe the air. Never got to be alive. Not really. Now she's a pinkish, swollen sack of meat and flesh. Isn't that what we all are, when you tear away the skin and hair and nerves? See the white of her eyes, the rolling slope of her muzzle. Like a mountain."

Her gray eyes flicker over the crowd, carefully, methodically, until, I swear to God, they land right on me. Even though I'm all the way up here in the nosebleed section.

"Her mother cried for days," Caroline goes on, the feedback from the mic so shrill it's like knife blades slicing down my eardrums, drowning out the growing chatter, the crying, the scattered, frightened laughter.

"Is this a prank?"

"What the hell is going on?"

"She refused to eat for weeks. Her screams sounded like the wails of a broken woman. She was a mother who did not deserve to see her foal have its life sucked out of it before it had a chance to stand and walk and run and play. A mother who went through unspeakable horror. Heartbreak. Loss. Life can be cruel. Fate is often cruel, but with wisdom, we can learn and—"

Caroline keeps speaking, but her words turn to water. To mush. Even from all the way up here, so far from the foal fetus, I can clearly see its unborn eyes. The squishy whitish sockets where they should've been, should've formed. Staring me down. Unseeing. All-knowing.

Caroline lifts the fetus close to her face, plants a gentle kiss on its forehead of soft pink-and-blue-veined squishy flesh, and then carefully places it back in the burlap sack.

I shudder, along with the rest of the amphitheater. A shudder that ripples through us all collectively.

Caroline leans so close her lips nearly kiss the mic. "Remember what I've told you, my dear campers, and have a safe, productive, wonderful summer," she says into the microphone. She slips her mask back on. The robed figures—the owl, the deer, and the horse—all take a bow. Then they exit the stage, disappearing behind the billowing red curtains.

The stage lights dim.

"I'm gonna be sick," I moan. I lower my head into my knees and cradle my arms around my head, pretend this isn't happening.

That it isn't real.

"*Shit . . . ,*" Winnie hisses beside me.

"*I want to go home!*" someone screams.

"Fuck this shit! My parents didn't pay for this!"

"What the hell *was* that?!"

The microphone whines again. Forever Freya speaks calmly into it. "Please, everyone, stay in your seats as your counselors count you down. Caroline has informed me tonight would be part of a special Camp Rockaway tradition. I know this was strange. Different. But please, there is no need to panic."

As people stand and huddle together, uneasy, unspeakably tense, counselors initiating count-offs and comforting crying campers, Olive's words of warning echo through my head: *I mean, it's beautiful here. It's . . . almost like paradise. But there's something off, too. You know?*

∘ ∘ ∘

There was this one time when I nearly hitchhiked home.

I was almost fourteen. It was really late. Far too late for anyone so young to be out on their own, especially in late winter, the ground blanketed in snow. The roads slicked with black ice. Air so cold it fogged up my glasses every time I breathed.

It was nearly a year after Dad left us. After what I did in the woods. That first secret I kept from Mom.

I was failing nearly every class in school. I'd stopped going to piano lessons entirely, and Mom didn't have the strength or care to argue anymore. She was a ghost of the mom I had known, especially that winter. She'd come home from work, take off her beautiful blazers, and toss them onto her bedroom floor, the bedroom that used to belong to both of my parents. She'd change into sweatpants, wipe off her expensive eyeliner, micro- wave a frozen dinner for each of us, then drink wine right from the bottle while the glow of the TV screen lit her tired face.

After the woods, after what I did . . . I stopped taking my friends' calls or answering their texts. I quit the poetry club. Threw my math worksheets in the trash when the pages blurred together as I tried to work on them. Fell asleep at my desk and went to school in the same pair of rainbow pajama pants that I wore over and over, barely ever washing them.

Kids laughed at me. Passed notes about me right in front of me. Called me all kinds of names. Tossed gum at my hair. Of course they did. I was a disaster. I thought, *I deserve this.* After the woods especially, I thought, *They can see me for who I really am.* The monster inside me. The wild animal. The sick twisted girl who deserves all the ridicule in the world.

My former friends were upset at first that I'd ditched them, but being middle schoolers, they didn't have the capability to under- stand or really empathize as much as they could've. Not that it mattered. Like I said, I deserved their disdain.

I could never sleep that year. I no longer cared about school. About cliques or cool girls or upcoming auditions for our school's dinner-theater show. It all felt so . . . fake. Plastic. I began cutting classes, walking to a nearby shopping plaza hours before the school day ended and people-watching on a bench across from a Wendy's drive-through.

By the time Dad called me, I was so listless, so lost in my own ennui, in my house that no longer felt like home, that I immediately said yes when he asked if I would come over to his place that night.

"I miss you, kiddo," he said. He sounded so sincere on the phone, and it was like being colored in again after spending so much time living in black-and-white. An overwhelming burst of relief and gratitude. "I'm just so sorry for everything that's happened. I want to make it up to you."

I trusted him.

He was living about fifty miles outside Raleigh, in a neighborhood no one really wanted to be in, and I agreed before asking Mom.

She was furious when I told her I was going. She screamed at me. Threw a wine bottle against the wall so hard it shattered, shards of glass cutting her skin and leaving blood on the kitchen floor.

"If you go see him, you're *betraying* me!" she yelled in my face. Her face was pinched with fury, but her eyes were wild with fear.

"You can't stop me," I told her. "Dad wants me, not you. Deal with it."

I packed a bag and waited for his headlights to shine into our living-room windows. Mom stomped upstairs and locked herself in the bedroom that once belonged to her and Dad. As I left the house, I could faintly hear her crying.

Dad gave me the biggest hug when he saw me, and I relished the warmth and comfort of his strong arms. Maybe I didn't need Mom. Maybe I'd never needed Mom, or Raleigh, or anything at home that I used to think I did.

Maybe she'd deserved to be left for another woman.

He looked older. A lot older. He'd grown out an untamed beard and gained wrinkles around his eyes, but he'd brought me mint hot chocolate with whipped cream. My favorite. I sat blowing on the lid as he drove us down a dark highway, slowly enough so we wouldn't slip on the black ice.

He asked me about school. Piano. I lied and told him I was acing everything. Killing my recitals. On my way to winning another state music award.

"You'll come, won't you?" I asked him as, an hour later, we pulled up in front of a dumpy apartment complex right off the highway. "To my next recital?"

He looked pained when he answered, like it hurt to speak. To fake that smile. Dad was always a terrible liar. "Of course I'll be there, kiddo."

I could hear sirens blaring even from inside his fourth-floor walk-up. It smelled like cat piss in the hallways and I could hear neighbors arguing and having loud, wild sex. We passed a dead roach, belly-up, and I nearly puked up the mint hot chocolate.

I haven't been able to drink one since.

Dad's unit was even more depressing inside. Barely any furniture. A mattress on the floor, covered in greasy stains. Pizza boxes and beer cans cluttering the Formica countertop.

"Well," he said, trying to sound happy, "here we are."

"Where do I sleep?" I asked. I could do this, I told myself. It was pretty grim, but I could make a life here. Start over. Eat pizza and do my homework as Dad read the paper. Maybe I'd start doing my homework again.

"Oh, well . . . ," he muttered, rubbing the back of his neck. Dandruff flecks came flying off. "I figured I'd drive you back home after we had dinner. You like ramen noodles?"

A cockroach skittered across the threadbare carpeting.

I didn't know what I'd expected. I guess not this. He'd left me and Mom for that shiny woman, and now this hovel. For this sad, horrible excuse for a life . . . and he wouldn't even let me stay the night.

"Arlee?"

I tossed my drink into his filthy kitchen trash pile and bolted. Dad called after me and began to chase me, but I was faster. I ran into the darkness in zigzags, then stood shivering and sobbing on the sidewalk as an icy wind picked up and I held out my arm, desperately trying to flag down a car, but for so long everyone ignored me. No one stopped. Someone even honked at me, splashing freezing water that soaked through my sweater. I remember screaming.

My phone buzzed in my pocket. Dad was calling me, over and over, frantically texting me, too. I ignored it all.

Instead, I walked a mile or so down the long, lonely highway until I reached a gas station, which is where I called Mom.

"I need you to come and get me," I pleaded.

"Drop a pin," she said. I could hear her tearing open the closet door, getting out her coat and boots. "I'll be right there."

That night, she hadn't downed any wine. She'd switched to sparkling water instead, and we both got lucky.

When Mom pulled up in front of that gas station, she *was* smoking a cigarette. I'd never seen her smoke before. When she opened the door and came toward me, there was wildness in her eyes, that same fury from before. I thought she might slap me across the face, but then she enveloped me in a hug that was even stronger and truer than the one Dad had given me earlier. A hug that killed every bit of icy cold that night.

"Never leave me again," she sobbed, holding me so tight to

her I thought she might break me in half. "You're all I have, Arlee. Never leave your mother for a sad excuse for a man. Promise me, Arlee Samantha Gold."

"I promise, Mom. I'm so sorry. I promise."

Dad kept calling, but finally gave up after Mom reamed him out over the phone. He did call me again months later, on my birthday, but I let it go straight to voicemail.

CHAPTER ELEVEN

Sundown Ceremony is officially over.

Unit Seven stands huddled together, looking to Bea and Chantal and the rest of our counselors for guidance. Answers.

They have none.

Normally mellow Bea looks absolutely petrified. She keeps pacing around our group, counting us over and over to herself even though we've done a count-off twice. Even our mild-mannered test-prep teacher Ruth seems shaken.

Porter has stopped crying, but her eyes are still red and wet, Uma's arm wrapped around her. Some of the girls in our unit are demanding a phone call home.

"You know that's against the rules," Chantal reminds them, firmly but gently. *Except for me*, I think. *Caroline said I could call home anytime, day or night.* She doles out a few stiff hugs and words of encouragement. "Let's go back to the unit. We'll make s'mores, sing some songs."

No one seems interested in either of those things.

"This is utter *horseshit!*" Uma snaps. "*Pun very much intended!*"

"Seriously, so sick. What was she thinking?!"

"That was disgusting! Traumatizing!"

"It's never been like this before. . . ."

So I keep hearing.

There's another faint, distant rumble of thunder on the horizon. The darkened clouds inch closer, a breeze catching in the air, whipping back our hair and sending shivers down our spines.

I stand with Jane and Winnie, both of them looking as horrified as I feel.

"Guys?" I ask weakly. "What the fuck was that?"

"I don't know," Jane mumbles, staring down at the shoes she picked out special for tonight. "I . . . really don't know."

"Porter? You said it always means something? What do you think it means?"

I'm still drunk, and I can hear my voice is coming out too loud, too aggressive. Porter doesn't respond. Uma shoots me a dirty look like I've done something wrong and steers her away from me.

Most of the other units have filed out and gone back to their cabins, though plenty of counselors have stopped to exchange concerned words with campers. Counselors I recognize from the barn party, including the boy who wore the antlers on his head. Campers like Paula, the girl who threw a drink in Lisha's face. She's crying, too, another girl comforting her.

I catch a flash of blue-black hair as Lisha runs up to me. "Arlee!" she says, pulling me in for a hug. Jane stiffens beside me. "Are you okay? That was wild, wasn't it?"

"I'm fine," I say. "What do you—?" Before I can finish, she slips a wad of crumpled paper into my hand, then disappears back into the crowd that's moving up the hill like river water flowing backward.

The first raindrop hits my cheek like a slap.

I tuck the paper into my pocket, suddenly elated at the idea of another chance to see my sisters.

Though something about the timing, and the weird look on Lisha's face, feels off.

And I'm pretty certain she wasn't wearing the yellow nail polish.

A jagged bolt of white lightning streaks through the sky. Someone shrieks. We're all on edge now, our nerves collectively frayed.

"Let's go!" Chantal yells, clapping her hands together, rounding up the rest of us who've lagged behind.

Winnie takes my hand and we make a mad dash back to Unit Seven as the rain comes pouring down in torrents. We're soaked to the bone by the time we get inside, but the cabin feels like a sanctuary. Warm. Dry.

Safe.

Even though my bunkmates won't stop talking about the horse fetus, peppering Chantal and Bea with questions they don't know the answers to. I've started to get the spins, the room tilting like a seesaw.

I plan on curling up in my bed and sobering up in the form of sleeping forever.

Instead I retreat to a corner and carefully unfold the note.

Meet at the barn at midnight. Wear sensible shoes. Tell no one, as always. If you do, I'll know. —Pale Mare

o o o

Midnight.

Once again, I have to wait until midnight.

I can do this. I can chug enough water to make the spins stop.

I can ignore the taste of metal crawling into my mouth, the static starting up again in my ears.

I have my bunkmates.

Chantal is making her rounds around the unit, meeting with other counselors about the circulating chaos. Some girls are *demanding* to go home. One is even threatening to tell her lawyer about how the camp is holding her hostage in an unsafe and psychologically perilous environment, or that's what Uma heard. Bea snores from her bed, earplugs stuffed in her ears, as if her way of dealing with the horrors of existence is to completely zonk out and pretend none of this is happening.

Namaste, I guess.

I envy her. I wish I could sleep, too, but I have to stay up. Stay focused, even though my head aches from the alcohol that's still making its way out of my body, and I'm crashing hard.

I've already chugged one of Uma's Red Bulls, but it's only made me feel more ill and anxious. I'm snuggled up in a big blanket with Winnie, my head resting on her shoulder—because right now, it feels safe to do this, it feels okay—luxuriating at the sound of her heartbeat in my ear as I fight to keep my eyes open. We're sitting with Ginger, Uma, and Porter on blankets and pillows in the middle of our cabin.

It's 9:30 P.M. *Two and a half more hours.*

Inevitably the storm will end, and then I'll get to see my sisters again.

Or at least, I'll see Lisha. My Pale Mare.

The thought brings a blooming warmth in my stomach, but the warmth is turning sour, like a pill I swallowed down that hasn't settled and is making me nauseated.

I push away the thought of her in the hollow horse skull, the way her eyes bored into mine through the holes in the makeshift mask.

I do my best to think about the love. The arms all around

me. The way I felt held and seen and loved on the night of my initiation.

Surely, it will be like that again, won't it?

Why won't my heart stop racing?

Rain pounds on the roof of our cabin, humidity hanging in the air along with the general sense of residual dread from Sundown Ceremony. Jane is curled between her sheets on her bed, her head throbbing once again.

"I just want to know why they're back," she moans, meaning her migraines. "Aside from, you know, being traumatized by whatever *that* was." We all shudder at the thought of the baby horse, but no one wants to mention it again. It's a dead end. A rabbit hole with no bottom. "I thought my meds were working," Jane goes on. "They *told me* they would work." They being the doctors she's seen, the ones who, like mine, probably shrugged her off. Maybe even told her that it's all in her head, so to speak.

"Could be air pressure–related," Porter offers wisely. "Some migraines are triggered by changes in weather patterns and the like."

Uma gets Excedrin from her stash of pills and gives them to Jane, while Porter wets a cold washcloth for her to put on her forehead. None of it works. Nothing helps. Not even the doctored concoction of vitamin powder, lemonade mix, and filtered water Ginger put into Jane's water bottle. We've even turned the lights off, two of Winnie's contraband candles glowing in the dark.

"Want me to massage the stress spot on your hand?" Porter asks, sitting down on Jane's bed.

"Anything," Jane groans. Porter nods and begins to rub circles around Jane's palm. "Mm, wait, that's nice actually. That helps. You guys can talk and all. Don't let me ruin an already shitty day. Just . . . please keep it down."

Winnie has made us all yet another flask of whiskey stolen from the vacant cabin, mixed with soda she swiped from the dining hall. We pass it around on the floor, but I decline.

I've had enough alcohol in the last few days to last me a lifetime.

"I used to make this drink for my dad," Ginger says, nodding to Jane's half-drunk water bottle filled with her homemade medicine. She laughs and takes a swig of the whiskey and soda. "The vitamin lemonade, of course. Not the booze. My family isn't *that* dysfunctional." We all laugh, even Jane. "Anyway, he has chronic pain, and I always tried to make him feel better, so one day I made up Hurt No More Juice. The actual recipe includes fresh ginger—naturally—and much higher-quality lemonade, but I tried."

"Thank you, Ginger," Jane says weakly. She's on her back, one arm over her eyes, curled up under her blankets. "And thanks, Porter. This . . . feels really lovely, actually."

"On the subject of dads, mine taught me this hand-massage technique," Porter says. "You know, it's funny, he would always teach me things, always encourage me, but he's never once looked at me and said, 'I love you.' I guess that was always his way of showing it."

"My dads constantly tell me they love me," Uma says. "And honestly, I know it sounds like I'm bragging or something, but it's not quite like that." She tugs hard at a loose thread on the blanket wrapped around her. "It's like they don't want me to forget. Like they're afraid I'll wake up one day and decide they aren't my real parents after all. They've always been this way, ever since they brought me home."

"Where were you before?" I ask.

Outside, thunder rumbles. An omen, perhaps. I tense up, but then feel Winnie's hand moving under the cover, coming to rest on my knee, and begin to relax.

"London," Uma tells her blanket, so quietly it's hard to hear her, especially over the sound of the rain. All her normal snark and bravado is gone, replaced by a girl who now just looks vulnerable, sad. "They adopted me when I was seven. Before that it was foster homes. Awful stuff, really. I'm beyond lucky they came along." She takes a deep breath. "But America is . . . no offense, really fucking weird." She chuckles. "It was hard to adjust, even with the language being more or less the same. I remember sitting on the plane in a seat between both of my new dads on the way to Boston, watching the in-flight movie with my headphones on. I think it was *American Beauty*, something I *really* shouldn't have been watching, but they let me because I liked that 'American' was in the title. I remember thinking, *Wow . . . so this is it, these are the people I'm meant to live with, meant to love. I'm American now, too.*"

"I didn't know that about you," Winnie says. "Like, I knew you were adopted and from London, but I didn't know it was when you were seven. That's . . . older. That must've been hard. Scary, even. Like, who are these people? Why me? Why now?"

Uma nods and pulls at another thread. "That's exactly what it was like. School was strange, too. All this funny slang I didn't know, music and movies I'd only seen bits of that no one could shut about up. The kids made fun of my accent, but this one boy, I can't forget it, he looked at me in class one day and asked, 'Why don't you have a mom?' He was only curious, I'm pretty sure, but it hurt all the same. I already felt like such an . . . other."

"I feel like that, too, in my own way," Jane says. She rolls over on her side to face us, squinting through the pain in her head. "My parents are so famous, and you'd think that would be cool, but it's really not. When Mom ran for office, she told me to delete Twitter from my phone, stop reading the racist comments about our family. Hold my head high in school or on the street, no matter what anyone said to me. It's fun to live in D.C., but it's also kind of a nasty place. Mom thinks I don't know the depth of the corruption in our government, but I have *seen* some things."

"I'll bet!" Uma says. "Like I said, America is fucking weird, man. The UK is probably not much better but, *man* is America weird."

Winnie raises the flask. "Amen to that!" She drinks before handing it over to me. I've refused so far, but now I drink down a huge gulp that burns my esophagus. I sputter, cough, wipe my mouth on my hand.

It slips out before I can stop it. "I never knew my father."

They're all staring at me now, with their pity, their shock. I clear my throat and shake my head, cheeks burning. "I mean, I did know him. He lived in our house most of my life, but I didn't really . . . know who he was." I sound so ridiculous. Tongue-tied again. I stare down at my hands and realize that they're trembling. "Why he was the way he was, if that makes sense?"

"It's okay, Arlee," Winnie says gently, and it feels good to have her here, her body solid against mine. She's a safe place to rest my head against, to let myself fall into whatever it is I need to feel right now.

I've never talked about this before. I want to. I can trust them with it, I know I can. I can feel it in their patient silence, the way their attention is fully pinned on me. I don't have to give them everything. Don't have to relive it all, but I can offer them a crumb. Maybe then some of it will finally get off my chest. Out of my system. Let my heart feel a little lighter and less broken.

I know I'm bad and wrong, but I'm dying for things to hurt just a little less.

I take a deep breath and let myself go under.

"It's like there were two versions of my dad. The one I desperately needed and wanted him to be, and the real him. The one it took me a while to start to see. The one I wanted was the dad who told me how talented I was at piano, how he couldn't wait to come see my recitals. He never did, though. He never came. He'd always promise and promise, tell me he'd wear his best tie that night and we'd go out for ice cream after, but the night would come and my stomach would clench up and Mom would get so tense and weird and I'd know he wasn't coming after all. There were always excuses. Work ran late. Car trouble. Emergency at the office. It happened with everything, not just piano. Birthdays. Holidays. He had to work. He had to go out of town. It couldn't be helped. They piled and piled on, the lies, the excuses, until I stopped believing any of them. I expected he'd be gone. He wouldn't show. I got used to it."

Thunder claps and the wind whistles through the trees. The wind is growing stronger, now and then sending light mists of water shooting through the window screens, tickling at our skin. I pull the blanket tighter around me. I want it to stop. I need it all to stop.

"But one time, he did come. It was my end-of-the-year piano recital. I'd won a county award, some major certificate of achievement. I don't remember. Mom was so insanely proud. She was glowing from her seat in the front row. All her friends were there. They were like my aunties, I guess you could say. What I remember most is that Dad actually came, and he sat front row next to Mom, and I could barely believe it when I saw him. It was like I was hallucinating, like he was a hologram. I played better that night than I'd ever played in my entire life." I squeeze my eyes tight, bracing myself against the pain. As if I can undo what's been done. "At the end, he gave me a standing ovation. He finally took me out for ice cream, and we had this long, long talk about how he was sorry he hadn't been there more. How he wanted to be in my life, as if we lived in different houses, in

different timelines. How he'd never let me down again. That
was late winter." There's the taste of metal in my mouth. It's
overpowering, so strong I could gag on it. The static in my ears
begins to buzz.

"Arlee?" Winnie's voice is nervous as I pull away from her.
Afraid. Of me? The trembling has gone up from my fingers and
traveled into the rest of my body, into every nerve and tendon.

"He . . . he dropped me off at the house. Said he was going
to go pick up some milk and he'd be back soon. I was buzzing. So
happy. With love. I believed him. I believed in everything. I began
to walk up the driveway to our house. We had a long, winding
driveway that went up a hill, and I did think it was strange, how
he dropped me off at the very beginning of it. How he didn't
park in the garage and go in and at least say hi to Mom. Or . . .
bring me with him to get the milk." The metal taste grows stronger, like blood is there in my mouth. I swallow, forcing it down.
"I remember all the snow, shiny like glass on the concrete under
the light of the moon. It was so cold. Bitter cold. I should've gone
inside. Should've just gone upstairs and stayed in my bliss . . ."

I want to sob. I want to scream. I know the girls are asking me
if I'm okay, if I need anything, but I'm not, and nothing will ever
make it okay.

"But something was wrong. I could hear his engine growling,
even as I began to walk up the driveway to our house. So I did
something I shouldn't have. I turned around and followed him,
followed the glow of his headlights at the bottom of the hill. He
drove slowly up the long road, and I trailed behind him until he
parked in front of our neighbor's house. Right in *fucking front*.
And then she stepped out, wearing a dress made of red sequins.
They sparkled in the porch lights. She was . . . so beautiful. And
she got in the car. I saw. She kissed him before they sped away. A

real kiss. A grown-up kiss, like they were devouring each other. He didn't see me. He didn't know I was standing there in the cold with my whole world shattering before me. And . . . I know he saw me in his rearview mirror, if only for a moment, because he sped away, so fast his tires squealed, and very early the next morning he came into my bedroom, crying, and kneeled beside my bed and begged me to never tell Mom. Never, ever tell her what I saw. That it would destroy us, destroy our entire family, and that he might never get to see me again if he did. I held it all inside until I felt like I was going to break, all the rest of that winter and into the spring. I thought maybe this could be our secret, even though it broke my heart every time I saw him lie to Mom. She found out eventually, anyway, and he never came to another recital. Never took me out for ice cream again. Never looked at me the same. As if maybe I'd ruined it, by standing there in the snow and seeing him. Seeing the woman in the red dress and all his ugly truth."

There's a horrible crash, a booming sound that rattles the earth and makes us all jump. Then the faint smell of smoke.

"Oh, shit!" Uma cries, leaping to her feet and racing to see out the screened window that overlooks the campfire circle and the lake beyond. "One of the trees caught on fire!"

I made it happen, I think. *I set that tree on fire.* It's wild, irrational, but in this moment, it feels true.

Before they can stop me, I rip myself away from Winnie and the comforting circle of girls. They call my name as I slam the screen door behind me and run out into the rain. I need to feel the cool water shattering down on my skin. An oak tree beside the campfire circle is indeed on fire for a brief while from where the lightning struck it, but the rain pounds on it until that spark of flame goes out. I race down the hill, past the tree and the campfire circle, until I can sense I'm alone enough. Until all I can hear is the rain thrumming in my ears.

Then I let out a long, bloodcurdling scream.

o o o

The storm is over. The moon is high in a now clear night sky.

Its light brightens everything before me, illuminating the damp summer campgrounds. Downtown in Raleigh, there were always so many unnatural, artificial lights. I never used to notice the contrast between the brightness of the full moon and the blanket of darkness.

I snuck outside at 11:45 P.M., unable to stand tossing and turning in bed any longer. I did my best to avoid the creakiest parts of the floors, and I put on my oldest, rattiest pair of sneakers.

I love the way the air smells after it's rained. As if the earth itself has been cleansed. Especially in the summer. Crickets sing and I can't help but wonder where they go in the storm, how they don't drown.

I make my way down the long winding forest path until I reach the barn. The doors are open. I take a deep breath and enter.

It's damp inside, musty. Dark but for a light bulb dangling from the ceiling that flickers several times, the waning electricity buzzing like a frenzied insect.

"You're early," I hear Lisha say as she emerges from a shadowy corner.

She isn't dressed for a ritual. Without her Pale Mare mask, Lisha no longer looks so terrifying. She's in black sweatpants and a gray T-shirt, her hair piled on top of her head with a giant clip. It's the kind of thing she usually wears, though normally there's no black dirt beneath her fingernails, which I certainly didn't see earlier.

And she isn't normally holding a pair of plastic gloves. She slips them on.

"The others should be here soon."

I swallow. "What are we doing, exactly?"

Her lips turn up into a grin that frankly scares me. Her eyes are wild, too wide. Too empty. "You'll see, Arlee Gold."

Here are the barrels, hay, and—as I can see better now—large cloth sacks filled with something stacked against one wall. An assortment of spades and shovels and farm tools. An axe. Cobwebs are gathered in corners of the ceiling. I can almost feel the spiders crawling across my skin.

Moments later, three other girls file into the barn together: the new sisters of the Order of Equus.

Then Lisha slides the barn doors shut, sealing the five of us inside. Her long shadow splays out across the barn floor, the four of us standing within it. Once more, the bulb hanging above us buzzes, clinks, and flickers.

I can feel the eyes of the three new sisters flickering over me, too. Curious eyes. One is dressed in purple pajama pants and a baggy T-shirt, her hair up in a ponytail. Another wears a thin tank top and cotton shorts with white horses printed on them. Both of them wear flip-flops. The third girl wears fuzzy rabbit slippers and a sleeping jumpsuit, a neon-pink choker around her throat.

I suppose none of them got the memo about sensible shoes.

I wonder how they were chosen, why they were selected. As a legacy, I understand why they picked me. Are they legacies, too? Did they have any idea this was coming?

Do they know more than I do about what happens next? Why us, tonight? Sure, we're all new, but . . .

"Where is everyone else?" I ask.

"My new *sorors*, I need your help with something," Lisha tells us, ignoring me. "It is, very, *very* important, and it's very much a secret. Can I trust the four of you to keep a secret?"

The three girls nod, but I hesitate. None of this feels right or safe.

But if Lisha is aware of my hesitation, she doesn't show it. She's too focused on something else, some thought bubble floating above her head.

"We'll do anything you need us to, Pale Mare," says the girl in the neon-pink choker. She's shorter than all of us, but stands tall and proud as a flagpole. The others chime in with their agreement.

"We're here for you, sister."

"Whatever you need, Pale Mare."

"What *is* it you need?" I ask Lisha.

Any trace of worry or fear on Lisha's face vanishes completely. "You'll find out when we get there," she tells me, voice icy. A warning. "And you'll help me with it, Arlee. You'll all help me and you'll all keep quiet about it. This is your first task."

I sigh and check my watch, suddenly fighting to keep my eyes open, even though my pulse is pounding so hard it sounds like a thunderstorm in my bloodstream. How am I simultaneously so wired and exhausted at once?

Really, I just want to leave. Get out of here. *Run.*

Yet a part of me also doesn't want to run. A sick, twisted part of me wants to dive right in to whatever happens next. It almost feels inevitable.

Lisha's nostrils flare at me the same way that Velvet's do. "You want to be part of the Order of Equus, don't you, Arlee Gold?"

I thought I did, but my thoughts are jumbled now. My mind has turned to mush. To Jell-O.

I feel a million different emotions and thoughts spinning through my exhausted brain.

I'm in too deep.

"I'll help you," I say cautiously.

"Yes," Lisha says, her expression stone cold. "You will. Each of you: grab a shovel."

° ° °

The five of us wade back into the tall wet grass of the horse field. A strong breeze whips past us, carrying with it all the smells from the stables. The familiar sharp brackish scent of the Echo River catches right on the tail end of it.

The three new sisters march ahead like soldiers, shoulders back, heads held high. I trail behind, yawning, stumbling a little, trying to wake myself up again as we walk deeper and deeper into the field beneath a black ocean of unseeing stars backlit by a spotlight moon. What we come upon, minutes later, is better than any jolt of caffeine could've ever been.

It begins with the flies.

Horseflies don't come out at night. That I know. I've spent too many hours online going down my endless research rabbit holes. Horseflies prefer sun and heat, and they usually won't enter barns or go where there's shade. Sometimes the nasty little torpedoes graze at night, though it's not their usual pattern.

Same thing with deerflies. They prefer the brightness of day. Both kinds of flies only feast on blood if they're females.

Female horseflies have a stabbing organ that works like two pairs of cutting blades. Their blades cut deep, while another mouthpart of them soaks up the blood like a sponge. Deerflies have mandibles like sharp scissors. They use these mandibles to make careful incisions before lapping up the gore.

With the blood coursing through their bodies, they make their eggs.

There're dozens of blowflies in this part of the field, the kind that are usually the first to come after death. The kind that come out to feast after dark. I hear them before I see them, but they come into view all the same. The next thing that hits me, though, and nearly has me doubled over is the smell. It's putrid. Horrible. There's nothing else like it.

It's worse than what I smelled all those years ago in the woods. It clings to everything, that smell. Powerful. Pungent.

The smell of death.

Right now, even with my glasses on and vision intact, the world feels so damn out of focus.

Lisha leads us to its source: a pale, broken corpse, its limbs splayed in all directions in the tall grass. Not the corpse of an animal. No, this is no game. No gimmick with masks and cloaks and chants. No blood ritual.

This is the corpse of a human being. A freckled boy. Around our age.

"*Zach*," I whisper.

He's right in front of us and he's dead. He's dead. *He's dead.*

An arrow sticks out of his body, like he was shot right through the heart.

I retch.

Neon Choker lets out a piercing scream. It flies up into the black sky and around those unseeing, silent stars. The stars do nothing. God does nothing. Lisha is the one who quiets Neon Choker's scream in seconds, wrapping her hands around Neon Choker's throat like a vise, forcing her into silence. The other new sisters stare, wide-eyed, terrified, clutching their shovels. The ground beneath me tilts like I'm on a seesaw, and everything before me goes fuzzy and gray like television static. There is no more oxygen left inside me. I am stiff and I am frozen, but I can smell it all the same. The smell of a recently murdered boy.

A dead boy that I knew.

I realize now what Lisha wants us to do. She doesn't have to say it, but she does anyway, in a voice as bitter and cold as the waters of the Echo River at midnight.

"Dig."

o o o

It happened in the woods all those years ago. I was only thirteen.

It was midsummer. The summer after I saw Dad in the car with the woman in the red sequined dress.

Mom and Dad had woken me up again with their fighting. Roaring voices. Ugly, garbled words traveling through the walls. I'd lain awake in bed, blinking up at the ceiling, my stomach twisting and turning with sulfuric acid.

It went on and on until I snuck downstairs in my Minnie Mouse pajamas, listening from the top of the staircase.

After their screams settled, Dad left us with the slamming of the front door and the sound of his car engine starting, the garage door cranking open before he sped away.

I found Mom in the darkness of the kitchen, clutching at her chest, eyes red and hollow from crying, her expression vacant.

"He's gone," she whimpered, though if it was to me or herself, I couldn't be sure. She wouldn't look at me. I stood there in a daze, waiting and willing for this to be some elaborate practical joke. Dad would turn the car around and walk back inside, apologize with a sheepish grin, pull us both into a big bear hug. Tell me he can't believe I almost fell for that. Mom would laugh and snap on the kitchen lights and we'd all joke and rib each other.

The lights didn't turn on. Mom didn't move.

Dad didn't come back.

In that moment, I felt that first tinge of rage. I *hated* Mom. Hated her for yelling and letting him leave. For driving him away, just like she'd been driving me away from her all these years. Critiquing me. Controlling me. I hated her for finally shattering the fantasy of the woman in the red dress and making it real and consequential. Why was she just standing there, doing nothing? Like Dad did fucking nothing when I threw the rock at the squirrel and she screamed at me and grabbed me, called me a wild animal. He didn't fight for me then. She's not fighting for him now . . . or me.

Why wouldn't she look at me now? Why *couldn't* she? I was furious with her, but just as much, I was scared of losing Dad. Of everything falling apart before my eyes, which was happening now, and all I wanted to do was make it stop.

I stepped into the kitchen. "Mom," I said, voice breaking. Desperate. "Mom, we have to go after him."

It was as if I were a ghost, and she couldn't see or hear me. She stepped to the kitchen sink and turned on the faucet. Began washing the dishes.

"*Mom.*"

"He's gone, Arlee," she told the plates and the kitchen soap and the sponge. "There's nothing we can do to make him come back."

"You don't even want to try."

"No," she said, then finally met my eyes. "You're right. I don't."

White flashed before my eyes. I was no longer thinking, just feeling. Just burning up like a nuclear fusion made of white-hot rage. I opened a kitchen cabinet, pulled out Mom's favorite dinner plate, and smashed it to the floor. I felt her flinch, but I felt nothing inside me as I stood and watched it shatter into a billion pieces.

She made a small sound in her throat, then bowed her head and kept scrubbing the dirty pots and pans.

Then I heard it under her breath. She choked it out like a cry. *"You animal."*

It was like my heart was ripped from my chest. I slammed the screen door behind me and stepped out into the night, tears blurring my vision, my throat aching with an animal cry that wouldn't come. My bare feet were cold on the soft, damp, cool ground as I walked deep and deeper into the woods behind our house.

I remember first the flies. So many of them. Angry little torpedoes, screaming in high-pitched whines. As angry and buzzing as I felt.

And the smell. The smell of rot, of blood and stinking shit.

A deer corpse lay before me in a small clearing like an offering, its broken body splayed against the dirt and broken twigs and branches. The flies screamed and hummed, laying their eggs in the gashes of its torn flesh.

I could've cried out in disgust, but instead, I began to laugh.

It was wild. Animal.

Raw.

I thought of Dad, his relentless broken promises, his constant lies, the way he tore my heart to pieces, over and over like the world's saddest song. I thought of Mom, her constant denial that anything bad was happening, until it was too late. Her refusal to tell me what was going on between them, to tell me the fucking truth, even though I damn well knew.

Her forcing me, all those years, to play and play that fucking piano.

Then I was full-on sobbing, gasping for breath. I reached for the open wound in the deer's stomach and slid my hand in deep. It was warm and wet and the smell grew worse. I choked and gasped and laughed again and nothing made sense and the flies buzzed and buzzed and they were in my ears and on my face. I reached deep inside, deeper and deeper, fishing for its heart.

Then I screamed, and the lights went out inside my mind, the glass shattering in my brain. I needed more than the deer's heart. I needed to make someone, something else hurt like I did, even though the deer could no longer feel pain.

Every inch of me was trembling, my heart and lungs searing with panic.

I could've killed someone—something—right then and there. It was maybe a brief moment, a flash of rage and grief that flooded my veins, an instinctual need to hunt down something weaker than me. Something that I could make weaker than me.

The deer carcass smelled of shit and decay, yes, but it also smelled beautiful. It smelled honest. There were no lies here in its dead flesh, no promises to break. Everything in its life had already been broken.

What I did in the forest with the deer . . . I remember parts of it. My body was pressed up against it. Its blood covered all of me, my Minnie Mouse pj's, my skin, and I tasted raw deer flesh and blood and bone in my mouth. I was an animal then, a feral predator. I can't recall all of it, but I know I woke up from some kind of blackout minutes later, heart thrumming, my blood-soaked arms wrapped around its cold dead body, sobbing. Shivering. In spite of the heat. In spite of the summer air.

And the flies. There were so, so many flies, and they covered my body, too.

CHAPTER TWELVE

The blade of my shovel is the first to hit the soil.

Lisha doesn't even have to prompt me.

The ground here is thick, but there's enough give that I can begin to loosen it up. I put my back into it, sweat pooling down my neck, my chest, every part of me. I dig and dig until my hands are raw and nearly numb, blisters popping on my palm.

The three other new sisters—before so valiant, so devoted to the secret mission of their dear Pale Mare—they've been crying a lot. Asking question after question. Purple PJ Pants babbles a mile a minute, begging for answers, an explanation. A way out. Horse Shorts just stares out into the abyss, her eyes focusing on nothing and no one in particular. Neon Choker pukes up her dinner.

None of us run to get help.

Me and my Accomplice Sisters.

"He deserved it," Lisha keeps saying over and over, as I continue to dig his grave, arms searing with pain. "He had it coming. Don't waste your tears and cry for him. Don't ever cry for a boy. Not even a dead one."

I do my best not to look too long at Zach's face, or pay too much attention to that horrible, familiar smell of death. Only this death is fresh. New. I know it's seeping into every hole in the fabric of my shorts and sleep shirt, and that I can never wear these clothes again.

"That's right, Arlee, keep digging," Lisha growls, though there's a purr beneath that growl. Like she's really enjoying this. Enjoying watch me uproot the soil for the body of the boy she—

"Did you kill him?" I ask. The still air seems to grow cold for just a moment. The three new girls gape at me. Horse Shorts is sobbing. Neon Choker wipes puke from her mouth. Purple PJ Pants rocks back and forth.

"Like I said, he deserved it," Lisha says, as if we're discussing the weather. "He more than deserved it." She points accusingly at Zach's body, the blowflies buzzing and humming in swarming circles above, landing on every inch of his flesh. Drinking. Eating. Laying their eggs. They start so early, even before the rot settles in. Hungry worms crawl through the soil. Horse Shorts sobs even harder. "He's lucky he left the world this way. There are things he deserved far more than death. Agony. Pain. Burning in the fires of hell, if that even fucking exists. I hope his soul is there now. I hope it's real." She spits on him. One of the girls gasps. Lisha whirls on her and slaps her hard across the face. Horse Shorts. Even I flinch at this. "Don't you *dare* act as if his body can be desecrated! You have no idea! None of you do! Dig, Arlee!"

I resume my digging. I focus on the smell of the fresh earth, the soil, but the scent of death overpowers everything. Overwhelms me.

"You all will dig," Lisha warns the other girls. "You'll dig, you'll help me bury his sad excuse for a sack of flesh, and then you will not ever tell a soul. You won't cry to your counselors or to Caroline. You won't cry to Mommy and Daddy, either. You won't *ever* go to the goddamned police. If you even *think* about attempting it, you will no longer belong to the Order of Equus, but that will only be the beginning. First, you will be kicked out of the camp for good. I know which of you are here on scholarship. You can kiss your chances at getting into college goodbye. Your futures will be over. The police will come and arrest you, because I will tell them that *you* did it. Your fingerprints are on those shovels, *sorors*. You are just as guilty as I am. I will tell them you killed him, and I saw the four of you do it, and that I tried to stop it, but I was *scared*." Her voice wavers rather convincingly on this word. She's a good actress, I'll give her that. "I'll tell the police whatever they need to hear. Trust and believe that."

"Please, Pale Mare." Horse Shorts sobs. "We won't say a word. Please don't get us arrested."

The two others nod in fervent agreement. They're just as terrified. Shell-shocked.

Lisha strokes Horse Shorts' hair, gently, like a mother soothing her unruly child. "Shh, don't worry," she says gently. "I'll keep you safe as long as you keep me safe. Understand?"

Horse Shorts nods and bows her head. She continues her digging, her crying muffled, muted.

We were chosen carefully, the four of us. That much is clear. These girls are young. Naive. Desperate for Lisha's approval.

Lisha and I lock eyes. She smiles. Her eyes, I realize, play tricks upon the viewer. They are not a window to her soul, but two wide, empty black pits.

She murdered Zach, reduced him to bones and raw, stinking meat. She feels no remorse, and maybe he did deserve it, but she murdered him all the same.

"Do the others know?" I ask her. "The other *sorors*?"

Her smile flickers like the flame of a candle. "No, and they don't need to know, Arlee Gold. Because . . . if they did find out . . . Well. What happened to Zach can happen again. Quite easily, and quickly. Keep digging. We don't have long before sunrise."

I could run right now. Hit her over the head with my shovel and sprint back to my cabin. I am stronger and older than the other three girls.

But . . .

I realize that I won't.

And I don't exactly know why, but I feel it. Lisha's eyes may be empty, but they see me all the same. There's a recognition there, as if we're two kindred spirits in horror and gore.

Every now and then, I look back toward the stables, where the horses sleep. Where Velvet is resting peacefully in her stall. My innocent horse.

And so, we dig until our palms ache and the tears recede and our bodies feel raw and broken open.

Until the great blinking, unseeing eyes of the stars begin to disappear as dawn inches closer.

Until, I swear to God, Zach's corpse twitches and spasms now and again beneath the spotlight of the bright full moon.

Until the light of dawn skims the sky and Lisha deems the hole ready. She digs, too, but with a ferocity, a feverish kind of glee. And all the while, the horses whinny and snort and stomp their feet, and the flies land on my arms and legs before going back to feast on the corpse.

The corpse of a boy. A boy whose grave I dug.

A grave Lisha snapped that she would finish after we helped her push his dead body into the ground. Skin that will never feel the kiss of embalming fluid, that will never turn soft and still again.

And all the while, I don't feel a single fucking thing.

So it goes.

So it goes.

So it goes. . . .

∘ ∘ ∘

I walk myself home, filthy, exhausted, and smelling of death. I walk like this all the way back to Unit Seven. It's half past six, the sun burning pink and gold in the swollen early morning sky. Inside my cabin, everyone is asleep. Their bodies so still . . . but breathing.

None of this can be real.

Everyone is here, including Chantal and Bea, curled up in their blankets. Chantal's mouth is slightly open, a puddle of drool forming on her pillow.

Quickly, carefully, and quietly as I can, I gather my towel, my robe, and a clean change of clothes from my footlocker.

Winnie stirs in her bed. "Arlee?" she asks, her voice sleepy and groggy. "Why are you awake?"

"Just showering," I whisper. "Go back to sleep."

She moans and rolls over. "What's that smell?"

I rush out of there.

In the shower I make the water as hot as it can go, so hot it scalds my skin. I scrub off the dirt and grime and the smell of death. The tiny red ants march across the wooden panels. In my fevered state I see them salute me.

I start to sing to myself, softly, *"The ants go marching one by one, hurrah, hurrah . . ."* My voice doesn't sound like mine.

After my shower I slip into a clean tank top and shorts, toss my soiled nightclothes into the outdoor trash bin, and practically crawl back to bed, where I collapse into a dreamless sleep.

When the Monday-morning bugle calls, I find that I cannot move. The sunshine is strong in my eyes as I lie on my back, but I don't stir. Everything in me weighs heavier than a thousand bricks. Even my eyeballs feel like massive paperweights, though they see the bottom of Winnie's bunk above me all the same. So many lines and grooves and patterns in the light-colored wood.

The other girls yawn and stretch. They dress and chat and head to the bathroom to brush their teeth and shower. I don't budge.

I stay like that until I hear Chantal's voice.

"Arlee? Are you all right?"

I don't move or speak.

"Are you sick?" Her tone is softer, far less cold than it normally is. Certainly not mean or angry.

I use every last bit of my strength to manage something like a small shrug.

To my surprise, she gently reaches out and touches my forehead with the back of her hand. It feels nice and cool on my hot skin.

"You're burning up. Go back to sleep. I'll bring you a croissant from breakfast. Don't worry about test prep. If you're still feeling sick, I'll take you to the nurse after, okay?"

I'm absolutely stunned, and this small unexpected kindness from Chantal of all people makes my eyes go wet with tears. Jane and Winnie and Ginger and Porter and Uma keep asking if I'm okay, but Chantal shushes them and hurries them out of the cabin, telling them to get to breakfast.

I need to sleep.

I can't move.

I close my eyes.

I drift back into a sleep so deep and dark it's like I've slipped off the edge of the world.

○ ○ ○

Hours later, Chantal brings me a croissant as promised—a chocolate one—and a hot mug of tea.

She sits at the edge of my bed, her long wavy hair falling in front of her eyes. In the midmorning light, her brows don't look as sharp. Her gaze doesn't seem as harsh, and she doesn't feel so hard. Just as she looked when she was with Eric by the river, or with Winnie when she was vomiting in the bushes.

She really is beautiful.

"How you feeling, camper?"

"Bad," I say. My voice comes out flat, affectless. Dry. I barely recognize it. I should drink something. My throat is as parched as desert ground.

"Poor thing," she says. If there's an air of condescension there, I can't hear it. "Maybe you should see the nurse."

"No."

"No?"

"I just need to sleep."

Chantal holds my gaze for quite some time. I stare back at her, unblinking, daring her to tell me otherwise. I know it's probably very warm in the cabin under my blankets, but right now I don't feel particularly warm. I feel . . . nothing. Like I am made of emptiness and floating through space, and where I am now is merely my spirit drifting among the stars.

Chantal leaves the croissant and the tea on a tray on the floor beside my bed. The other girls return from what I guess is test prep, chatting, their voices loud and spirits high. They are girls who have not seen death.

Not like I have.

"Arleeeeeeeee?"

Winnie leans down until she's at eye level with me. Today she looks stunning in a bright yellow T-shirt and ocean-blue shorts. Her medium-short hair is tied back into as much of a fishtail braid that the length will allow.

"I'm dying," I say.

She snorts and frowns. "Liar."

"She still on her deathbed?" I hear Jane ask, biting into another piece of candy. "Ugh, that was me last night. Do you also get migraines? We have Excedrin, remember? Arles, you missed the worst session we've had so far. Ruth would *not* shut up about binomial probability."

"If she has the flu or whatever, don't let her near me," I hear Uma snip. "I can't afford another summer spent with a sinus infection."

"She probably just has sun poisoning," Porter adds. "My aunt got it once and couldn't leave her bed for days, she was so sick. Her skin was all scaly and hot like a lizard's."

From her top bunk, Ginger plucks a few guitar chords and adds, "I could make some Hurt No More Juice."

They're all so kind to me. I don't deserve their kindness.

"Her skin looks *fine*," Winnie says. She rolls her eyes in their direction and grins at me. "You missed breakfast, and the eggs were honestly *impeccable* this morning. Now if you stay in bed, pretending to be dying, you're gonna miss everything else, including lunch, and *also* archery. With me." She says this like that would be the worst thing in the world . . . but she seems to mean it, her fingers tracing circles around my wrist. "You've been working so hard on your aim. I know you wanted to improve your score before the end of the week. Don't you want to beat that douchebag Michael in the next practice round?"

That finally coaxes a tiny grin on my own face. Michael really is a douche. Always giving the girls in our elective backhanded compliments when they miss or score worse than he does. Things like *"Damn, Beth, I didn't think you'd hit the bullseye twice in a row. Nice job."* Or *"Wow, Winnie, do you usually hold your bow like that? I didn't expect it to be so effective."*

Scumbag. The prettier the girl, the worse his backhanded compliments seem to be. No wonder, since he's friends with Zach and . . .

Zach.

Oh, shit.

No. No. No. *No.*

"Arlee? What is it?

An urgent thought flashes through my mind so loud and bright I can feel it screeching at me, *Act normal.*

I swallow down every dead and dying part of me and force myself to sit up in bed. Stars flash before my eyes because I did it way too fast. I swipe the to-go cup Chantal brought me off the tray on the floor and take a sip of the now-cold tea.

"There you go," Winnie says, smirking. "Proof you're not dying. A dying girl can't drink, can she?"

My body is still full of lead and bricks and paperweights, but I manage to crawl out of bed. "I just need a shower," I tell her. "I'll be okay." I already showered earlier, but I don't think anything will ever make me feel clean again.

"She's healed!" Jane cries. She flounces over to me and waves her arms dramatically around. "It's a miracle! The power of Winnie compels you!"

"Shut up." Winnie laughs.

"Seriously, though, Arles, how you feeling?" Jane asks. "You want me to walk you to the nurse or whatever? Chantal told me to keep a close eye on you."

Before, I might've snarked, "*I bet she did,*" whether out loud or in my head, but now that kind of comment holds no implication. Chantal maybe being moody with me no longer feels like anything worth worrying or thinking about.

Plus, she didn't seem moody this morning at all. She seemed genuinely concerned.

"I'm good," I lie. I chug the rest of the tea and gobble up the croissant, though they taste like nothing. My head is still fuzzy from dreams I don't remember, but the way they made me feel when I woke was horrifying.

If I act normal, like everything is fine—like I'm fine—then it will be.

It must be.

○ ○ ○

At aquatics, Eric takes us for a long walk down to the Echo River. Past the black lampposts with lanterns now free of moths both dead and alive, the challenge course with the zip line and ropes and its dizzying array of equipment. A hummingbird flutters past my face, her feathers cerulean, and the sunshine warms some of the numbness that's sunk into every part of me.

At the river we pick out life jackets from a toolshed. We're supposed to work on the techniques we learned in the pool, but most of the campers clearly see this as an excuse to horse around. If anyone has realized Zach is missing yet, the news hasn't reached our group.

As I wade into the water, watching the others laugh and splash one another, I find myself staring back at the strange yellowed piano that haunts the beach.

There's a feeling bubbling under the surface that I can't deny. The one that ripples through me right now.

Disgust.

I do my best to block it from my mind as I carefully step across the slippery river rocks. They are sun-soaked, warm on my feet, pressing into every nerve and muscle like a massage. Out here in the baking sunshine I almost feel peaceful. Whole. For a little while, some of the broken, tattered parts of me are woven back together through the magic of sunlight, cold water, and fresh air.

I don't hold my breath when I unclip my life vest and go under.

The river is murky, brown, with soft mud underfoot. I stay there as long as I can without passing out, then surface and swim to the bank.

"Arlee! You know you can't do that!" Eric scolds from the beach. "Put your life jacket back on. You know better."

I did it with Winnie, when your hand was sliding up Chantal's thigh, I think. *We swam without life jackets and no one watched over us and you didn't say anything then.*

"She's new. She's also a fucking grade-A weirdo. She doesn't know shit," one of the boys says—the one who called me a bitch, I think—and a few other kids snicker.

Before the horse field, before I saw and smelled and buried the fresh corpse of Zach, comments like this would've set off a fire in my belly and my face aflame with shame and rage. But now I feel nothing. Their words ring empty and hollow, as does the laughter of the others.

I've seen death in more ways than any of them. I've held it. Tasted it in my mouth. Warm and wet.

I no longer care about the things that do not matter.

During horseback riding, we embark on our first trail ride through the woods. On the way across the field, we walk our horses across Zach's grave, and I begin to shake uncontrollably, like Velvet does whenever she's covered in flies. The heat presses down on me and I'm sweating so hard in my jeans and thick helmet, my stomach churning at the site where the horseflies linger. There are so many of them in that spot now. Ravenous.

I pat Velvet's soft neck, doing my best to focus on the horse in front of us and staying at least six feet apart, as we've been instructed. Horses get scared easily, after all, and might kick when they feel threatened.

Velvet makes a low nickering sound, and I imagine maybe she's comforting me . . . but maybe she knows everything. She was there, after all, in the stables last night, and the night of the raucous party. She sees everything we do under the cover of darkness, every sinful moment caught between the whites of her eyes.

Maybe she's afraid of me.

Some of the horses are stopping now and then to munch on leaves, slowing down the train. One girl kicks furiously at her horse's sides. Much too hard, I think, and our asshole instructor only encourages her.

"Yank the reins, Gina!" Cara barks. "Hold tight to the reins! *Kick her!*"

"Stop it," I say, too quiet for her to hear. "You're hurting her."

Velvet huffs as if in agreement.

Olive's horse never stops to graze. She keeps her reins tight but not too tightly held. She navigates the creeks we step through and hills we climb with perfect form. She is the depiction of a controlled yet easy rider. I wonder if she knows what I did, or has any inkling, even though Lisha said none of the others know. I want so badly to talk to her, to confide in her like a real sister would. Would it change her mind about being my sister? Did she know somehow this would happen to me? I'm not sure what I'm more afraid of: Lisha's wrath, or Olive's judgment.

She tried to tell me this place had an underbelly. Tried to warn me, even if it was only to scare me. She wasn't wrong. The long clanging church bells that ring in the morning as we sit and wait in the campfire circle before first count-off. Sundown Ceremony. The odd figures, and the dead baby horse dangling from Caroline's hand that would never breathe this air or move through life. Initiation. The gray robes and wooden horse faces with empty black eyes. Lisha holding my mouth down to the bleeding skin of my new sister, forcing me to taste her blood.

This was far worse than any "silly blood ritual" could ever be.

After our trail ride, I'm hanging Velvet's things in the tack room when I hear a girl say to her friend, "This is bad. This is really, really bad."

I keep my head down but listen in as the conversation continues. I recognize these girls from the party with Paula. They're Unit Eight girls. Likely friends with Zach.

"Where the hell would he have gone?"

"It makes no sense, right? Apparently, he's been missing since this morning. Or, at least, last night was the last time anyone saw him. Michael said his bed was perfectly made, like no one had even slept in it."

"Jesus Christ, that's creepy."

My hands shake as I hang Velvet's bridle on the tack wall, then accidentally kick over a stirrup. It goes clattering to the floor. The girls whip around for the source of the sound. I scurry out in time to hear one of them mutter, "*Ugh, that girl gives me the creeps.*"

Lunchtime is full of similar nervous chatter, though now I can blend in with my table and focus on tearing my paper napkin into tiny pieces. I half expect to see Zach sitting beside Lisha, cracking jokes with Michael and their doofus buddies. The boys are unusually sullen and quiet today. No laughter here.

I feel a sharp pang of guilt.

I could tell them what happened. Tell a counselor. Pass an anonymous note to someone . . . anyone . . . but Lisha is watching me out of the corner of her eye, as she always does. Vigilant as a hawk or a god. All-seeing. All-knowing.

Before we eat, Caroline appears like an apparition in the center of the dining hall between the two conjoined rooms. She looks elegant as ever in a bright red sundress that shows off her shoulders. She folds her manicured hands and clears her throat until we quiet down.

"My dedicated staff, my wonderful campers . . ." *Oh God. Oh God.* "I have some troubling news, though I urge calmness and focus. As some of you are now aware of, Zachary Clark of Unit One has not been seen since last night. We have taken the necessary steps to report him missing, though God willing, he is somewhere on the premises. Rest assured I've assembled a professional search team that will comb the grounds from sunrise to sunset until he is located. If you have any information about his whereabouts or the last time you saw him, please tell one of your counselors—"

The rest of her sentence is drowned out by the chorus of fear, panic, horror. Zach. *Missing.* I spot one of my Accomplice Sisters. Neon Choker. She stares blankly ahead.

Lisha smiles at me across the aisle. Her fangs look extra sharp today.

During archery, Zach's absence is an open, gaping wound in the fabric of our normally easygoing elective class. Strangely static without his bravado and constant commentary, as obnoxious as it was.

All of us deal with it differently. Heather does her best to feign normalcy, to pretend this isn't happening. She keeps blurting out random facts while practicing her shots. "I bet you guys didn't know that archery is one of the safest sports!" she says loudly to no one in particular, since most of us aren't really listening. "It's true! Even safer than bowling. Funny, right?"

Zach's devoted fan club huddles together by the shed, their voices running over one another as they fight for airtime in loud whispers.

"I'm honestly convinced he ran off with that girl he made out with last summer at Midsummer Concert. What's her name? Jenna McIntire?"

"Uh, then she'd be missing *too*, genius."

"God, it's so scary! What if he's *hurt*? I can't even imagine him in pain. Alone. Terrified. We should organize our own search, don't you think? What's taking so freaking long?"

"Yeah, why isn't there a helicopter scouring the property *right now*?!"

"Zach's parents are gonna sue the *shit* out of this place."

"It's a serial killer, y'all. I'm telling you, we need to go home. This is bullshit. We can't stay here."

"There's no serial killer, Hailey. Chill."

Michael tries shooting, swearing loudly each time he misses. Finally, he gives a garbled shout like an angry wild animal and tosses his bow and arrow across the field, then slumps down to the grass. His friends approach and comfort him.

"They'll find him, dude."

"Mike, it's gonna be fine."

"Just leave me alone!" Michael shouts. He swats them away and buries his head in his knees. I almost feel sorry for him.

Heather keeps talking to herself, like she's the host of some podcast no one is listening to. Beads of sweat drip down her face and her muscles twitch as she aims and shoots and rambles on.

"Archery was the first Olympic sport to allow women to compete. Wild, right? Like, *imagine* the world without Khatuna Lorig?!" She laughs way too loudly.

Winnie and I sit together in the field making chains of clovers, this time our knees barely touching. Her face looks ghostly pale today, in spite of the warm, relentless sun, and she keeps biting her fingernails, her leg jiggling nervously.

"Jesus Christ, Arles," she says with a deep sigh. "This is all such a mess, huh?"

"Has . . . this ever happened before?" I ask, trying to sound genuinely concerned. At least I don't have to pretend to be calm. "Someone going missing?"

She shakes her head and holds her wrist out to me so I can tie a clover chain around it. I think of how safe and good I felt last night, resting my head against her shoulder. Before the storm was over. Before a new storm began for me.

And now . . . Winnie feels so far away. She can barely maintain eye contact with me, even though we're sitting so close, and talking, and just being together.

I had her, if only for a little while. We kissed. We laughed. I felt love radiating through her. I tear a handful of clovers from the ground and squeeze them together, the green juices staining my fingers. It makes me so anxious, thinking of how fragile every relationship is. How someone can be right there with you one minute and then gone the next.

Or *dead*. I shudder.

"Not that I know of. Though I guess it was a matter of time, you know? The counselors here are drunk or stoned half the time. There're woods for miles. It's easy enough to wander off . . . get lost." She presses her lips together. "His parents could sue for gross negligence, honestly. You've seen what happens here after-hours. I think we all sort of operated under the illusion that we were invincible until now, you know?"

I can read the traces of fear etched across her face.

My heart thuds in my chest. I want to tell her that everything is going to be okay. That even though Zach was a douche to her and to me, she shouldn't have to worry about him anymore. Or herself, really.

She's certainly not the one in danger.

Instead I do my best impersonation of a comforting friend, if that's what we even are. I have no idea how to define us in my mind. Winnie and me. Me and Winnie.

I fake a smile and tie another knot around her new clover bracelet. If only she knew who I really was, what I was capable of doing. The secrets I can hide from her and everyone else. I barely understand why she likes me at all, why she and my bunk-mates and Reyes and Gabe accept me—or at least pretend to—when the rest of the camp acts as though I have rabies.

Maybe they feel sorry for me.

Ugh, that girl gives me the creeps.

She wouldn't let me touch her like this, I think, if she knew what I did last night. Wouldn't ever look at me the same again. She's too pure. Too perfect.

I swallow down my secrets. I'm exhausted and dizzy, the colors of the day beginning to blur together like a watercolor painting. Mutable and surreal.

I'm floating through reality, hanging on by a thread. As if I'm dead asleep with my eyes wide open.

"Anyway," she goes on, and I realize she's rambling like I do when I'm really anxious, "I really do hope he's run off temporarily or something, maybe got drunk last night at some under-age party with townies and is still sleeping off the hangover."

She chuckles to herself. "He always used to talk about doing that."

Always used to. I clear my throat and struggle to speak. "Were you . . . ever close with him? Like friends?"

She rolls her eyes and tears a blade of grass in half, her lower lip trembling slightly. "I wouldn't call it that. I've just known him a while, is all."

I nod and shut my eyes so hard I see stars. All I want to do is go back to the cabin and go back to sleep, but I have to pretend I'm close to being fine. I have to stay off everyone's radar, especially after earlier today.

I nearly doze off in yoga class as Bea leads us through a sun-salutation series. It's burning hot in here, the sun beating through the screened windows, but it's the kind of warmth that almost feels like a soothing bubble bath.

"Remember to *breeeathe* . . . ," she instructs. "Keep a calm, steady mind, even if you don't feel okay right now. That's all right. Focus on the present. In this moment, you are safe. In this moment, you are—"

Someone is whimpering. Crying quietly.

It takes me a moment to realize that it's me.

CHAPTER THIRTEEN

The rumors continue to evolve and take shape throughout the day. I can't get away from any of it, not even in my own cabin before dinner, pretending to nap while my bunkmates bat around speculation in urgent voices that buzz in my ear like horseflies. All the while Ginger strums her guitar, creating a twisted soundtrack to all this chaos.

"Honestly?" Jane says, chomping on her tenth Twizzler in the last ten minutes. "My money is on runaway, but like, the wealthy, poor-little-rich-boy kind. Zach always acted like he was too good to be around the rest of us peons. I bet he's *Eat Pray Love*–ing it up right now somewhere."

"Unlikely," Porter chimes in, her voice laced with worry. "I would guess he went on a walk and suffered some kind of head or bodily injury and is trying to make it back now. If that's the case, the search party should find him soon."

"The serial-killer-in-the-woods theory intrigues me more." Uma's crunching loudly on what sounds like chips. God, I wish she'd stop. Every sound is agonizing against my already frayed nerves.

"*Uma!*" Porter scolds.

"What?" *Crunch crunch.* "It's possible."

"Don't even joke about that," Porter says stiffly. "It's not funny. It hasn't been that long. He's not . . . he can't be . . ."

"Shit, I'm sorry, Port. You're right, we should try to stay positive." I catch the hint of sarcasm in her tone. "Arlee, what do you think? *Eat Pray Love*–ing or injured off the grid?"

I pretend I'm sleeping.

At dinner, Zach is still all anyone can talk about at our table.

I glance over at Lisha's table. Michael sits staring at the wall, his eyes haunted and faraway, while she's casually plucking crumbs off a muffin, chewing them slowly. Savoring every bite.

Psycho, I think. I may have been the one to help bury Zach, and I may have weirdly enjoyed it, but I sure as hell didn't kill him.

"I've changed my *Eat Pray Love* theory. There's no way he just *left*," Uma argues, sprinkling sugar over her filet mignon instead of salt by mistake. She curses at herself when she realizes what she's done.

"Maybe someone kidnapped him," Porter adds, her eyes wide with fear behind the frames of her glasses. "Stalked him until they got him alone. Maybe we're all in grave danger. I keep thinking about the serial killer on the loose people keep talking about." She shudders.

"Statistically, the odds of a serial killer being on campus are slim to none," Reyes says in between bites of his potatoes. They don't look remotely appetizing this evening. None of it does. Even the taste of the food here has seemed to change, at least for me. It was once rich and full of flavor, but now everything that touches my tongue is kind of soggy. Sour. Like it's been cooked with dish soap.

"I don't even want to think about it," Gabe groans. "I just hope he isn't hurt."

"Me, too," Winnie echoes. She reaches out for Gabe's hand

and gives it a reassuring squeeze. "He's not my favorite person, you all know that, but I wouldn't want anything bad to happen to him."

I drink down the rest of my coffee. It still tastes like dirt.

A woman enters the dining hall. A hard-looking woman, if there ever was one, face pinched and tight, as if she's served in the military, survived some truly nasty things. The kind of things that can make even the most positive person spiral into utter despair.

A sheriff.

Her hair is gray, and like Caroline's, braided long down her back like a horse's mane. She walks with a cane and a bit of a limp—old army injury, Reyes supposes—though she moves with an air of pride.

She's older, possibly in her fifties, much like Caroline Rhinelander. Unlike Caroline, she wears no makeup. She doesn't smile or speak in a bright, lilting tone. She is mostly silent, actually, standing stoically in her tan uniform and campaign hat with one hand grazing the gun clipped to her belt. As soon as she arrives in the middle of the meal, everyone stops speaking.

People stiffen with anticipation when they hear Caroline's heels click on the hardwood floors of the dining hall. She stands between the front and rear rooms and rings her creepy little cowbell. Deep concern is painted on her face along with some bright red lipstick and sparkling gold eyeshadow. She flutters her long fake lashes at us so dramatically it's almost comical, and when she speaks, there's a hitch in her voice like she's trying not to cry.

If only they knew what we did last night. . . .

"My Rockaway campers, my wonderful staff, I have good news, though the circumstances are certainly troubling. Zachary Clark has been located." The dining hall erupts in frenzied chatter, but she raises a hand and gently shushes them. My stomach turns to ice. *Oh God.* She found the body. *Oh fuck.* The uniformed woman's hand comes to rest atop her gun holster. Can she see the guilt in me? I begin to tremble.

"I recognize this has been a very difficult time for everyone here," Caroline goes on, "but we were able to confirm that . . . Well, Sheriff Dupont? Would you like to tell them?"

The hard-looking woman gives a curt nod and steps forward. When she speaks, her voice is deep and guttural, like tires crunching on a gravel road.

"He brought a contraband cell phone onto camp grounds, which we were able to track to the town right outside camp. We have eyewitnesses who saw him there in multiple locations, and have confirmed he is a runaway."

What?

There's no way I heard that correctly, though when my eyes scan the room, I see that I didn't. Because everyone in here heard it, too.

Runaway.

Jane mutters, *"Knew it."* Porter sighs in relief. Beside me, Winnie makes a low, whimpering noise deep in her throat.

My face flushes hot. I'm so dizzy I could vomit. I clutch at the edge of my seat to stop the dining hall from spinning.

"I urge all of you to please remain calm and patient as we continue our search to find his exact whereabouts. If you have any information at all that might be helpful to us, including how he was acting before he ran away, what he was talking about . . . please do report directly to your unit head or to me. No matter how small or seemingly insignificant a detail, we do want to know."

Caroline nods in fervent agreement. She locks eyes with me, holding my gaze. "You all know that my door is always open."

Day or night.

Fuck.

"Our entire department is fully committed to quickly locating Mr. Clark. And you can be sure you're in the best hands with Missus Rhinelander. I've known her since she first became camp director, and can vouch for her ever-present professionalism and diligence concerning the safety of her campers."

Runaway?

I begin stacking squares of cheese on top of one another like Jenga blocks to give my shaky hands something to do, my eyes something to focus on.

Caroline gives her a thankful smile. "Out of concern for the general safety of our campers, we will also be keeping the grounds secure until the end of the summer," she says. "Therefore, all alumni events are hereby postponed. Our Midsummer Concert will go on as scheduled, but without help from any outside vendors. I realize this is unprecedented, but we must keep calm and carry on, as the Brits say."

This gets a few laughs. I can feel the relief flow through the dining hall. *A* runaway. *Probably somewhere in town. Maybe out partying with friends. Missing, but presumed safe.*

"If you need to speak with me, I will be at my usual office hours, but will also extend them—" she goes on.

For a moment, we lock eyes, and I just know when I see it.

Caroline is not just part of the Order.

She is the head of the horse. She has to be.

Very likely, Sheriff Dupont is somehow part of it, too. I can't trust her.

Caroline must know what I did. What *we* did. Maybe Lisha told her—though Lisha warned us not to tell anyone.

Stars dance before my eyes.

No one can help me.

Winnie leans in closer to me. "We'll look out for each other from now on, Arles," she says softly. "No matter what happens next. Promise me?"

She wraps her pinky finger around mine under the table, where the others can't see. "Promise," I say, even though I don't know how to promise something encased in a lie.

Across the aisle, Lisha continues to watch me eat out of the corner of her eye. She isn't as sneaky as she thinks she is. I use my fork to carefully spear my chicken breast and imagine using it to stab her in the eye, before taking a massive bite.

o o o

That night, in an attempt to cheer us up, Chantal organizes a campfire sing-along.

Ruth hugs and comforts the remaining frightened, upset campers, keeping her demeanor outwardly calm. Sweet Ruth. Well-intentioned Ruth. I could never really call myself either of those things.

Winnie breaks out the booze yet again, as do other girls in my unit. That night, all the adrenaline of the day reaches a fever pitch, only this time, it's not crying and speculating and worrying. It's booze and cigarettes, joints smoked openly, girls running around screaming late into the night, and no one stopping us.

Winnie uses a stick to trace circles in the dirt. Only a few nights ago, we were using these sticks to roast marshmallows. We were singing camp songs with abandon, and she was sitting beside me, her laughter a concerto in my ear. The air smelled of woodsmoke and happiness and freedom. The promise of a long, beautiful summer.

Now that beautiful summer is laced with fear.

"Are you okay?" she asks me, voice quiet and sweet, eyes glassy from drinking. "It's okay if you're not. This is . . . a lot."

"I don't know," I admit. "I don't really know how to feel."

"Well, we have each other, right?"

She gazes at me as if I can help guide her through this madness, be her beacon of light and hope. Winnie holds out her pinky finger for me, and I take it in mine. It feels like there are razor blades slicing down my throat when I swallow.

Tell her. Someone. Anyone.

I can't.

I won't.

It sends electricity all the way down my spine and into my toes.

Even amid all this chaos, this pandemonium, she's still so caring. So . . . nurturing. Even as the world seems to lose more color by the second, it's like Winnie still emits glowing rainbows. She remains impossibly beautiful. I lean my head against her arm the same way Chantal leaned her own arm against Eric's, and it helps a little. She doesn't back away but rests her head against mine.

Like friends do, I tell myself. Like girls do.

Even I know that's a lie.

We kissed, after all. Under the lights. On the makeshift dance floor. She kissed me back and it was powerful and charged.

I wish I could feel like that again. I ache for it, even the painful bits.

Because I'm beginning to feel even more numb than I did before. Emptier. Blanker. Like whatever Arlee was there before is slowly but surely getting whited out.

I wrap my arms around Winnie and inhale that intoxicating mix of liquor, sunscreen, and shampoo.

The party rages on late into the night until Anna snaps at us all to get back to our bunks. My own bunkmates are tipsy, chatty, and bursting with energy.

"All of you should get to sleep," Chantal murmurs in agreement from her bed. "For the love of God, it's been a hard enough day. Oh, and Winnie, put the flask away. I can smell the bad vodka from here. Not tonight, girlie."

I shut my eyes and will myself to fall asleep.

But I can't.

The night stretches on eternally, and as tired as I am, I toss and turn in bed for hours.

Restless. Listless.

Guilty.

Wicked.

I should tell someone. Anyone.

But who?

Sure, I could run and tell Caroline, but she's in on it, I know she is. She has to be. I know she's the one calling all the shots. Fabricating the lie.

But why? To avoid a lawsuit? To continue camp as normal at all costs?

To cover up for someone? For me?

But the body . . . I know where Zach's body is, and it seems like she doesn't.

Or does she?

I shiver. Part of me doesn't want to know, as if the truth around that were more frightening than anything else I've experienced here so far.

I check in with myself, do a full-body scan the way my meditation app always tells me to do. I feel . . . a strange cocktail of emotions. On the one hand, I feel numb, like this isn't real. Like I'm not really here. On the other, I feel the reality of what I've done—of what that makes me—slowly moving up from beneath the soil that's crawling with earthworms. . . .

I drift in and out of fevered sleep. My dreams are strange. Vivid. Lucid, almost.

When the morning bugle finally calls, I startle as if someone's doused me in freezing water.

Even with a popular boy gone missing, life at camp inexplicably goes on.

The sky last night was a mourner's veil.

After all, a boy is missing.

After all, a boy is dead, everyone here wrapped around the finger of a murderous lie.

Everyone but Lisha and my Accomplice Sisters and me.

And Caroline.

Runaway.

∘ ∘ ∘

At the campfire circle this morning, we sit and wait for the familiar toll of the church bells. This morning they almost sound comforting, though also fittingly macabre.

"Unit *Sev-en!*" Chantal calls, in a voice markedly weaker than normal.

"Unit Seven," we mumble in unison. "Unit Seven countdown."

No one else looks particularly rested, either. Chantal keeps pacing back and forth, as if she's counting and recounting us over and over even after we've finished. Bea can't stop yawning. Anna lights yet another cigarette.

Winnie loops her arm through mine and we walk like that all the way to breakfast, each footstep I make on the dirt path sounding like *liar, liar, liar* pounding in my ears.

During the meal, I steal a glance across the aisle at Michael. He sits slumped forward, head in his hands. Not eating a thing. Lisha chews her cornflakes, her expression blank. Unreadable. Fury churns inside me. She knows damn well what happened to Michael's best friend—what she did to me and my Accomplice Sisters that night, what she put us through—and yet she sits there, perfectly fine. Eating her fucking cereal. No remorse. Nothing.

She's sick. Cruel.

But so are you, the voice in my head hisses at me. *You wanted to bury him.*

"Shut up," I say under my breath, digging my nails into my wrist. "Shut up."

You enjoyed it, you sick fuck. Your shovel was the first to hit the soil. Don't you remember how it felt?

The catharsis?

I close my eyes and I'm back in the horse field, the air stinking of death . . . and all those fucking flies. The way they swam through the moonlight. Yes, I felt disgust. Horror. But I also felt . . . as I dug and covered his remains . . . that strange sense of relief. Vindication.

"Arlee . . . ?"

I come to and Lisha is standing over our table, a smile of sympathy painted on her lips like poison. Immediately I recoil from her, nearly knocking over my water glass, like she did to me days ago. My hands shake as I steady it. I won't let her fool me with that shit again.

"Are you okay?" Her voice is as sweet as the syrup on Reyes's pancakes. Sticky and oversaturated. "You were talking to yourself and you seemed so upset. Kind of out of it, maybe? I wanted to check on you."

Fuck off, bitch. I imagine my hands around her throat. I imagine squeezing . . .

"She's *fine*," Jane says curtly, regarding her with suspicion.

I don't know how much Jane knows about Lisha, but I should've trusted her distrust from the beginning.

"Well, technically, none of us will be fine until we've resolved the missing—"

Jane kicks at Reyes under the table. "We're fine, Lisha. Thank you."

"I'm only trying to help." Lisha pouts. She kneels down so we're at eye level. "Seriously, Arlee. You know I'm here if you need to talk about anything. We're friends, right?"

She slides her hand across the table toward mine and . . . shit, she's wearing the yellow nail polish. No. *No.* I can't do a ritual tonight. I can't.

I can't be here anymore. Can't do this.

But I have to.

It's now a matter of life or death.

"I'm going to the bathroom," I say, shoving Lisha aside and making a mad dash for the very back of the hall, ignoring the stares, the whispers, the way I think I hear someone say *"guilty"* as I pass.

Once inside, I collapse to the tiled floor and cradle my head in my arms. I can barely breathe. I'm hyperventilating so hard my lungs hurt. My chest constricts like a snake is squeezing it shut. *It's okay, it's okay, it's okay.* If I tell myself this enough, maybe I can make it true. *I can handle this. I'm safe.* But I'm not. Not while I'm here. Not after what I did, what I continue to do: lie by omission. Hide the truth.

The truth that I helped bury in the ground.

But Lisha is watching me closely. Listening. A predator

stalking her prey. She could do what she did to Zach to me, or to one of the other Accomplice Sisters. She said as much. She knows which unit I'm in. It wouldn't be hard to figure out where I sleep.' . . .

I cry out and slam the heel of my hand against the floor so hard it leaves a big bright red spot. It will probably bruise.

Something skitters across the floor and I nearly stop breathing. A cockroach.

The dirtiest, most disgusting insect I've ever seen in this pristine palace of a summer camp. I leap up from the floor and stare it down, even though I want to cry out, even though I want to run.

I pretend it's Lisha when I stomp it to death with a sickening crunch.

For a moment, I feel a flicker of a grin appear on my lips like the flicker of a tea-candle flame.

o o o

Winnie sits with me during test prep, in the very back of the amphitheater. As Ruth drones on about the differences between connotation and context and the minutes drag on, I drift off into a kind of half sleep, half trance.

I watch her lips move. Her voice sounds familiar and soothing . . . until it doesn't.

"Mistakes, mistakes, mistakes," Miss Teresa says, her voice coming right out of Ruth's mouth. "Again and again, Arlee, you make foolish mistakes that cost you everything. You could've placed higher at that recital in seventh grade. Don't you remember? You could have done better, and maybe then your father would've stayed. Why do you make these mistakes? I'll tell you, Arlee. It's because you're a wicked girl deep down. A wicked, nasty—"

"Arlee?"

Ruth's voice is her own again. I see it in her eyes: the pity. I can feel it from the Unit Seven girls.

Pity and . . . something else.

Weirdo.

Freak.

If only they knew.

"Why don't we, um . . . take a break?" Ruth says. "Call it a morning." She shuts the textbook she's been reading from with such force it reverberates throughout the amphitheater. "It's been tough, huh?"

The other girls mutter in agreement.

"I'm sorry, I can't concentrate," Porter moans. "I know he's okay, and I'm so thankful, but right now it's too much, Ruth. I'm so overwhelmed."

"Aww, honey, I know."

Beside me, I feel Winnie gently slide her hand down to my thigh, resting it in the same place Eric left his hand on Chantal.

I am wicked.

I am sinful.

Yet I feel things that aren't.

And I want her hands to travel deeper . . . into darker places I've never let another person go.

CHAPTER FOURTEEN

It's extremely difficult to keep myself awake tonight.

I don't know if it's all the physical activity, the many late nights with my bunkmates catching up to me, or the fact that I'm most definitely suffering some kind of horrific trauma from seeing Zach's corpse and helping to bury him.

Perhaps it's a combination of all three, Arlee, Miss Teresa snips inside my mind.

Listen to Miss Teresa, Mom adds. *You can learn a lot from her.* I clench my jaw and bunch my fists, remembering how she forced me to keep going to piano lessons, over and over, even though it was absolute torture for me. Even though I cried and begged for her to let me stop.

Why didn't Mom ever let me stop?

Winnie snores softly above me, but otherwise the night is tranquil with its lullabies of crickets and owls. I'm so cozy under my blankets, and all I want to do is close my eyes and sleep forever. Maybe if I sleep long enough, I can wake up and pretend that none of this was ever real. That it never happened. That there isn't a horrible, animal part of me that's clawed free once again.

The truth is, I'm terrified of her. Of that Arlee Gold. The ticking time bomb within me. Maybe even more terrified than I am of Lisha or what's waiting for me and my sisters tonight. I huddle under the covers, fighting to keep my eyes open until my watch says that it's a quarter to midnight.

Time to move.

I grudgingly get out of bed, grabbing my miniflashlight and slipping on my glasses. Bea is passed out; Chantal talks in her sleep.

I gently slide my footlocker out from under my bed and rummage around for a zip-up hoodie, quietly as I can—though it's not quiet enough, because Winnie moans and rolls over.

"What're you doing?" she murmurs.

"Bathroom," I whisper. "Go back to sleep."

"Want me to come with you?"

My heart flutters at the slight suggestion in her tone. I want her to, I really do. I want to run off into the woods with her and kiss her ferociously and never come back here, but I can't. She can't be part of this. Not when bloodthirsty psychopaths like Lisha are waiting for me where the horses sleep.

If I can make anything good out of all this horror, I can at least keep her safe, like I promised myself I would.

"I'm good. Night night."

I wish I could see her reaction in the dark, if she's mad or hurt, but she gives me nothing to go on, not even a "good night" in return, so I slip out of the cabin as quickly as I can.

It's much too warm and muggy for a hoodie, but I keep it on like armor, sweating as I make my way down the hill and along the dark forest path, my little flashlight lighting the way.

I should never have been so naive, to think joining this society would be a good idea. That it wouldn't bring me such agony, leaving me cold and empty inside. Shades of dark blue where vibrant colors used to be.

I buried a body.

My shovel was the first to hit the soil.

You wanted to, remember? a voice hisses in my ear, and I whirl around, panting, my skin flushing hot, thinking something is behind me. Maybe in the trees. In the bushes. There's a rustling. A snapping branch or twig. It's so dark, and my flashlight only lets me see so much. I freeze, listening for footsteps. Someone. Anything.

There's nothing. No one. Just the crickets and cicadas. The owls and the forest that never sleeps.

I'm helping to cover up a murder.

It's choking me, holding me by the throat. Squeezing the air and life out of my lungs, or whatever is left inside.

By the time I reach the barn, most of my sisters are already there, cloaked and masked. They stand around chatting happily, as if this were an ordinary evening, as if this were the barn party and a night worth celebrating.

As if a boy weren't missing.

My Accomplice Sisters are here, too. Neon Choker nods when she sees me, but the two others avoid my gaze and skitter away from me like roaches.

I feel another surge of anger. Lisha did this. Lisha made those girls feel like I do: dead and empty inside. Afraid.

Wicked.

It's not their fault.

"Arlee!"

Olive runs over to me, beaming, and pulls me into a warm hug. "Come, *soror*. You can help me in the barn with the baby."

"The what?"

She beams at me. "Lisha gave me the key." She takes my hand and beckons me inside, my mouth filling with the taste of metal as we walk across the damp floorboards. Just as she said, Olive pulls a key from her cloak and unlocks the secret closet.

I finally get a good view of what's inside.

Our shovels and spades from that night are gone, but there are golden crests and emblems mounted on the wooden walls, all containing the symbol of the crooked star. Gray cloaks and white horse masks hang neatly from a makeshift coatrack, and on a shelf beside a collection of tea candles is a bundle of knives.

Knives of all shapes and sizes. Some long and thick, like the hunting knife Danielle used to cut open her arm. Others are small, with fine points that seem impossibly sharp.

Olive hums to herself as she selects a serrated knife with jagged edges.

Pushed back into the corner of the closet, beside the cobwebs crawling with spiders that make the bile reach my mouth along with the taste of blood, is a bulging bundle, tightly wrapped in white cloth.

Olive hands me the knife and lifts the bundle into her arms.

"The baby," she coos, cradling it gently to her chest.

"No. Oh, fuck, no . . ."

"Yes, Arlee. Don't be afraid. Look at her."

She pulls back the cloth, revealing the face of the dead fetus horse.

I cry out, but Olive touches my shoulder. "Don't worry, Arlee. She feels nothing anymore. She's safe now. Do you understand? I think our Pale Mare has plans for her tonight. Why don't you grab a cloak and mask and meet me outside? Pocket the knife. We'll be needing that. The others will bring the candles and arrange our circle. I'll take the little one. We only have an hour or so before . . . well, before the flies get to her."

"The flies?" I ask weakly. I can't take my eyes off the dead baby. Up close, it's even more horrible. Milky white-pinkish blue and wrinkled, and a strong chemical scent wafting from her translucent skin . . .

"Yes. She was frozen, I think? We have to return her as soon as possible."

I watch her hum and rock the fetus gently in her arms as she walks across the wide barn to the door, past the bales of moldy hay and beneath the rafters where the disco balls once twirled and mirrored back everything and everyone in this awful, twisted place.

There's no doubt in my mind now that Caroline is the one in charge, that she's running this.

Even if she wasn't the one who killed Zach.

◦ ◦ ◦

1865.

This was the year our society was founded. Or so these girls are saying.

Long, long before the camp existed. When it was merely woods and swampland and a river with another, older name.

It's starting to sound like bullshit.

The love, the feeling of being held . . . it's beginning to slip out from under me.

The warmth is growing cold.

"For centuries this land was run by women," a sister reads from a booklet, her voice partially muffled by her wooden horse mask. My Accomplice Sisters and I kneel in the tall grass of the horse field, wearing our masks and cloaks, as the rest of the *sorors* encircle us. They shine their flashlights down on us in place of a full moon. "Before the white settler men came and dominated it and made it into what we see today. Before it was capitalized. Uprooted. It was made of women. Pioneer women who had fled the bondage of marriage and cruel homes, riding here on majestic feral horses from the coastline. Emancipated women who were once enslaved. Native women who had been ripped from their homes and families and found new family here.

"It was not always a peaceful group, the original Order. I won't lie to you or sugarcoat it, new *sorors*. Nor was it perfect, as we all came from different places and with different life experiences. There were many disagreements. Women who had to be banished for trying to take more than they were owed, or thinking they deserved more than they did. But through it all we remained united by a common goal: *protection*. We vowed to protect one another, always and forever, from the men who wished to harm us."

The sisters begin to place the tea candles on the swath of leather fabric we saw during our initiation, once again using them to form the shape of the crooked star. We learn its meaning: *Light the way for your sister, and hold out one arm to shield and protect.*

One by one, they each light a candle, and the grass itself seems to glow.

"The Order evolved over time," another sister reads next. Anna's voice, I recognize. As the sisters speak, Olive cradles the dead baby horse in its white bundle as if it were a living, breathing child. "What began as a place of refuge for women of the Carolinas slowly became smaller, more secretive. Sisters left to start families and businesses. To homestead elsewhere. Over time our numbers dwindled, yet the core of the Order remained and we kept to our duties. We tilled the land and nourished her, growing our own food. Building our own shelter. Fighting off the men who learned of us and tried to infiltrate and destroy everything we had built. We held their heads under the river water until they gasped their last pitiful breaths. We put those heads on spikes and let them rot in front of our encampment as a warning."

There are soft footsteps behind us, and then a long shadow

casts itself over me and my Accomplice Sisters, splaying out across the burning symbol. The long shadow of a horse's skull.

"When we eventually were taken over," Lisha says from behind us, "when we were made into this camp, this place where wealthy white men sent their sons to be prepared to follow in their footsteps and accumulate their riches with each passing generation, many of us worked in the kitchens. The camp laundry. We waited patiently. We watched and observed the men when they didn't think we were looking or listening. They underestimated us. Eventually, girls were allowed to join the camp, too, to till the soil of their own families' riches. We watched them, too. The way the boys interacted with them. The things they did to them. We chose our *sorors* carefully. Together, over time, we designed a new Order. A stronger Order. A better Order. A more united Order. *Soror* Olive, please place the child in front of our sigil."

Olive nods and carefully lowers the bundled baby to the center of the leather. My face drips with sweat beneath my mask. I can hear the sound of my own ragged breathing. I can smell the formaldehyde.

"When they stole our *soror* in the dead of night and maimed and ravaged her, what did we do?" Lisha asks.

"We destroyed them," the others chant in unison.

"When they drank too much whiskey one night and set fire to the cabins we lived and worked in. When they dragged our sisters from them and beat them for the sport of it. When these men assaulted those girls who only worked to serve them, groping up their skirts, squeezing their breasts as they moved past, a sick smirk on their lips all the while. It may have happened before, but it is always happening, my *sorors*. The past is always present. We are there in spirit, and so I ask again: when they held *us* down. Forced us. Hurt us. Slapped us. Demeaned us. We plotted. We waited. And what did we do?"

"We destroyed them."

"No. We *annihilated* them."

How could you possibly know that? I think.

Lisha meanders around the circle of sisters, holding a long wooden staff in her hands affixed with what looks to be an old cracked human skull.

"My *sorors*. You know this ritual. You know it well. A mare miscarried her beautiful daughter earlier this summer. A daughter she could not protect. As custom, we will pay homage to the baby's suffering, and to the mother's. Who will do the honors?"

The sisters whisper back and forth; some volunteer.

"I will, Pale Mare!"

"I would be glad to, Pale Mare!"

"*She* will." Anna growls this as she shines her flashlight in my eyes, a finger pointing accusingly at my masked face. "I say make her cut it open and eat its heart. After all, she didn't want to taste her *sorors'* blood. She showed no interest in anointing with the Order. Have her atone for her sin that night. Have her see what it really feels like to—"

"Enough." Lisha holds up a hand, her massive skeletal mask casting strange, frightening shadows over all of us. "*Soror* Anna, you are right. Perhaps *Soror* Arlee should atone. But we mustn't be cruel to one another, my sisters. We have to show mercy. Kindness. Understanding. *Soror* Arlee, please stand."

I do, even though my legs feel weak and wobbly as a newborn filly's.

"Come closer, my sister." She beckons with a long, yellow-painted fingernail, then points at the clothed bundle on the leather swath.

I gulp and approach her, moving carefully to not kick over the tea candles, or disturb anything that might set her off further.

"Closer," she says roughly. "Come, Arlee Samantha Gold."

My ears fill with radio static, and everything and everyone suddenly seems very, very far away.

"Produce the knife *Soror* Olive handed you."

I reach into the deep pocket of my cloak and pull out the serrated knife.

"Remove the cloth from the baby's body."

Knees trembling, mouth full of metal and bile, I kneel down on the swath and tear the cloth away from the baby's flesh like skin being ripped off.

"Cut. Out. Her. Eye."

Each word is a slice through my heart. The helpless, innocent baby, her eyes sealed forever shut, seems to stare up at me . . . pleading.

No.

"No." I shake my head again and again. "I . . . I can't. I can't do it."

"She is dead, *soror*," Olive pleads with me. "She cannot feel pain. We are not desecrating her."

"Silence," Lisha commands. "Cut out her eye, Arlee Samantha Gold. Prove to us that you want to be part of this Order. That you would do anything for *praesidio puellae*."

"*Praesidio puellae*," the others chant. "Protect the girls."

Now I'm back in the woods with the deer, my hands deep in its warm, wet flesh . . . but that flesh was decomposing. This baby is no dead deer. She's been dead far longer, frozen in time, and that somehow makes it all the worse.

As I lower the knife to her skin, my sisters chant it over and over, like a hymn.

"*Praesidio puellae. Praesidio puellae.*"

I could pretend that it's Zach. Or Lisha. Or my father. That I'm cutting out the evil. Cutting out the bad.

"I can't," I cry, my tears spilling onto the baby's flesh. I cover her body with the cloth, like she's naked. "I . . . I can't hurt her. I have to protect her." My voice is rising in pitch, my throat straining. "Isn't that the point?! To protect the girls? Why would I hurt her? She's a baby! A child! She did nothing! She—"

Lisha grabs my wrist with such ferocity even most of the other sisters gasp.

"Give me your arm," she commands, leaning down until we are at eye level, the gaping eye holes in her skeleton mask staring directly into mine.

"No. *No.* Please don't hurt me."

"Do you want me to cut your neck instead?"

"Please," I cry. "I'll do it. I'll . . ."

"You'll do it," Lisha says, and her skeleton nostrils seem to flare right in my face. "You'll do it, or you're telling me that you won't do anything for the Order. Or for me."

Every part of my body flashes hot and cold. There is no doubt what she is implying.

I lower the serrated knife, slowly trying to make the incision, and my vision goes white and when I come to, the knife is pressed instead to Lisha's throat.

"What the fuck are you doing?!" Anna screams in my ear.

Lisha is standing still and solid as stone as I sob and wheeze and hold it there and press so hard it draws a trickle of blood.

Her eyes flash madness.

She's going to kill me.

She'll kill me . . . leave me dead like the baby horse in the field and bury my body in the soil. . . .

"I'm sorry," I choke out. I drop the knife to the grass. "I'm so sorry. I didn't mean . . ."

"Take her back to the barn, *Soror* Anna. Lock her there for the rest of the ceremony."

"No! I'll do it! I'm sorry! Don't lock me anywhere! Please!" I struggle out of Anna's grasp and kneel down over the dead baby foal, then frantically began to slice apart her eye, frenzied, shaking, pretending that none of this is real.

o o o

When it's over, Lisha says nothing more to me. No commands. No pronouncements. Her silence is terrifying. I stand in the circle with the other sisters. The ceremony continues, but I only remember bits and pieces. Blurs.

They hum. They sing. They chant. Hold hands right over left.

And in turn, they cut pieces of the baby away until she is nothing more than a sack of mutilated horseflesh.

o o o

I cry all the way back to Unit Seven, alone.

After handing over my cloak and mask, I left. I didn't stick around for "libations," or whatever bizarre fucking after-party they seemed to be throwing with red wine and strange sugar cookies shaped like baby horses.

I ignored Olive and Forever Freya and the rest of the others who all tried to comfort me and assure me that what we did was okay. I avoided Anna and the wolfish grin on her face, as if she's won some dazzling victory.

I left before Lisha could say another word to me, or decide to put the knife to my throat instead.

This absolutely wasn't worth it, joining the Order. These girls aren't my friends. They're certainly not my family. Anna clearly hates my guts and enjoys seeing me tortured. Lisha is out for my blood. Olive's drunk the Kool-Aid, and the others . . . Well, if that's the kind of shit they do, I'm not sure I want to be a part of it.

Even though I do things just as bad, if not worse.

I'm shuddering and wiping tears from under my glasses by the time I get back to Unit Seven. Climbing the hill, my flashlight in hand, I stumble on a jagged rock and cut my knee, hissing at the pain. The air smells rich with pine and fresh-cut grass.

No more formaldehyde, at least.

It feels safer here. Like a kind of sanctuary.

I pass beneath the wind chime on our cabin's awning, accidentally stepping on the creakiest floorboard as I head to my bed.

Chantal groans and rolls over in her sleep. I freeze for a moment, worried she'll catch me—before realizing my alibi is an easy one: I went to the bathroom.

I strip out of my clothes and slip into an oversized T-shirt that still smells like Mom. I inhale the fabric deeply and nearly burst into tears again. I miss her so much. I want to go home more than ever. I want this all to be over: a distant, horrid dream.

"Arles?" Winnie whispers, making me jump. She's lying on her back, head hanging over her bed, upside down. "You okay?"

"I don't know, I—"

"Shut up!" Uma murmurs from her bed. "Some of us are trying to sleep in this godforsaken hellhole."

I move closer to Winnie, smelling of shampoo and some sweet lavender moisturizer. "It's okay, Arles," she says softly, more quietly.

"I'm . . . probably not okay," I admit, my voice cracking over the whisper. It's the most honest I've been with her so far. "This whole situation has . . ."

She sighs. "It's hard for all of us. Want to go for a walk with me?"

All I want to do now is maybe silently cry myself to sleep, dreaming of home. Of Raleigh. Of the girl I was before.

"Nah," I say, doing my best to keep my voice steady. "Thanks, though, Win. I'll see you in the morning."

I can feel her crooked grin, even in the darkness. "It's already morning. Okay, night, Arles. Love you."

Then she plants a slow kiss on my cheek, inches from my lips, her lips lingering seconds too long. My stomach explodes with a gold rush of frenzied butterflies, and none of them frighten me at all.

I kiss her back on the lips, hard and deep.

An upside-down kiss, like the famous one in *Spider-Man*, only way hotter. I pull away, breathless.

"Good night, Winnie," I whisper back.

I crawl into bed and wait until I'm fairly sure that she's asleep. I do my best to control my heavy breathing as I slide my hand down my pajama shorts and bite my pillow to muffle any moans, imagining Winnie's fingers down there instead of mine.

CHAPTER FIFTEEN

M oments turn into hours that stretch out and wrap around
me like long-fingered river reeds. For the next few blurry
days, everything is horrible, yet everything is also sunshine and
cool rain and goodness, my blood pumping, skin softening,
mind melding back to the rhythm of the camp.

If I keep pretending nothing is happening, that nothing has
happened, maybe I can will myself into forgetting completely.

Winnie continues to touch my thigh or arm or linger too long
with her head resting on my shoulder at the campfire circle, and
I imagine tracing every inch of her skin with my lips. We still
don't talk about the kisses. We don't talk about what's always left
unsaid, always burning beneath the surface.

At least I have Winnie, I think. *At least I have her.*

I try my best not to think about Zach. About Caroline. How
she lied to all of us, how she said her door is open—*day or night*—
and other campers have gone to speak to her, coming back reas-
sured. How can she continue to lie? What is she getting out of all
of this? Part of me wants to go see her, demand an explanation
to everything, but I feel stuck in my fear. Frozen. What if Lisha
finds out? What if she kills me? What if Caroline stands by and

lets it happen, like she did with Zach, and covers up my death with more lies?

Instead I eavesdrop on conversations in the dining hall or during electives. During yoga, as Bea leads us through a sun salutation, I hear two boys whisper fervently back and forth, interrupting each other.

"Apparently he ran off to be with some girl in town? Like, they'd been sexting all summer on his secret phone, but—"

"*Oh, shit,* so that would really embarrass him if we found out. If his family—"

"Yeah, plus the camp would be in deep shit, obviously, since I don't think anyone here has gone missing since, like—"

His last word is drowned out by Bea's sudden long deep chant of "*ohm*" that she leads us all through for what feels like forever. I do my best to chant along with her, with the rest of the class, even though I am anything but relaxed, centered, or calm.

Ginger teaches me a few more chords on the guitar and tells me I have a real ear for music, and maybe even songwriting. She likes the lyrics I think up on the fly. They're surreal. Metaphorical. Strange. A little scary.

A girl from Unit Eight who's won state equestrian championships falls off her horse midjump and nearly crushes her skull.

The barn parties continue raging on, wild, into the night. They happen more often now. I don't go, but I hear about them. Smell the weed and alcohol on Unit Seven girls' breath, see the stars in their eyes when they speak about the lights, the music, the dancing.

Jane and Winnie and I stay up late eating candy and sipping beers we steal from the minifridge in the vacant cabin. I pretend to laugh at their jokes and end up laughing at the wrong times, my mind adrift in thoughts of horse fields and blue-and-pink-skinned foals.

Whenever I spot one of my Accomplice Sisters at a meal or on my way to an elective, they're wearing the haunted faces of women well beyond their years. They move slowly, quietly. Keep their heads down like they did the night of the ritual. Speak in soft voices. One of them barely speaks at all.

I sit in my test-prep sessions and draw fields spilling over with blood. In every drawing, the blood comes from the sun that sinks over the land. I write lyrics to songs I know I'll probably never finish. I sketch horses and their skeletal faces. In one of my drawings, half the horse's face is alive and the other is nothing but bones. In another, pieces of the baby horse are painstakingly stitched back together by my sisters, forming the shape of a crooked star.

○ ○ ○

That Saturday is cloudy and humid.

After brunch, I walk down to the Echo River alone.

No one stops me. I pass by other units. The campers and other counselors ignore me entirely, as if I'm a ghost girl walking through the world in an invisible body.

I suppose that I am.

I love evening the best here. I pass creeks full of bullfrogs croaking among the strange garbled mating cries of other amphibians. The air is thick with humidity, fireflies winking in the nearing dusk. The flies scare me, as do most bugs, but for some reason, these little flying light bulbs do not. Maybe it's because I can squint and pretend that they aren't really bugs at all, but hazy string lights suspended in midair.

Now that I am mostly numb, everything is covered in a dull gray filter. Things that once struck me as lush appear flat, all the color drained out of them. My brain feels fuzzy, and there's always that static humming in my ears, so faint that I barely notice it anymore.

The sun is beginning to set across the Echo River. On the beach, the old yellowed piano sits and watches me, waiting for me to come and stroke its keys. It's trying to frighten me. Entice me. It wants a reaction. I know it.

I ignore it and take off my flip-flops, wade into the cool water.

"Fancy meeting you here at this hour."

I turn and there's Chantal, sitting in the sand with her knees pulled to her chest, smoking what looks and smells like a joint.

She takes a deep drag, that smell now so familiar. Skunky but no longer strange. The river breeze blows back her long wavy hair, and I can't help but think that her side profile is achingly perfect. High cheekbones. Pouty lips. I get a quick flash of Zach's freckled face, his cold white corpse drenched in moonlight before I covered it with worms and dirt.

Chantal doesn't smile often, and I've decided I like her better for it. I imagine the many men who've nagged her to look happy, brighten up her pretty face with a smile. I assumed it, too, that because she wasn't nice to me from the beginning, because she was hard and suspicious, she hated me.

I look out at the wide expanse of water and consider diving headfirst into the crushing cold, but Chantal's pull is far more magnetic. I come out and sit beside her in the cool sand.

She offers the joint. I take it and inhale.

"Why do you think Zach would run away?" I ask her, blowing smoke out at the river waves that lap onto the bank. I'm curious, is all. She hasn't voiced her opinion on the matter, hasn't weighed in on any rumors one way or the other. All she's done is encourage us every hour to stay positive, stay calm, which I know is her job, but it can't be how she really feels.

She laughs darkly. "Well, that's a way to open a conversation. I don't know, honestly. This has been one of the weirdest summers of my entire life."

"*One* of them?"

She smirks at me. "I've had stranger, believe it or not. Summers where my parents forced my siblings and me to attend exclusive island parties full of executives rolling on MDMA while getting lap dances from local girls. Most of them probably were underage. I don't know, I was so young when I went, always watching from the shadows. And then, paradoxically, those summers my siblings and I were forced to attend Bible camp, where we learned about how every part of us is inherently defective, and the only way to fix this is to pretty much deny everything you really think and feel. It's like our parents used *us* to purge themselves of their own sin. So, strange? Ha. This place is nothing." She reaches for the joint and I hand it back to her, surprised she's telling me this. Her eyes are bloodshot and she's clearly baked out of her mind, but this feels genuine. "This place is a bit of a paradox, too, though. I'll give it that."

I think again of what Olive told me: *Almost like paradise. But there's something off, too.*

"And Caroline?" I ask, my throat aching as I say her name. The head of the horse. "What the hell is up with her? Everyone seems to love her, but . . ."

Chantal taps some ashes out onto the sand. "I know. I felt that way, too, for years. I idolized her like she was my own mom, but the stunt with the dead baby horse was . . . weird as hell, even for her."

"But why? What's the point of it all?"

Chantal shrugs. "I'm starting to suspect it's part of how she stays in power here. I know Anna is scared of her. She told me a few nights ago." This surprises me. Anna always seems to regard her mom with contempt. "But we keep coming back to this place, because I guess we want the pleasure, so we accept the pain. The weirdness here. The asshole rich boys who get away with everything because their parents make massive donations to the camp. Pricks."

"I had an intuition about this place," I admit. "When I first got here. I don't know why, but I was terrified." I grab a fistful of sand and squeeze as hard as I can. "I'm . . . honestly not really terrified anymore. It's like I've already seen the worst of it, the darkest corners of it, and it no longer frightens me." *Shut up, Arlee. What are you doing? You're going to spill any second.* I force my lips closed.

I want to tell her so bad about Zach. I want to tell someone. Anyone. Maybe then the fog would lift a little and life would start to color me in again.

But it would mean risking my life.

After a long pause, Chantal looks closely at me and says, "You're a very strange girl, Arlee Gold."

It loosens something inside me and we both laugh a little.

"But you are afraid." Her eyes soften. "You're afraid of the bugs. I've noticed."

I shut my eyes tight. "I . . . yeah. I am."

I suppose I'm not dead inside. Not really, not when the fear of insects lives within me still. How can a dead girl fear anything? I glance over at the piano again. Watching me.

Waiting.

I know what you did, it whispers, in a voice so eerily familiar. Miss Teresa's. I shake my head. *No, no.* Leave me alone.

Why won't she leave me alone?

I clear my throat and change the subject. "Where's Eric tonight?"

Chantal shrugs. "Busy with his unit, I guess. A lot of them

are still upset about Zach's . . . vanishing act. A lot of them are friends with him."

The trees beyond the river blur together until I realize that I'm crying. Shit. Out here on the beach, I'm no longer numb. It almost feels like relief.

"I'd ask you if you're okay, but I think we both know the answer to that," Chantal says. She kills the joint and buries it deep in the sand. A breeze, brackish and sweet, carrying with it the faint scent of river rot, blows back our hair. "I don't think any of us are okay right now. It's all right. Not to feel okay. This whole situation is supremely fucked up."

I wipe my eyes, sniffle and nod, but say nothing. If I open my mouth again, I'll tell her. I just know. I'll start to unravel, piece by piece, and then . . .

Then what?

"I'll tell you a story," she says. "It's not a happy story, but it's a doozy. I met Eric at Camp Rockaway. We spent every summer together until he graduated from high school, and then became a counselor here. My last summer here as a camper, we had to be careful. Sneak around everywhere. On the night before I was supposed to leave for college, my parents found Eric and me together, naked in my bed. They lost their fucking minds.

"They had me kidnapped in the middle of the night by transporters who forced me on a plane to Utah. I was so scared I thought I was going to die. That the world was ending. In a way, it was. It was this ultrareligious place in the mountains meant to set me straight. To embrace the *virgin* in me. I was seventeen at the time, so technically, my parents could sign away custody of me. Even though I had gotten into Yale. Even though I had exceeded every expectation they ever had of me, been the good girl they wanted me so badly to embody." She squeezes her eyes shut, as if trying to suppress the horror of the memories.

"Utah was a wash, of course. A hellhole full of perverted men pretending to be preachers, and staff who tried to get us to confess our every sin because, you know, it probably turned them on. I told the people there what they wanted to hear so I could go home. It didn't matter. They were relentless that I was a sinner, that I needed their help in finding my 'sacred feminine heart' again through God," she scoffs.

"So as soon as I turned eighteen, I left. I started Yale a semester late, and I didn't tell anyone why. I lied to my friends and said I'd gone traveling for a few months to 'find myself.'" She sighs and tucks a lock of her perfect hair behind her ear. "I spend my summers here to help cover the debt I'll be in, since my parents kicked me out and cut me off after I left that place. So, yes, to answer your previous question from that first day when I interrogated you, Arlee Gold, I *do* go to college, and I plan to graduate with honors. Eric goes to USC for pharmacy school, so this is the only time we can spend together until I'm done."

"Wow," is all I can say.

"Yeah, wow is right."

"I had no idea you . . . I thought . . ."

"You thought I was a completely heartless bitch, didn't you? A spoiled rich girl who's never been through a damn thing. Most people do when they first meet me." She grins at me but it's clearly not funny to her.

"Well, no," I say. "The night you took care of Winnie. That's when I knew. I . . . I'm sorry I was so rude to you that night. That I was so angry. I shouldn't have taken that out on you."

"Oh," she says, "I forgot about that. It's okay." It's not. Shame burns through me. I'm evil. I'm a monster. "I was pretty rude to you when I gave you the lowdown on day one. I'm sorry, too, by the way. It's just because—"

"My mom," I finish in a small voice, the sadness so thick it could choke me. I almost wish I felt numb again. "I know. Some people hate me because of her."

"No. They don't hate you, Arlee. They're just afraid. Like you're afraid of the bugs. It's not rational. You did nothing wrong. It's not fair to you." She reaches her hand across the sand to mine, putting a finger on top of my own.

As if on cue, a massive horsefly buzzes right past my ear, landing its nasty feet on my bare thigh. The urge to scream and vomit is so strong that I almost do both, but Chantal merely swats it away.

"Flies are gross," she says gently. "I agree. You act like they're about to kill you, even though you could easily kill them yourself." She says this matter-of-factly, without judgment, as if she sees me in a way no one else has been able to. She's right. I was too scared to kill the spider, but I killed the roach. "You know what the Bible tells us about flies, Arlee Gold? They represent everything bad and evil in the world. They are, essentially, little demons. If they infest your life, you will never know peace or happiness. Friends will cut you off. Family will leave you. Everything you love and cherish will fall through your hands like sand. The longer they follow you, the longer they are present, the longer your sins will linger beside you." She smiles slightly. "That is what the Good Book preaches, though, to be frank, I never did believe in it much." She draws little circles in the sand. "Be careful who you tell your secrets to, Arlee Gold. Who you share parts of your soul with. Some people seem as harmless as bumblebees, but really, they're stinging wasps."

She stands and dusts the sand off her shorts. "It's getting late, and I'm getting cold. I should be with my girls. Want to come back with me?" She reaches out a hand to help me up. An offering.

I should take it, walk back with her up the long winding wooded path to Unit Seven.

It's the safest thing to do, though, really, aside from Lisha and possibly Caroline Rhinelander, I realize I have no one to fear but myself.

You deserve this pain, Miss Teresa whispers through the magic, evil piano. *You deserve to feel remorse for everything you've done. Your father left because of you; you do know that, Arlee Gold?*

Listen to Miss Teresa, Mom whispers, too. I shudder. *She knows best.*

"I just need a minute by myself," I mumble, and Chantal leaves me to it as the sky goes pink and gold with the last inches of sunlight.

As the crickets sing and frogs croak and sound like alien creatures, I bury my head in my hands and sob.

o o o

In my dream that night, or maybe I should say the one dream I keep having over and over, I am walking barefoot through a field covered in powder-white snow.

It is summer, yet snow frosts the ground like cream on a wedding cake. It hurts to walk on it. Even though it should be freezing, it almost feels like hot coals or fire.

It is neither day nor night. The sky is an aimless gray, everything around us half lit by a muted sun. Not a sun, a light bulb. The bulb dangles from the ceiling of the sky. I try to pull on its string. I want to switch it on or off, see if I am in day or night, but I can't reach it.

I keep walking. My feet ache and burn, but still I press onward into this empty, unending stretch of white until I find the deer.

She is grazing in the snow, eating chunks of ice as if it were grass. Behind her is a massive grand piano, black and sleek, the kind I used to play in the big open recital halls. The deer lifts her head and parts her lips. I can see that she has fangs, sharp as knives. Serrated. They sparkle in the off-white hazy gray of the in-between limbo we've both found ourselves in.

I step closer toward the piano, so strange yet so comforting in this off-white world. The bench is inviting. I sit down on it, lift my fingers over the keys to play, but the keys are already moving, a beautiful song spilling out of the grand instrument.

Then the scent of sandalwood grows so strong I nearly choke on it. I feel a hand grip my shoulder.

I wake up shivering each time, even though I'm clammy and warm, like I've been running for miles.

Even though I feel like I need a shower.

o o o

Birds sing sharply and off-key from outside our screened windows. I put on flip-flops and walk down the hill to the bathroom. The air feels damp, the sky still heavy-lidded with lingering darkness. In the bathroom, I catch a glimpse of myself in the mirror.

I look beyond exhausted. Dark, heavy under-eye circles. There is something wrong with me. Very wrong. I can smell myself under my sweater. Sweaty and . . .

I sniff. I smell like horses.

CHAPTER SIXTEEN

On the fourth of July, we play our best pretend yet.

After sleeping in until ten thirty, we munch cupcakes decorated with American flags, those good old stars and stripes. We eat hot dogs and burgers and drink lemonade. Winnie spikes hers with whiskey and shares it with me. I embrace the burn going down my throat, the way it mellows me out and takes away some of the edge and numbness.

"We're standing on their bones," Porter says. She bites into her hot dog, ketchup splattering onto her clean white T-shirt.

"The what?" Ginger asks. Her beautiful Taylor GS Mini is slung around her shoulder on a pink strap, and I itch to grab it and strum it. Run off with it, since Mom would never buy me one.

Fuck her, I think. It's a sudden thought, like the jab of a needle. It surprises me a bit.

Porter chews for a while before speaking. "We're out here dressed in sparkly colors, celebrating the birth of America, but we're standing on the bones of the Native Americans, and probably enslaved people, too."

"How do you know that?" Uma asks, though she sounds uneasy. "What if there's nothing underneath but more dirt and lots of wriggling worms?" She wiggles her fingers at Porter, but it doesn't get her to laugh.

Porter shrugs and finishes off her hot dog. "I just know."

Uma tosses the rest of her burger bun into a trash can and huffs out a sigh. "Suddenly I'm not hungry anymore."

Most campers and counselors are dressed in red, white, and blue. A group of college-bound, all-American kids. White teeth, beautiful clothing, perfect smiles. Reyes and Gabe are dressed in a rainbow of colors, holding hands almost every moment.

We mingle out in the archery field at dusk, sparklers in hand and glow-stick bracelets stacked on our wrists. Counselors hand us little books of matches even though they probably shouldn't. I pocket one in my shorts.

Gabe keeps murmuring something to Reyes, who in turn comforts him with a kiss or a hug, holding him tight.

He's uneasy, but he shouldn't be. None of us should be, just like we're pretending that we aren't. Because Zach is alive, Caroline told us. Zach is at least alive.

Yet still, a boy ran off. Went missing. Vanished.

Counselors set off fireworks at dusk that hiss and pop into the sky, and we're standing so close we can feel tiny embers raining down on our skin. Gabe and Reyes kiss in front of everyone, their hands in each other's pockets. I think about kissing Winnie again.

I think she's thinking about kissing me, too.

All day, from morning campfire circle to rounds of outdoor games like ultimate frisbee and flag football to camp-song sing-offs in the archery field. From firecracker popsicles to dancing together as the concert bands rehearsed in the Grand Amphitheater, the pulsing speakers carrying the sounds of their music all across the grounds, Winnie has been glued to my side.

It's more than small gestures and coded winks and grins now.

It's her arm around my waist, or her hand resting on the small of my back. It's the way she whispers a joke in my ear that sets us both giggling. The way her lips touch my bare arm when she rests her face against it.

It's the way she sits so close to me on the grass, our knees more than touching now. They're pressed together, warmth traveling through every part of me. The way she runs her fingers through my hair, or brushes crumbs or stray blades of grass from my face.

It's the way she can't stop looking at me, finding little ways to touch me. She doesn't do this with anyone else. Not even Jane, who I thought was her best friend here.

She's no longer far away like she was in the archery field when we made the clover bracelets. No, it's like she's hanging on to me for dear life, soaking me in like at any moment, she might never see me again.

The Midsummer Concert was supposed to be a celebration full of camp alumni and donors and former staff in attendance. Maybe even a few college-admissions officials to mingle with us over mocktails.

But tonight, there is nothing to celebrate except the fact we've survived the latest blow to our summer. The mood grows dourer as the sheen of playing pretend wears away, the sunshine and the fantasy going with it as the sky grows darker. Campers break out their flasks and not-so-secret joints. Counselors openly smoke and drink with them. Everything is fully out in the open now. The simmering energy pulses with the music as we head to the Grand Amphitheater to watch the start of the show. Within minutes, the air smells like weed and liquor, clouds of smoke rising to the stars.

Several camp bands play onstage in turn, and we stand instead of sit, swaying, watching, singing along to the covers of songs we know. Some people are crying, tears of relief or joy or drunkenness. Others keep looking over their shoulder, as if the imagined serial killer in the woods is still lurking, waiting, gleeful now that they've got us all in one spot out in the open. Easy targets. Easy prey.

When it's Ginger's turn to perform with her band, she connects her guitar to the speakers and stands in front of the old-fashioned mic, the same one they used during Sundown Ceremony. Besides her, her band consists of a drummer, a bassist, and a keyboardist.

"How is everyone doing tonight?" she asks the crowd, and they holler back with excitement as her drummer plays the cymbals to keep the hype going. "I know things are rough right now, so I thought I'd play us something a little sweet. A little more personal. Is that all right?" People cheer in return. She's a natural on the mic. She glows onstage, her hair shiny in the outdoor lights along with her megawatt smile.

That could've been me, I can't help but think. *If I'd stuck with piano. I could've made a crowd hold their breath as I played. Could've charmed a concert hall full of people.*

Then I think of Miss Teresa watching me closely during each recital and competition, a permanent scowl on her face, keeping tally of every mistake, every fuckup that she'd later remind me of. Mom insisted Miss Teresa's methods, though harsh, came from a place of love. I never felt that love.

Not really from Mom, either.

All I ever did was attempt to please her. How is that love?

Jane passes me a joint and I take a hit. Winnie holds me in her arms, her chin resting on my shoulder, and from a few feet away, Reyes turns and winks at me, his own arm around Gabe.

Just for now, right now, I can play pretend, too. Winnie and I begin to sway in time to the music as the band starts up the opening of Ginger's song. It's full-bodied with the live instruments, the driving guitar, and drums. A living, breathing artwork come to life.

Ginger begins to sing. It's the most achingly beautiful sound I think I've ever heard:

Fields of white and wild and green
No one ever heard me scream
Standing alone, daring to dream
I tried so damn hard to be a good girl

Summer sunshine in my eyes
Bright as hell, those blinding skies
They say this is where good girls go to die
Too bad I've never been a good girl

I grab Winnie's neck and kiss her, hard. I need to feel something. Anything. I need her.

She moans and kisses me back ferociously.

In this moment, I am whole again. I am healed. My fingers in her hair, her arms around my waist. Her warm tongue on mine. The softness on her cheek against my own.

I want her so badly it could kill me. She's my everything here. My rock. My solace. I want to forget, and forget with her, if only for a night.

"Let's slip away after Ginger's set," she whispers urgently in my ear. "We'll finally be alone. They'll be partying out here all night."

"Good idea, I'll be there," I whisper back in her ear before nibbling it, and she giggles and bites playfully at my neck, leaning in for another hungry, animal kiss.

I feel a tap on my shoulder. Winnie pulls away from me, and everything is shattered.

"Arlee!" Lisha croons. She stands before us, dressed in her

usual all-black: a tank top and frayed cutoff shorts. Her smug smile is enough to make me want to punch her right in the mouth. She's enjoying this, interrupting me in my happiest moment here. "I need help with something. *Now.*"

"Go," Winnie says, kissing me again, and Lisha's sick smile widens. I don't need to hear her say a word to feel the implication behind it.

Oh fuck, no. Not Winnie. Don't come after my Winnie.

"I'll meet you later tonight," I whisper again to Winnie, then kiss her on her perfect nose and grudgingly break away from the crowd, from the music and the love and peace of tonight, the counselors all too drunk and stoned and drained to notice us leaving as I ball my fists and put on my invisible armor and slip away with Lisha down to the river.

∘ ∘ ∘

It is happening again.

The first thing I notice is the pale, swollen head. The head of Michael, eyes wide open and slightly crossed, his tongue lolling out like he's some grotesque animatronic.

His head has been sewn to a sack stuffed with straw. It swings from the sturdiest branch of the great willow tree, suspended with two pieces of thick rope. The sack has two stuffed tubes of what I imagine to be straw for arms, and two for legs.

God only knows where the rest of him is.

The second thing I notice is that my Accomplice Sisters are here, though they don't seem so shaken anymore. They've come alive anew. They wear gray robes and hold tea candles that burn and shimmer against the dark river waves. On the ground there are many other lit candles, forming the shape of our crooked star.

Just as there were the night of our initiation, and the night we cut open the baby.

"Pale Mare!" Horse Shorts cries in delight. Her eyes are glassy and distant, her smile not quite matching them. "You've returned!"

"Pale Mare!" the other two chant.

Neon Choker picks up the skeletal mask and helps to put it on Lisha herself as if it were a crown, adjusting it with care, while the others help her into her gray robe.

"Thank you, *sorors*," she says from behind her garish mask. "You are loyal sisters."

Her nails bite into my skin as she guides me to the old, dusty piano beneath the willow tree.

"Sit."

I do, staring down at the fading yellow keys.

"Play."

"What should I play?" I ask, my heavy tongue weighing down each word.

I can feel Lisha smile at me behind her Pale Mare mask. "Beethoven's Piano Sonata No. 14. Otherwise known as the 'Moonlight Sonata.' We know things, Arlee. We know that your mother had you trained you in piano. Many of us were. She wanted you to be ready for nights like these. This piano belongs to the Order. It always has, and it always will. Play the whole thing. Don't stop until the very last note."

For a moment, my vision goes white again. It's like all the air has been sucked from my lungs. It's the fifteen-minute piece Miss Teresa made sure that I knew by heart. Every turn, every suspension. Every diminished chord. The one she had me practice over and over, for hours a day, while other kids played outside and threw snowballs at one another's heads. The piece she trained me to memorize all three movements of, beginning at the age of seven. Practicing and practicing until my hands went numb and my wrists ached. Until my brain felt fuzzy and all I could hear were the notes in the movements again and again, over and over, echoing through my mind. Until I could play it all in my sleep, in my dreams, my fingers dancing over the keys as I drifted off each night.

The three sisters place their candles on the ground along with the others, as part of the shape of the crooked star. They hold hands and sway and hum. They are dancing, I realize. Joyfully.

One of them is laughing, brightly like the stars, her head thrown back. Neon Choker.

She spins and twirls, her robe flowing all around her like water, her mask concealing her face of joyous emotion. Joy or terror. They've become one and the same.

"Did she kill him . . . ?" I begin to ask, my eyes darting between Michael's mutilated corpse and her own body, vital and alive and breathing right beside me.

"It doesn't matter. You will play the sonata now. Play it for your sisters, Arlee."

"I don't know the third movement," I say weakly, and it comes out in a cracked whisper. I start to tremble. "It's too complicated." It's half-true. I remember most of how it goes, but it's difficult, all those lightning fast, arpeggiated chords.

Lisha moves closer. I gasp as she presses the serrated knife to the base of my throat just as I did to her, hard enough to sting, to draw a tiny drop of blood that trickles down and drips onto the keys. "You know it, Arlee," she says softly, almost gently. "And if you forget, look." With her other hand, she pulls a stack of papers from the pocket of her cloak and arranges them neatly on the piano stand. The sheet music to the entire sonata. She flips to the first movement. "Now play."

I begin.

The river breeze blows and the air smells of sharp musk and gutted fish as the sack with the head swings in half time to my music like a botched metronome.

Tears spill down onto the keys as I play, but I continue on through the second movement, fingers flying over the slipperiness of the old keys, a deep moan building inside my chest, pumping up like black bile from my heart and into my throat.

My sisters stand in their circle holding hands, humming one low note that grows louder and louder until it seems to vibrate the woods and the river and all the death and horror that surrounds us.

They begin to sing:

Praesidio puellae
Praesidio puellae
Protect the girls
Protect the girls
Kill the boys for they must die
They have made all the sweet girls cry

I play and play until my hands are numb and every note sounds like roaring static in my ears.

Until I am back in the field, shoveling soil over Zach's lifeless body.

Until I am back on the cold lonely highway, running as fast as I could from my father and back into Mom's clutches.

Why did you never let me quit? I plead in my mind to her. *Why did you force me into this? You knew. You knew I'd play for dead boys and traumatized girls.*

I play the third movement of the sonata imperfectly, stumbling, frantic, until I am back in Miss Teresa's old house and she is hissing in my ear that I must start again until I am no longer the worst pianist in the history of the world, her voice like nails clawing across my skin.

Until I am in the woods again, the ones behind my old house, my hands deep in the flesh of the sacred deer, my mouth full of the blood and taste of it.

o o o

Afterward, Lisha has us lower Michael's body—or what's left of it—from the tree branches and guide it into the river.

As my Accomplice Sisters carry it further and further until a tide catches it and it begins to float away, I stand on the beach, refusing to be part of this anymore.

Lisha stands with her hands together, observing the sisters, observing my willfulness, my insubordination.

Hatred fills me to the brim, as raw and pure as the love I felt for Winnie hours before.

"You will come with me now, Arlee Gold," Lisha says behind her mask. "Just you."

"Sure," I say, grinding my teeth together, tensing up my entire body.

I'm going to end this once and for all.

I'm going to fucking kill her.

o o o

On the way back from the river, Lisha in her mask and cloak, me in my tie-dye T-shirt and cotton shorts, I see the moths again illuminated in the glow of Lisha's flashlight, their bodies caught in the spiderwebs of the lanterns.

The sight no longer repulses me.

It fuels me.

When we arrive at the horse field, the distant sound of music echoing past us, the smell of manure and wet grass and hay and horse, Lisha removes her mask and cloak and lets them fall to the ground.

"Follow me, Arlee," she instructs.

I follow, trailing behind with her flashlight in my hand, scouring the ground for sharp rocks or a stick, anything to hit her with and crack open her skull. I'm salivating at the thought of it, of hurting her like she hurt me. Like she hurt Zach and Michael, and my Accomplice Sisters when she brainwashed them into aiding in another burial.

We arrive where the flies are thickest. Buzzing so loud and angry. They want what's beneath the soil, the flesh they crave from the hole that we carved in the earth.

I'm not even sure if it was six feet deep, after all. It was likely not much shallower than a pioneer woman's grave on the trail to Oregon.

What bullshit stories our *sisters* spun for us, to trap us. It was all a lie.

"The plan has changed. We're going to dig him up tonight, Arlee. We are going to burn him, then throw his bones in the river. Orders from above."

"You mean Caroline?"

She snorts. "You played so *beautifully* for us, Arlee, and now, you're going to help me. Retrieve some things from the barn for me and wait here until I bring the other *sorors* back. They'll be assisting us, of course."

"No."

Her eyes narrow, the flashlight shining into them. "What do you mean, *no*?"

"No as in *no way in hell. Fuck you*, you psycho bitch."

I move toward her, grass crunching beneath my sneakers,

stars singing down to me from an unseeing sky, until I'm so close to Lisha I hope she feels my hot breath on her face.

"You don't protect girls, you *hurt them*."

"How dare you, Arlee? I do more to protect the girls here than any officer of the law *ever* would."

"You killed an innocent boy."

"He wasn't innocent."

"Then what did he do?"

"That I can't say."

"You're a liar."

"I'm not lying, Arlee," she says through gritted teeth. "You're too disillusioned to see what's really been going on. Too much of a coward. A follower. A liability. I should never have let you into the Order. I'd think long and hard about what you do next, especially where your sweet little girlfriend is concerned."

No. Not Winnie.

Not my Winnie.

She spits at my feet, and then at my face.

I knock Lisha to the ground with a force that surprises me.

My blood is shimmering and alive with energy and rage. She struggles against me, kicking and squirming uselessly, but I punch her as hard as I can in the mouth, then hit her head with the flashlight so hard I hear a crack. Blood splatters on my lips and she goes slack. I wrap my hands around her throat and press my thumbs against her windpipe, harder, harder, harder, until her face turns blueberry blue as her hair. I see red. I am red. Red and white-hot rage and terror and a thunderstorm of every emotion that's been swirling inside me. She is the dead deer in the field. The corpse of Zach and the mutilated body of Michael. She is my father, leaving me, abandoning me. My mother, controlling me. She gasps, chokes, whimpers as I press and press. I grind my teeth together so hard I see stars behind my eyes.

"Stop," she croaks. Her windpipe sounds as though it's snapping in half like a twig. "Arlee. Please."

I feel a sharp, sudden pain in my head and fall to the ground on my side. I touch at my scalp and feel wetness. Blood. Lisha stares at me with wild, frenzied eyes, panting, choking and coughing and sputtering. In her hand she holds the bloody flashlight.

"I didn't kill Zach," she sputters in between raspy, painful gasps for air. A bruise is already blooming around her throat. "Michael knew too much and was going to talk, but I didn't kill Zach. Is that why you're trying to kill me?!"

I don't move. The breeze picks up a little, bringing with it the smell of leather and tack and manure into my nose. A horse whinnies from the stables.

She tosses the flashlight aside and sits up, rubbing at her swelling throat, and gives a few wheezing coughs. "*You're* the psycho bitch. Anna was right about you. She tried to warn me."

I'm so dizzy, the blood dripping down my neck and back, leaving the gash in my head. The horse field tilts sharply, but this time, it's not just from a glitch in my mind. My eyeglass frames are broken. I pick them up from the grass that's wet with my blood. Our blood. I put them on. They fit crookedly now. "What the hell are you talking about?"

Lisha struggles to stand before stumbling back onto the grass. From the stables another horse gives a sharp, high-pitched whinny. I swear that it's Velvet's. It sounds just like hers.

Even though I just tried to choke her to death, even though she just called me a psycho bitch and hit me over the head with a flashlight, Lisha extends her hand to me. "Sister. Help me up."

All the rage has boiled and simmered, leaving my body like the warm liquid blood that seeps from my head and speckles the grass. I stand, woozy, head throbbing, and help Lisha off the ground. We face each other, and as my eyes fully adjust to the darkness, I see in her eyes that she isn't lying. Not about this.

"Who killed Zach?"

She stares down at the spot where we lay and tried to beat each other to death. "Michael was a mercy kill. It needed to be done. To protect all of us, even you. Trust me on that."

I swallow hard. My voice comes out as raspy and pained as hers did when I ask her again, "Who killed Zach?"

She doesn't speak for quite some time, then turns and spits a massive wad of bloody saliva at the grass. "Go ask your fucking girlfriend," she mutters, before stalking off into the night.

CHAPTER SEVENTEEN

When everything unravels, time starts to slow.

Minutes stretch into aching hours. Seconds feel eternal. The closer I get to Unit Seven, the more the hooting of owls and symphony of crickets is drowned out by the pounding bass and not-so-far-away music from the Midsummer Concert.

My sneakers crunch against the gravel. It's been just over a week since the night I was initiated, since my spade was the first to hit the soil and dig what would become Zach's grave.

Now that all the pieces of the puzzle have revealed themselves to me, I no longer feel human. I move through the night air like it's water, or something out of my freezing fever dreams. My legs move and yet I do not feel them. So, too, do my hands hang numbly at my sides, buzzing, prickling with pins and needles. I'm not sure how my heart is still pumping so hard, still circulating blood through my veins. It seems an impossible task for such a shattered thing.

The wind chime hanging on the awning of our cabin clangs and tinkles as I reach the steps of our cabin. The light inside is off, but still, with the aid of Lisha's bloody flashlight, I can see the edge of Winnie's silhouette. She leans back on the edge of my bed, grinning to herself in that beautifully crooked way only she seems to have perfected. She wears nothing but a sports bra and lacy red underwear, her medium-short black hair slicked back.

When she hears me open the creaking door, she purrs, "I thought you'd never make it."

I'd dreamed of this night so many times. I'd replayed it in my mind, over and over, hoping and willing and wishing for it to happen. I thought about every move I'd make, how the air would feel soft and sweet like it does tonight, how we'd somehow end up together alone in here against every single odd there could be.

Every curve of her body beckons to me, drawing me closer. I feel a sudden terrible thirst. I want to drink her in, her skin and every freckle dotted on it like a sea of constellations.

How can she lie there like that, so coy and waiting and wanting?

How can she smile after what she's done?

I could tear off my clothes and run to her. I could press my lips to her lips, her neck, let this fever dream we've found ourselves in swallow us both.

But I am no longer the girl that believed she loved Winnie.

I am no longer human. I am no longer anything.

Arlee Gold is dead.

When I snap on the lights and snap off the flashlight, the dream shatters. She gasps at the sight of me and sits upright, shocked.

"Arlee? What the hell? Why are you bleeding—what the hell happened to you?"

I know how I must look, standing there trembling, covered in dirt and grass and bruises and scratches, my glasses crooked, eyes wide and sunken from all the horror I've witnessed. It's not what she expected when she whispered for me to meet her here. It's not what she imagined when she asked Arlee Gold to finally come to her in the secret of night.

"Lie to me," I say. My voice comes out as shaky as my limbs, scratchy and rough, as if it were my own windpipe I'd choked instead of Lisha's.

"Arlee, I—I don't understand." She shakes her head, and God, she looks so gorgeous when she does that. "What are you talking about? Are you okay?"

I swallow the barbed wire crawling up my throat. "Lie to me and tell you didn't kill him."

All the color drains from her face. I imagine the haunted look on hers reflects the one painted across my own.

I take one step closer, even though it feels like the arrow she shot through his heart is going through mine now, too. Even though I am no longer alive or even human, even though Arlee Gold is a dead girl walking. I choke back a sob and plead, "Please, Winnie. *Lie to me.*"

Tears drip down her cheeks. She covers the parts of her body she's exposed to me with her arms, as if ashamed now for me to see them.

"Tell me you had a good reason," I beg, even though there really is no good reason I can think of for murder. "All along, I thought it was Lisha. I thought Lisha was sick and twisted, and honestly, I still think she is, since she fucking killed *Michael*." Winnie raises her head in alarm at this. "Yes, Michael is dead, too. His body was hanging from a tree by the beach. Well, not his body. His head . . . was attached to a . . ." I clutch at my abdomen, which suddenly roars with pain, as if the flames of hell themselves have sprung from the soil to lick at my soul.

"I didn't know!" Winnie shrieks, hysterical. "I swear I didn't know Michael was dead! I had nothing to do with it. It was only Zach. I swear, Arlee, it was *only* Zach."

I shake my head. I can't meet her eyes, even though this cuts deeper than any knife could. "Lisha said he deserved it. She said never to cry over a boy, not even a dead one. I don't cry for Zach, but you . . . Winnie . . . *why?* Why didn't you tell me?" I'm full-on sobbing now.

"I didn't think you'd understand!" she pleads. "Lisha told me to never tell a soul. Not a single soul, as long as I lived." She takes a shuddery breath. "She said it would seal my fate if I did, but it's too late, isn't it, Arles? Both of our fates sealed now. No matter how hard we try to bury this, it's only a matter of time before the truth gets out."

I feel as though my body is being ripped clean in two different directions by two impossibly strong, opposing forces.

We don't have to, I think. *We can leave the truth buried with Zach's body. We can forget this.*

But I still don't know the truth.

My voice hurts when I ask her, "What happened, Winnie? What happened between you and Zach?"

To my surprise, she comes over and wraps her arms around me.

She strokes my hair and lets me rest my cheek on her neck. It destroys everything inside me to let her touch me like this, but I do. "Come sit with me, Arles," she says gently. "Come sit and I'll tell you everything. First, though, please, let's—" She reaches over and flips off the light.

Perhaps it's better this way. In the dark.

We pull apart and settle onto my bed. Awkwardly. Unsure of what to do with our bodies, our hands. This time, our knees don't touch and our arms don't press together. The love is still there buried in my heart, but everything is ruined now. We sit inches away from each other, me dirty and bruised, her exposed and untouched, and inside me everything is cold and barren as the snowy horse fields of my dreams.

Winnie takes a deep breath. A bit of moonlight splashes through the screen window and across her face. *She's like a painting,* I think. *A beautiful, unbalanced painting with the colors all wrong, though it's harder to see that here in the darkness.*

"It started two years ago, when I was a rising freshman in Unit Five," she says quietly. She keeps her eyes on the floor, as if she can't face me. "He was always into a lot of girls here, flirting and following them around, but he was *really* into me.

"He would come to my cabin at night . . . and I—I would sneak off with him." She winces, and my heart breaks a little more. "We were sort of an item that summer, but then I realized maybe I like girls better than boys—especially boys like *him*—or . . . maybe I only like girls, I don't know, and by the time we went home, I'd cut things off. Or I tried, at least. He didn't believe I was over him. He kept sending me messages on Instagram, asking how I was doing, what I was up to, commenting on and liking all my photos. I did my best to ignore him. It was annoying, and more than a little weird, but I wrote it off because I thought that's how boys can be. I thought maybe he'd grow tired of it, or find some other girl to latch onto." She takes another deep breath.

"And that next summer, when I was in Unit Six, he did. He found a shiny new naive Unit Five girl who believed all of his bullshit, though he still tried to talk to me every chance he got. Again, I did my best to ignore him, but then he weaseled his way into one of my electives, just like he managed to do this summer. He was the best archery player in his *county,* Arlee, maybe even the whole state. He has—*had* a private coach, lessons paid for. Everything. I don't have any of that. This is one of the few places I get to practice. He joined archery to harass me, to get under my skin, just like he did when he joined the in-line skating elective I took for fun last summer. That asshole didn't even *like* any kind of skating. He would always skate too close past me, 'accidentally' brush against my hip or touch my thigh." She

shudders, as if recoiling. "At the time, I didn't say anything. I
could've. But who would believe me? We'd dated before, I was
always outwardly 'nice' to him, and Zach was cool and popular
and . . . hot, I guess. Ugh. Even most of the counselors adored
him." She rolls her eyes. "They let him get away with everything, Arlee. *Everything*."

Winnie gnashes her teeth together and grips at my bedspread.
"I couldn't let him get away with *this*, though," she says, and it
comes out almost like a snarl. "Not this. He knew he couldn't
touch this."

I can feel it, that familiar rage, bubbling and rising like mol-
ten lava. Only it isn't coming from inside me, but from inside
Winnie. I'm seeing the Winnie I never knew she could be.

"What did he do?" I practically whisper. "Did he touch you?"

Winnie lowers her head to the floor, tears dripping down to
the dusty hardwood. "He didn't have to," she says quietly.

"Then what, *Winnie*?" I shake her arm, desperate for an answer that fits correctly in my brain. One that explains. That
soothes this nagging terror inside me, this voice that keeps re-
peating over and over, *You thought you knew her.*

But I buried his body, and I said nothing to the sheriff or anyone else. I lied by omission.

That girl is dead, I remind myself. She buried Zach's body
along with her soul. Whatever is left of Arlee Gold can steel herself against anything. She has felt everything there is to possibly
feel, and so her pain is dulled. She can handle the truth.

"His father owns shares in my dad's company," Winnie finally
says, letting out a frustrated breath. "A *lot* of shares." It's not what
I expected her to say at all. "Zach always loved to torture me.
Loved to hold things over my head. He never let me forget that,
even when we were dating. He held it above me like some kind
of threat. 'My dad basically owns your dad's balls,' he'd say." She

makes a face of disgust. "I'd tell him to fuck off, leave me alone. Stop texting me. Stop *stalking* me!" She hits my bed with her fist in frustration.

"'Or what?' he'd ask." Her impersonation of his voice is so good it gives me full-body chills, almost like Zach is still alive, in the room with us. For a second I think I see him in the corner, grinning, watching, eyes wild. "'*What are you gonna do, Winnie?*' he would taunt me, over and over, and for so long I said and did nothing about it because I thought, that's what boys do. That's what weak, selfish, petty boys do. But this summer, when he wormed his way into *my* elective, tried to make me look stupid at my own thing, the one sport he knows I love, I cornered him after class, and said I'd tell his dad he was stalking me. I'd tell everyone. He said no one would believe me. That I was *obsessed* with him. That he'd twist it around and make everyone think I was stalking *him!*" She grits her teeth harder, jaw muscles pulsating. All the sweetness and softness in her are gone, replaced by searing rage. "Then he made the worst mistake of his sad, pathetic little life: *he threatened my father's career.* Said not only did his dad own my dad, and could fire him at any time and tarnish his reputation, he owned *me*, and I would never be free of him. Not really. Not if I wanted to go to my 'fancy prep-school girl college' and get a 'nice little job' myself. The thing about me, Arlee, is you can fuck with me all day. You can tease me, taunt me, bully me . . . I'll take it. But the second you come for my family, you're *dead*."

The last word comes out as a snarl so ferocious I jump up, moving away from her. The cabin begins to spin around me. Everything feels so small and faraway, and it's hard to breathe.

"I didn't know what to do," she goes on. "But I knew there had to be a way to get through to him, at least. To scare him straight.

So I went to the best black widow I knew: Lisha. President of the deadliest secret society east of the Mississippi River. Or that's what people always said. That night, at the barn party, you were with me. I was there to talk to Lisha. To get her help. She said she'd help me. She told me to tell Zach to meet me in the horse field after lights-out. It was my idea to bring the bow and arrow. She said she knew that would get to him, being threatened by a *girl* he *owns* aiming his favorite toy at his heart. I told him to leave me alone or I'd kill him dead right here, right now.

"'You don't have the guts,' he said to me, and he *spit* at my feet. And I thought for just a moment, maybe he's right. Maybe I couldn't. Maybe I wouldn't kill someone, even someone who tried to have a hold on me, my life, my family. Even though I had a perfect shot set up. My stance was *faultless*. Heather would've *swooned* if she saw it, Arlee!" She laughs wildly. "He was so wrong, though, because it didn't matter what he said, whether or not he backed off, cried, begged for my forgiveness. I knew he wouldn't. I'd made up my mind about what I'd do to him hours before I did it. Lisha took care of the rest, as promised."

Her eyes meet mine. I don't recognize the girl who lives inside this familiar face.

Premeditated murder. Winnie. *My* Winnie.

No, this isn't right. This isn't real.

Winnie gives a long, bitter laugh. "Oh, don't look at me like that, Arlee! You *really* want to know what people say your mom did? You've been begging to know for days now, but once I tell you, I can't take it back." Something in her softens, and her tense body goes slack. She's looking at me like she's begging, pleading with me not to tell me—even though she also clearly wants to, because she still has to prove to me that she isn't bad. Not as bad as some people. "Are you sure?"

"Tell me," I say quietly, because the room is violently spinning and my heart is breaking and what could be fucking worse than this?

She takes my hands in hers, which are freezing to the touch, and they've never felt cold before, not even in the chilly morning camp air. Winnie leans in close to my face, so close our lips brush once more, electricity sparking between them, and rests her forehead against mine with a sigh of agony so deep it rattles me to the bones.

"They say she *skinned a boy alive*."

"No." I shake my head. The spins get worse and I stumble backward. "No. That's not possible."

She grips my hands tighter and squeezes until the cuts on them burn and the bruises throb and I yelp. "*Yes*, Arlee. That's what everyone says she did. Everyone knows it was her and those girls in the Order of Equus, and after that meeting with Lisha, I knew it was true." Her voice cracks.

"What did he do to her?" I ask in a shaky voice that is not mine, a girl's voice that I don't recognize. "Why did she try to do that to him?" I have to hear her above the static in my ears, the buzzing beneath the surface of it that grows louder and louder with each short breath I take. I want her to press a button and rewind time, back to when I first walked into the cabin and saw her lying there in her underwear, waiting for me.

I want to throw her on my bed and ravage her in all the ways I've been dreaming of. Like an animal. Like a wild thing. I want to forget.

I want.

"They say he raped one of her secret-society sisters. During a party in the barn. So, a few weeks later, the sister brought him to the horse field, pretended to seduce him, as if she had wanted it the first time, as if he hadn't fucking *assaulted* her, and then she watched while Sam Gold grabbed him from behind and slowly cut his throat with a knife. Slowly, so she could skin him, so he could bleed but still feel every bit of pain before he passed out, and the sister . . . they say she laughed the entire time, and the air was filled with screeching owls."

"*Which sister?*" I ask, frantic, horrified.

"The mother, Lisha said," she whispers, her hands shaking in mine, eyes wide with terror. "Lisha told me it was the mother of all this. The one who started everything. Who makes all this happen. She was Sam's counselor at the time."

The head of the horse. Caroline.

Yet Lisha lies. She lied about our history, about being my friend, caring about me. She used me. I can't believe anything that comes out of her mouth.

But still . . . my mother.

A killer? Is it possible?

Then the still rageful part of Winnie goes under like a wave and she breaks.

"*Shh*, it's okay, Winnie. It's okay." I hold her close to me and let her sob into my chest, cradling her head. Even though it's not okay, and it never will be okay.

Even though I love her.

A killer. A confessed killer. What does that make me?

She cries into my shoulder, soaking my filthy shirt through with her tears. She hiccups. "They did investigations, the police, but I—I don't think anyone's ever found the body. The body of the boy they say Sam Gold tried to skin alive." She glances up at me, as if in apology, all her words tumbling out fast and disjointed. "That's why it's a *rumor*, Arlee. A secret. Because no *body* was ever found. It remained an unsolved mystery. He . . . his parents sued, tried to press charges, but the Rhinelanders made it go away somehow. They have the best lawyers in the country. The best connections. I don't know how, but they did it. They can make anything go away. Arlee? Where are you going? Arlee, please come back! *Arlee!*"

She screams my name so loud birds go flying in a panic through the trees.

First, I stop in the vacant cabin, where I yank open the mini-fridge and pull out a giant bottle of vodka.

I feel for the pack of matches in my pocket. They're still there. Good.

Then I start running.

o o o

My feet carry me through the forest.

Down the dirt path, past the other units, the gleaming yoga studio and the soccer fields and swimming pools.

My lungs ache as my feet pound against the earth. With each step I can feel my heart cracking open little by little, my blood spilling onto the soil.

Finally, I can smell the manure and the sharp scent of fresh leather. I can almost hear the horseflies buzzing in my brain, see the afterimage of the party superimposed onto every spot outside the barn. I hear a loud hoot and startle, whipping around to find an owl staring me down from a branch with wide yellow eyes. I shiver. It seems to nod at me once before flying off.

I'm breathing so hard it's like there're knives in my lungs.

I grip the vodka bottle tight and head inside.

It smells more damp, mustier than before, if that's even pos-sible. I think I hear a mouse scuttle across the ground, squeak-ing as it goes. I know there are insects here, too, hiding in the molding hay. The walls. I bet if I used a crowbar to detach one of the floorboards, there'd be dozens of squirming black beetles underneath.

I want to scream. Cry. Curse the whole fucking world.

Instead I splash the vodka everywhere, starting with the door to that cursed, awful closet that's held so many of the Order's things. The masks and cloaks. The dead baby foal. I rain vodka down over the hay. The ground. The walls. *This is for all those drunken, twisted nights,* I think. *All those bad decisions made under the influence. Manipulation made easier with liquor under the tongue.*

This is for the chaos, the misery, drowned out with beer and whiskey and too-sweet sodas mixed in, trying to hide the bitter, the truth.

Fuck the Order.

Fuck Caroline.

This is the only way I know right now to tell her that.

Sweat is pouring down my back and face, pooling beneath my bra and between my thighs. Dripping down onto the vodka-soaked wood. I take out the pack of matches and strike one. The spark of fire looks like some kind of revelation.

I'm ready. I'm going to burn this barn to the fucking ground.

The doors squeak and I whirl around to find Anna, smoking a cigarette, her mouth open in surprise at the sight of me.

"Arlee." That's all she says for some time, before, "What the fuck are you doing?"

"You have to help me," I plead. Tears well up, the pain sharp and aching inside my head. "You know, don't you? You know about the murder. What Lisha did. We need to stop it. This needs to end."

She narrows her eyes at me, but takes a step back, as if she's afraid. "You're nuts. You don't know what you're talking about."

"Oh, *fuck you*, Anna!" I spit, advancing on her, tossing one lit match onto a bale of hay. It bursts into flames, and she startles, eyes wide, face pale as the moon the night Lisha held my head down and made me lick my sister's blood. "Stop lying to me!"

She is a deer. Frozen. Afraid.

I won't hit her. Choke her. I won't be like the others, let the violence take over again.

"Help me, Anna. Because I'm not going to stop, but I could use your help in ending it. It all needs to end now. I'm burning down the barn, the Order's closet and everything in it. Everything they love. Then I'm going to the police."

She winces, taking nervous puffs from her cigarette, which is turning to ash in her hand.

"You think that'll fix everything?" she snaps. Her eyes are welling with tears, voice cracking under the weight of them. "Huh? You think that'll scare my mother?"

"I need to do something!" I roar back. "You have to help me! Send a message!"

"No," she says. "I can't." She sounds afraid. "I've dealt with my mother my whole life. You don't understand. None of you understand what's it like!" She grabs at her hair with one hand and tugs wildly. Behind me, the smell of smoke rises into the air.

I think of what we discussed in the dining hall. The Jungian shadow. The darker part of ourselves that we push away and pretend isn't there, until we finally snap.

I see Anna now for what she is. Her cruel, vicious shadow self that emerged as a way to protect the terrified little girl that still lives inside her.

I am fight and she is freeze.

"Fine," I say, then do something that surprises even me. I grab that cigarette right out of her mouth. "Then stand back and don't try to stop me."

She swallows as if her throat hurts and nods. She steps back, tears falling freely down her cheeks.

I carry the lit cigarette like a torch and toss it into a particularly dry bale of hay.

I use the rest of the matches in the packet and light every patch of vodka I can find, letting it build and grow. Flames lick the floor, up the side of the barn. Outside, the horses whinny in fear. They'll be safe, I tell myself. The stables are far enough away, after all.

Finally, the air is so thick with smoke it's getting hard to breathe.

I walk out of there, out of the ashes, smelling like woodsmoke.

o o o

This time, I don't run.

I simply walk across the lush front lawn where the camp begins, where it all began—all the way to the pleasant, rustic cabin surrounded by milkweeds and towering sunflowers—covered in smoke and ashes and embers.

It's no use, simply burning the barn and the Order's things. It felt good, but it means nothing in the end if Caroline is still in charge, still the head of the horse.

I have to show all my cards and try to reason with her, try to explain exactly what happened. I have to try, for my sisters, for Winnie.

For me.

Even if it means I end up dead.

I no longer care.

I don't really expect her to be there. Not at five till midnight. I don't expect any lights to be on in the Welcome Center at all, but she told me, *Anytime. Day or night.*

And so, there is a light on, one burning red in a small window toward the back of the building.

I feel as though I have no other choice.

I am a moth helplessly drawn to her flame . . . and this may be the only way I can stop this. I don't know exactly what I'll say, but I know I'll start with the truth.

I pound on the front door, the one that was once open to the place Mom signed me in and bought me all those stupid, tacky souvenirs. It feels like it happened a trillion years ago. In another lifetime. I bang and bang again, but still, no one answers. Which makes sense, because many people would probably be home in bed at this hour, and yet I let out a scream of frustration. Of agony.

As the crickets sing me their haunted lullaby, I toss rock after rock at the burning red window, crying silently, until finally a face appears in the window, awash in crimson red.

Caroline Rhinelander's pale face smiles back at me. She waves a manicured hand and puts a finger up—one second—as if I come here all the time, at nearly midnight. As if I'm here for fucking dessert.

I hear footsteps. Shuffling. Other lights snap on from inside, and finally, the front door swings open, Caroline standing in a long white silk robe, velvet slippers on her feet, her snow-white hair down in her signature long braid.

"Arlee Gold," she says brightly, like she's been expecting me. "Come in, come in. Have some tea. I just made a fresh pot."

There's a boy who's been missing, and by morning there will be another, but she stands here soft and serene, as I stand here panting and shivering in the night, dirty, crying, ravaged.

And she's *smiling*, showing me the white of her perfect teeth. Just like she did during the Sundown Ceremony, when she dangled the dead baby horse by its neck.

I could turn around now, run right back to Unit Seven. Back to Winnie. Forget this whole mission I haven't thought through. I could run to the parking lot and follow the highway until someone stopped for me . . . but that could be just as foolishly dangerous as staying here, waiting for Lisha to find me and kill me, too. I could go down to the Echo River and try to knock some sense into my sisters—I shudder at the thought, because, no, I can never go back there again, and it wouldn't work anyhow—so I step inside and let her close the door behind us.

I shouldn't be in here. I should be grabbing a flashlight and a jacket, running out right past the exit and down the winding highway into town. Hitchhike a ride to the nearest police station. Tell the cops everything.

But I can't.

I can't turn in Winnie. Can't implicate myself, since I'm entangled in this web no matter how you attempt to unweave it.

No, not *can't*.

I won't.

Not until I try to talk to Caroline. I have to at least try.

"I set the barn on fire," I tell her. The story comes out rushed, half-finished. "It's burning to the ground as we speak. I'm sorry. I was angry. Furious. At you. At all of them. I buried Zach's body, too. I-I helped, at least. I just want it all to stop. I need it to. Lisha made us. Lisha killed Michael. I want my—*our*—sisters to be safe. This has to end. *Please*, Caroline. I need your help."

She flashes me a look of sympathy and beckons to me as if I'm a confused, anxious child. "Why don't you sit down, Arlee, and we can talk?"

I nod and follow her, even though I'm trembling. Even though I don't trust her.

It feels so strange and hollow in the Welcome Center, without the person selling souvenirs, without all the parents in their crisp polo shirts and sundresses who were here on the very first day, drinking cocktails and eating pigs in blankets. I can almost hear the ghost of their laughter. The main office is down the hall, or so I recall, but Caroline opens a door I didn't see before, leading me down a short dark hallway that smells of mothballs and must, and into a hidden parlor.

It's dazzling. Ornate gold curtains. Dark wood antique furniture, a forest-green sofa, and a magnificent red chaise with decadent trimming. Shimmering white-and-gold wallpaper with dizzying patterns. In one corner, a small old-fashioned stove top with a hissing tea kettle resting on top, maybe the most modern thing in the room besides the minifridge next to it and the laptop I spot perched on an antique writing desk. Above the stove top is a wide wooden cabinet with frosted glass.

"Is this where you live?" I ask.

Caroline doesn't answer. She hums to herself, a song that is neither happy nor sad. Something in a minor chord, something eerily familiar, though I can't quite place it. She takes her sweet time opening the cabinet and selecting two porcelain mugs.

"Green or black?" she asks me. "Or maybe you'd prefer mint. Hibiscus, maybe?"

"I want to call my mom," I say. It comes out pleading. I imagined coming in here calmly, confidently, to negotiate, level with her . . . but somehow in the surrealness of this room, in Caroline's potent presence, I suddenly feel stripped of that grit. My throat hurts when I speak, it's so raw from screaming. Fighting. "What's going on, Caroline? How do we make this stop? It needs to stop."

She chooses a tea bag from a glass canister in the cabinet and pours me a cup. "I think you'll enjoy this hibiscus, Arlee. Sugar? I also have honey, if you—"

I don't mean to, but the gentle way she's speaking to me, all her deflecting . . . any remaining patience goes out the window.

"I don't care!" I cry. "I don't want any fucking *tea*! This is

madness! I burned the fucking barn down! Do you not care?! I
burned down everything in the Order's closet! Two boys are *dead*.
Oh God, please, I want my mom. I told you everything and now
I need to know what's going on! It needs to end and—" I begin to
hyperventilate.

Caroline pours a cup of tea for each of us, then hands me
mine. It burns against my sore, scratched palm. I get this animal
urge to throw it across the room, to shatter it against the ostentatious wallpaper that's beginning to make me feel feverish. Like
I'm hallucinating. I must be. None of this can be real.

"Please sit, Arlee. Join me." She waves to the couch and takes
a seat on the chaise longue facing it, but I stay rooted to the floor.
"I can see how exhausted you are, honey. It really was so much
for you. Too much. I tried telling Sam. So much to put on a girl
your age . . . and with your, well, don't take this the wrong way,
Arlee, your disposition."

"*What?*"

She crosses her legs and blows on her tea, steam rising from
the mug. "You know, my daughter Anna was wrong about you."
She swirls the tea bag around and around, smiling up at me.
Fondly. "Won't you sit with me, Arlee Gold? You can call your
mother. Not to worry, dear. I only want to talk with you first, help
you understand things. I know it's been . . . quite blurry."

My arms and legs are shaking, my heart racing so fast I think
I could puke right now. Exhausted, delirious, I sink into the
comfortable green couch, spilling hot tea all over my bare legs. I
don't care. I don't care anymore.

Caroline takes a sip of her tea. "Sam always liked hibiscus
best. Won't you try it, Arlee? Your voice sounds very raw, as if
you've been screaming." She flashes her teeth at me once again,
and for a moment I see Anna's face instead of hers. "Drink up.
It will help."

I stare into the mug, now blooming with murky red water. It smells . . . good. Delicious, even. Fragrant and fruity. I hold it closer to my face, breathing in the scent of it, then take a sip.

I wince when it burns my tongue.

"Too hot? You must blow on it first, Arlee," Caroline says, chuckling to herself and recrossing her legs.

"The boy they say my mother skinned alive . . . ," I say, voice raspy. My head is pounding. I feel like someone's sliced me open, too, leaving my insides raw and exposed as the baby horse's. "How did you make it go away? Win—someone said you made it go away."

Caroline waves her hand, as if I just asked her why she traded a stock on the market. "Oh, Arlee, you shouldn't believe everything you hear. Gossip is the devil's plaything. That was only a scholarship boy, anyhow." She laughs a little. "Those are easy enough. I believe it was . . . some story about how he'd likely wandered off during a group hike even though he was warned not to and hurt himself. We manufactured several witnesses, of course, all of whom claimed they saw him ignore their counselor's orders. His parents didn't have the money to investigate further, and luckily, with all the prized students we continue to create, all the star athletes and Ivy League scholars and award-winning actors, no one else looked any closer. Mother was always . . . good with the police. Good with negotiations." She nods with respect at the corner of the room, and then I see it: a small black urn resting on a Victorian side table.

"Your mother was in the Order?" I ask, my voice nearly a whisper.

Caroline takes a drink of tea and cocks her head at me. "Oh, of course, my dear! Didn't they tell you? I'll have to have a chat with Lisha about this. They should be educating you girls on the full history from the beginning, not just the liner notes. It should be a top priority for new sisters. Well, I suppose this summer, it wasn't." She laughs openly, beaming at me, as if we're in on this together, as if I should be laughing and smiling, too. "Yes, Arlee, the Order has been here longer than the camp. This is old land. Very old. Haunted, you might say." She chuckles.

"It's a lie," I say. "Everything about its history."

She smirks at me and stirs her tea, a cat enjoying having a mouse caught between its claws. "Most of it, yes. Bad publicity is better than none, you know."

"So you know what Wi—what Lisha made me cover up. Of course you know. You've known this whole time."

Her face darkens. "Lisha is a foolish girl. She tried to impress me to get ahead, and I appreciate that, I do, but she's made such a mess of things that I've now had to clean up." She *tsk-tsks* to herself as she takes another sip of tea. "She will be reprimanded."

The threat in her voice makes my blood go cold.

"I could go to the local cops," I say. I set the teacup down on the coffee table in front of me, my hands shaking so hard I nearly drop it. "I could tell them everything."

Caroline looks, at most, mildly puzzled. Not the least bit alarmed. "What good do you think that would do? Sheriff Dupont already knows everything and is well involved. She is our sister."

They're everywhere. Black widow spiders, waiting, watching. Woven into every facet of the camp's web and beyond.

Preying on boys and girls alike.

"You psychopath! You've covered up the *murders of boys*! You brainwash girls to be indoctrinated into your fucking *cult*!" I shriek. It's all too much. All of this. This cloying room, with its scents and secrets and horrible, garish colors. Caroline Rhinelander, sitting with her teacup in her silk robe and slippers. Her long white hair braided down her back like a horse's tail. "And

I burned your precious barn down! Don't you care? About anything?!"

I wish she would react to me. Get angry. Threaten me. Tell me to stop screaming. She continues to watch me, carefully, as if I'm a fascinating specimen. The room does another spin and I hug my knees to my chest, letting everything inside me out with a wail until my throat is on fire from screaming.

"Oh, you poor, poor girl." Caroline sits beside me and wraps her arms around me like a vice. She smells like danger. Familiar danger. Like sandalwood and apple blossoms. The same way Miss Teresa always smelled. I struggle in her arms but she holds me tighter, stroking my hair a little too hard with nails that feel like claws. She sighs deeply. "I told Sam it would be too much for you, that you might not be ready." Then she adds, very softly, her voice like honey laced with poison, "In some places, boys are protected by the local law at all costs. No matter whose lives they destroy. No matter what they do. We like to do things differently around these parts."

I manage to squirm out of her grasp, my eyes darting around the room. I could run, but I don't have a phone. No way to call home, and it's the dead of night. I could hit her over the head with something—maybe her mother's urn—knock her unconscious, use her phone to—

No. I won't be violent. I won't be like her. Like *them*.

And . . . I'm growing impossibly drowsy. As if I've swallowed a bottle of NyQuil.

"Call my mother," I demand. I stand to my feet and hold myself, recoiling from her. "Right now. I'm going home."

Caroline smiles patiently at me. "In a minute, Arlee. When you've had your rest. You'll wake up and remember what happened."

"W-what?" The lines on the wallpaper begin to swim, time

moving like molasses. The clock on the wall ticks too slowly. The carpeting feels heavy, as if it's pulling me down, pulling me under . . .

I feel Caroline's hands gently pushing me back onto the green couch. I don't resist. My body goes limp, like a doll. Like a broken thing. My eyes flutter shut. They are heavy red curtains. Impossible to open.

I am floating through space, but still I hear her gentle voice as I drift among the stars. "There now." Her cold hand is wrapped tight around mine, squeezing. *The tea*, I think vaguely. *Why did I drink the tea?* I sink down, deeper and deeper, the stars and blackness swallowing me up like a black hole.

"Just a little rest . . . and don't worry about the barn, sweet girl. All is forgiven." She touches my cheek. Her fingers are ice cold. "We'll build another."

o o o

I can hear her voice, muffled behind the walls. Two raised voices arguing.

I moan. My head is difficult to lift. It's late morning, and I'm still in the room. On the green couch. An afghan has been draped over me, pillows propping my head up. My broken glasses are resting on the coffee table.

I reach for them, but I'm tired, so tired . . .

"—*to my own daughter!*" I catch the tail end of what Mom shouts as she storms into the parlor room, eyes red with tears when she sees me. "Oh, Arlee! Honey. Baby. I'm so sorry." She crumples to the floor beside me on the couch, her hands so warm in my cold ones.

My heart aches with relief. She's here. *Mom.* In a sharp navy blazer and pencil skirt, her neck and ears dripping with pearls.

Perfectly winged eyeliner, even after the tears came. She's going to take me to the police. Take me home. Help me fix this. Everything.

Then I remember . . . the rumors. Her control. Her lies.

All her involvement.

A knife twists deep in my gut.

"*Mom*. What the hell is going on?" When I speak, my throat is still scratchy. Quiet. I've lost most of my voice, so I drop to a whisper. "I'm so scared. I need your help. Please."

"I will help you, baby," she says, kissing my hands. "I can't even begin to—no, that's not right. This is my fault. It's all my fault."

Caroline stands in the doorframe, dressed in a cream-colored pantsuit and brown mules, a smile on her face and a tray of deviled eggs and toast in her hands.

"Good morning, Arlee Gold."

My head is still so heavy, and when I stand, I feel woozy.

"I can't leave yet," I argue weakly. My throat hurts. My head and neck hurt. Everything aches. "My friends. My sisters. The younger girls who—Winnie. Mom, you don't understand. You don't know what happened. We need to go to the police. Someone. Now. *Please*."

"Oh, Arlee, we *do* need to go, sweetie, but we can't involve the police. It's not possible, I'm afraid. They wouldn't believe you, anyhow, because Sheriff Dupont is in charge here, and baby, if the wrong people found out, they'd take you away from me. Do you want that, Arlee?" She gently strokes my cheek as she gaslights me. Her eyes harden when I fail to respond, fail to fall for it. Her voice darkens. She grips my chin tightly with two fingers and I wince. "Arlee Samantha. You need to think rationally. For once. Do you want to go to jail? Do you want *any* of us to go to jail? Throw away our lives? Your future? I brought you here. I worked so hard to bring you here. I spent *years* . . ."

"Winnie," is all I can say. My heart is breaking over and over. "What about Winnie? What happens to her?"

Caroline presses her lips together and says tightly, as if I'm a small child asking for a candy bar in the drugstore, "That all depends on you, my dear. You should listen to your mother."

o o o

I sit in Mom's air-conditioned car as we take the long, lovely drive back home to Raleigh, passing gas stations, drive-through restaurants, and open, lonely fields. None of it feels real in the slightest. None of it feels familiar.

I'm drifting in and out of sleep. "She roofied me," I say.

Mom grips the wheel, her jaw set.

"I know. I'm furious at that. I'm sorry she did that, baby. That was completely unnecessary."

I scoff. "You *think*?"

Mom winces. I don't ever speak to her like that. I don't think I ever have, since the night that Dad left.

I could apologize, but I have nothing to be sorry for. Not after what she did to me. What she put me through.

"You knew. That they'd make me bury a body."

"No!" Mom cries, shaking her head. "Arlee. Honey, I swear, I didn't know. I thought you'd join the sisterhood and be part of this wonderful family and—"

"And what? Be like you? *Skin a boy alive?*"

Her eyes wide, she nearly runs us into an oncoming car, swerving at the last moment.

"I don't know what you're talking about, Arlee Samantha," she says sternly.

"Everyone talks about it, Mom. Or at least, they whisper. They hated me there. Everyone except for my bunkmates and the people I ate meals with. A girl switched out of her elective because of *me*. I was the camp pariah, and now I see why. They were afraid that I'd turn into *you*."

Mom lowers her gaze for a moment before focusing back on the road. She flips on the radio, our favorite Fleetwood Mac song playing, but neither of us sing along.

"Please forgive me, Arlee. Please. I love you so much. I never wanted to hurt you. I never . . ." She gives a pitiful cry, and it tugs at my heartstrings. The desperation in her voice, the look of utter despair on her face, and that fucking kills me. I want to stay mad at her. I have so many questions. So many things racing through my mind, my thoughts overlapping at breakneck speed.

I know I won't get a straight answer about what really happened all those years ago. Not from her . . . and that terrifies me.

CHAPTER EIGHTEEN

We are back in our apartment in Raleigh.

The air-conditioning feels cool and good on my skin, and even amid all the horror, there's a bittersweet comfort in being home . . . though now, I'm not sure what home is even supposed to feel like.

While Mom makes us both coffees with almond milk—our favorite—I wander into my bedroom as if in a daze. This once-familiar space no longer feels like mine. Not the unicorn table lamp in the corner, or the band posters on the wall from concerts I went to when I was a girl who had friends and dreams. Certainly not the dozens of piano songbooks stacked on my shelves, taking up the space where I vaguely remember wanting comic books and sci-fi novels instead.

I have a sudden urge to burn them all, to burn down this whole apartment.

I want to cry, but I can't. The tears are trapped somewhere deep down inside me.

Mom did this to me. It wasn't just Lisha, or Caroline, or Anna, or any of the other girls who were lured like sheep to the slaughter into the Order.

It was Mom. She started this.

The walls used to feel like they were breathing, but now it's like their lungs have stopped working. Or maybe that's how mine feel.

I spot my cell phone right where I left it, off, tucked against the corner of my desk. For a moment, I'm afraid she disconnected it, and my hands shake as I try to turn it on. It takes a second, but it still works. Still gets a signal.

Good.

I need to end this.

"Arlee."

I startle when I hear my name, dropping my phone to the floor. Mom leans in the doorframe, a mug from one of our trips to Disney World in one hand and a tired, sad smile on her face. The kind of smile that says she wants to apologize to me.

"Coffee's ready. Come sit with me?"

I let her place a hand on my back and lead me to sit at the kitchen table, even though it makes me shiver. Recoil.

I don't think I ever want to touch a drop of tea again.

She stirs her spoon in her mug, again and again, blows on it, then takes a drink. I do the same with mine, but forget to blow first.

Once again, I burn my tongue.

"So, Arlee, are you going to go to the cops now? Tell them everything?" she asks me. Calmly. Patiently.

As if she knows what I'll say. How I'll answer, even though my body is no longer mine, and my mind and heart no longer belong to the girl who was once Arlee Gold.

This girl who is now nothing and no one, and no longer afraid of flies.

"I won't waste my tears on the boys who died," I tell her, like I'm reciting a prayer. "I won't ever cry for a boy. Not even a dead one."

"*Praesidio puellae,*" Mom whispers, eyes welling with tears of pride. Of love.

I whisper it back, my voice foreign to my ears. As my father's face flashes behind my eyes like an afterimage.

A phantasmagoria.

I'm lying to her.

As soon as she falls asleep, I'm calling the police. I'm telling them everything, confessing to my part in the cover-up of a murder, even if it means being ripped away from her, my home. My family. My bed and my things. My pink seashell lamp and my San Francisco poster, both of which now look like foreign objects.

Even if it means I get arrested, or go to trial, or even jail.

Even if it means the same for Winnie, or worse.

The girl I thought I loved.

It no longer matters.

I won't be one of them. I am now a corpse of the moth I once was. Hollowed out. Barely there, dangling on by a thread on the spider's web. But I'm alive, and my heart is pumping, and deep down, I know that Arlee Gold still lives inside me, her wings beating still. Struggling to survive even in the spider's clutch.

I can rescue myself.

And I won't let other girls get hurt. Even if they kill me, I'll fight for them. I owe it to them all.

When my mother is asleep, I tell myself, when my hands have finally stopped shaking, I will retrieve my cell phone from my room. I hope it's fully charged and waiting for me.

I will call the police. I will tell them everything.

I have to come clean. Even if it ruins my entire life, or puts it in jeopardy, along with Winnie and Mom's.

My shadow self can no longer win.

The Order can no longer win.

I can't stop hiding from what waits for me in the darkness, and I can no longer let anyone control me.

Protect the girls . . . for real this time, even if it kills me.

"*Praesidio puellae*," I dutifully say back. "Protect the girls."

This time, I fucking mean it.

THE CODA

". . . and this just in, disturbing reports from a Harriet County summer camp, Camp Rockaway, where a missing camper, seventeen-year-old Zachary Clark, was presumed to have run away, but thanks to an anonymous tip that he reportedly was buried in the camp's horse field, we are sad to report that remains matching his description have been found and exhumed as we await a coroner's confirmation. One main suspect is currently in custody: Caroline Rhinelander, camp director, and unfortunately at this time, that is all authorities are willing to share. Our thoughts are with the entire Clark family, as well as the rest of the campers who were removed from the facility and returned to their parents as the investigation continues, though two campers still remain unaccounted for: seventeen-year-old Michael Rodney Bearington and sixteen-year-old Winona de León . . ."